ALSO BY

NÉLIDA PIÑON

Caetana's Sweet Song

Republic of Dreams

VOICES of the DESERT

VOICES of the DESERT

a novel

NÉLIDA PIÑON

*Translated from
Brazilian Portuguese by
Clifford E. Landers*

Alfred A. Knopf
New York
2009

THIS IS A BORZOI BOOK
PUBLISHED BY ALFRED A. KNOPF

Translation copyright © 2009 by Alfred A. Knopf, a division of Random House, Inc.
All rights reserved. Published in the United States by Alfred A. Knopf,
a division of Random House, Inc., New York,
and in Canada by Random House of Canada Limited, Toronto.

www.aaknopf.com

Originally published in Brazil as *Vozes do Deserto*
by Record, Rio de Janeiro, in 2004.
Copyright © 2004 by Nélida Piñon

Knopf, Borzoi Books, and the colophon are registered trademarks of Random House, Inc.

Library of Congress Cataloging-in-Publication Data
Piñon, Nélida.
[Vozes do deserto. English]
Voices of the desert / by Nélida Piñon ; translated from Brazilian Portuguese by
Clifford E. Landers.—1st American ed.
p. cm.
Originally published: Vozes do deserto. Rio de Janeiro : Record, 2004.
ISBN 978-0-307-26667-5
1. Scheherazade (Legendary character)—Fiction.   I. Landers, Clifford E.   II. Title.
PQ9698.26.I5V6913 2009
2009011831

Manufactured in the United States of America
First American Edition

In memory of Carmen Piñon, my mother

9/09

Foreword

A thousand years ago, Scheherazade spent one thousand and one nights telling stories to the Caliph. In doing so, she saved the lives of one thousand and one maidens whom the ruler of Baghdad threatened to kill to avenge himself of the Sultana who betrayed him with her slave.

The tales of *One Thousand and One Nights,* from the lips of the most beautiful and cunning of narrators, have captured the imagination of countless readers, eager to learn what happened to Sinbad and Zoneida, and who, with bated breath, feared for Scheherazade's fate at the whim of the cruelest of listeners. A thousand years later, the time has come for another narrator, Nélida Piñon, to recount the internal adventure of Scheherazade as she confronts the man who holds the fragile thread of her life in his hands.

With empathy at once powerful and delicate, Piñon sees inside the woman of whom the fabled Middle Eastern creation had given us merely an outline, hidden behind the Muslim veil. Now we know who Scheherazade is, for Piñon reveals to us her deepest nature: she is the magical force that confronts oppression and death at every turn. Scheherazade is possessed but not loved. Yet sex alone does not satisfy the jaded Caliph; it is his thirst for words that is insatiable, and his desire to hear the unfinished story knows no bounds. It is this desire that saves the narrator and all the women for whom she sacrifices herself. It is a bizarre ritual played out by the sovereign, caught in his own web of power; Scheherazade's sister Dinazarda, the picture of crafty prudence; and her loyal slave Jasmine, on whom she relies. Piñon succeeds in extracting from this elusive figure the mine of popular fantasy on which the storyteller's fantasy feeds.

Foreword

With a subtle yet firm hand, Piñon makes us hear the voices of the desert, where the narrator's dreams came from and where they will go when she is finally freed from her self-imposed mission. Let all who have ears listen; let all who have been fascinated by *One Thousand and One Nights* have their fascination reignited.

Alfredo Bosi

VOICES of the DESERT

Scheherazade has no fear of death. She does not believe that worldly power, as represented by the Caliph, whom her father serves, decrees by her death the extinguishing of her imagination.

She tried to persuade her father that she alone can break the chain of deaths of maidens in the kingdom. She cannot bear seeing the triumph of evil that marks the Caliph's face. She will oppose the misfortune that invades the homes of Baghdad and its environs, by offering herself to the ruler in a seditious sacrifice.

Her father objected when he heard his daughter's proposal, calling upon her to reconsider but failing to change her mind. He insisted again, this time smiting the purity of the Arabic language, employing imprecations, spurious, bastardized, scatological words used by the Bedouins in wrath and frolic alike. Shamelessly, he marshaled every resource to persuade her. After all, his daughter owed him not only her life but also the luxury, the nobility, her rarefied education. He had put at her disposal masters of medicine, philosophy, history, art, and religion, awakening her attention to sacred and profane aspects of daily life that she would never have learned but for his intervention. He also gave her Fatima, the servant who, after the early death of Scheherazade's mother, taught her how to tell stories.

Despite the Vizier's protests when faced with the threat of losing his beloved daughter, Scheherazade persisted in this decision, which really involved her entire family. Each member of the Vizier's clan evaluated in silence the significance of the decreed punishment, the effects that her death would have on their lives.

Dinazarda, her older sister, had also tried to dissuade her, believing her incapable of swaying the sovereign's will. But why, then, accompany her to the imperial palace, as she had asked, and take part in an act that evoked her tears of anticipatory mourning?

The debate had gone beyond the boundaries of the rooms, the servants' quarters, to circulate in the Baghdad underworld of beggars, snake charmers, charlatans, and liars. In the bazaar they used obscene and mocking speech to spread the word that the Vizier's daughter, the most brilliant princess in the court, in an effort to save young women from the Caliph's grip, had decided to marry him.

News of the sacrifice, to which no one remained indifferent, spread throughout the kingdom. With no way to stifle the network of intrigue that the information had generated, the Vizier, it was rumored, after threatening his younger daughter with exile in Egypt, where a prince of that kingdom would make her his bride, once again found his plans thwarted. Disrespected by Scheherazade, he attempted to take his own life by slashing his wrists. He did not bleed to death, but only because of the providential appearance of both daughters, who, raising the scimitar he had used to commit the act, threatened to take their own lives with the same blade if he continued with his effort to kill himself. They could not accept the sorrow of burying him. Fearing the mad gesture of his daughters, though it was an expression of their love, the Vizier withdrew to his chambers, resigned to his fate.

Scheherazade's fate had become public knowledge, confounding the ancient medina so accustomed to seduction and fraud. The feelings the young woman inspired made the theologians and philosophers, the illustrious translators, and their masters, gather in distress before the doors of the Vizier's palace and, kneeling with their eyes turned toward Mecca, intone entire verses of the Qur'an, intent on dissuading her. At the mosque, not far from the Vizier's palace, the crowd of merchants and beggars, perhaps skeptical of her sacrifice, also prayed for the success of the young woman who dreamed of ridding the kingdom of the cursed decree.

In the beautiful courtyard of her home, Scheherazade reflected on her misfortune. At the fountain, water splashed onto her tunic and wet her long hair. At her side was Dinazarda, her constant companion since Fatima had left Baghdad forever. She was a prisoner in her garden, which had now become the stage for a family drama; it was there that the attention of the slaves and discreet members of the court focused, sharing the Vizier's pain. All around the young woman there was a feeling that a tragic end was imminent.

On the appointed day, Scheherazade got ready, indifferent to her father's suffering. He in turn refused to escort her to the door, not even to say good-bye. Scheherazade departed from the Vizier's house without looking back, taking with her Dinazarda, who was essential to her plan of salvation.

When she is presented to the Caliph, to whom she has been announced, he greets her with silence. She is quickly sent to the royal chambers, her face impassive. Though accustomed to the continuous gliding of slaves across the translucent marble floor, bringing and taking away delicacies, she faces a confinement amid luxury that disquiets her. Outside her home for the first time, Scheherazade realizes she is at the center of a drama that could easily escape her control.

The members of the court murmur as they observe her being led to the chambers in the expectation that she will be the Caliph's next victim. Their pallid faces recall masks from the grayish light of Babylon in the month of January.

Between those walls, the Vizier's daughters eat frugally. They embrace each other in shared unhappiness, avoiding mention of the fateful word that at dawn would take Scheherazade to the scaffold. She dissociates herself from the grave menace of being the next victim of the Caliph's tyranny. Assisted by Dinazarda, she makes their ephemeral time together, perhaps only a single night, bearable by telling her sister pleasant stories. When the Caliph is finally announced to them, the women's raiment, pastel in tone and without ornamentation, pales in contrast to the Caliph's sumptuous adornments, which make his white turban stand out, as do the jewels he wears from the Abbasid treasury, which gleam in the sunlight.

As part of her sister's cortege, Dinazarda adapts to the ceremony that precedes every movement. At the side of Scheherazade and the Caliph, she is part of a trio that moves almost mechanically. Each follows the notes of a silent ballad, in expectation of the carnal triangle's dissolving when Scheherazade is taken to copulate with the sovereign.

The Vizier's daughters sense their father's absence. A faithful servant of the Caliph, he stays away from the chambers, suffering from afar the loss of Scheherazade. From the instant when he watched his daughters leave, without the right to express pain or rebellion, a spirit of tragedy descended on him. At any moment, subject to the will of the sovereign, his daughters could be taken to the sacrificial altar, with no chance for him to revolt. In the name of what ambition had he shunned defending his daughters and immolating himself in their place?

The scaffold had been painstakingly constructed for the sole purpose of doing away with the Caliph's young wives, who were condemned to die at dawn. By order of the sovereign, no vile blood, criminal and treacherous, other than the young women's, would stain the marble floor prepared daily for the ceremony of the execution of his wives. The executioners chosen for this purpose were instructed to remain on permanent alert.

Away from the windows, Scheherazade closes her eyes, not wanting to see the silhouette of the city reflected in the gardens or to discover the shadow of the death chamber falling onto the wall beside the alcove. Dinazarda, however, even by turning her head, does not see the nearby scaffold. She is in love with the imperial gardens; from the arched windows she gazes at the tree-lined walks that, disappearing into the horizon, form a labyrinth that threatens to engulf her. Despite the spell of the flowers and their intoxicating aroma, her attention falls on the swooping birds that come to rest in the dovecote of the extravagant architecture.

Dinazarda wanders about the rooms, searching her memory for a recitative to express the agony of seeing her sister so close to death. At the same time, she laments being bound to someone laboring under the illusion that by telling stories she can redeem a man—someone who makes Dinazarda laugh and cry, and enchants her with the talent of transporting her so far away that at times she finds it hard to return.

Enclosed in the chambers, surrounded by slaves, she regrets having given in to Scheherazade. She feels like a passenger in another's dream, ready to occupy an irrelevant role in the daily life of the court, should the Caliph spare her sister's life. Immersed in a conflict she cannot escape, she decides to yield to Scheherazade's plan with a mixture of compassion and indifference that obliges her to follow her sister's fascinating steps.

Scheherazade seems not to notice her sister's mood. Focusing on her own salvation, which depends that first night on Dinazarda's actions, she is unaware that not even the foreign delegations visiting the court are typically spared the court's macabre spectacle. Crossing the gardens on their way to the sumptuous entrance to the palace, they must pass by the scaffold. The phantasmagoric presence, casting its shadow up the wall, advancing at different times of day toward the windows of the throne room, serves as notice to the kingdom's transgressors.

Intertwined by a shared destiny, the sisters wait for night to fall. In the chambers, Scheherazade can hardly disguise her nausea. The fear she feels accentuates her discomfort at being forced to live surrounded by slaves. Soon the Caliph will come to claim her body.

2

As night falls, Dinazarda encourages her sister to resist the Caliph when he comes to possess her. Since she and her sister occupy the same chambers, Dinazarda is unsure how to proceed once the sovereign arrives. Should she leave the bedroom before the amorous preludes between her sister and the sovereign begin? Or wait for him to dismiss her?

Dinazarda foresees the pain of the leave-taking, not knowing whether she will have time to embrace Scheherazade if the Caliph, refusing to hear the first story, condemns her to death. She would avoid watching them. Despite curiosity about the joining of naked flesh, one shamelessly penetrating the other, entwined like animals, Dinazarda cannot bear the thought of her sister bowing to the Caliph and would rather not witness the outcome of that union.

Scheherazade's serenity impresses her. Lying on the bed, her face inscrutable, she betrays no sign of her thoughts and exhibits no fear. Dinazarda doesn't want to think about the Caliph brandishing his member like an instrument of conquest when confronting her sister's nude body. To ease her anxiety, she reminds herself that it's natural for the Caliph, lying at Scheherazade's side, to move toward consummation. And each scene she anticipates joins the many others in her troubled imagination.

The bed, adorned with cushions and embroidered cloths, awaits the lovers. Among these magnificent brocades, Scheherazade relives in her mind the amorous stories that she often related to her nursemaid, Fatima, with the difference that now it is she who fornicates rather than her characters.

It has begun to grow dark. Dinazarda moves to comfort her sister, then decides against it. It is too late to add or subtract details in the drama that is about to unfold. The spiritless lamps spread shadows as the Caliph, preceded by fanfares, steps into the chambers. With each stride he looms larger, presaging his intention to possess the maiden's body without laying claim to her soul. Let it be known to his subjects, including the favorites there, that he has no need of the burden of intimacy. He executes the routine of sex certain that it will neither do him harm nor produce in him any indelible consequences.

For the first time Dinazarda sees the Caliph up close. Well along in years, with a thick beard and a corpulent body, he hides his opaque gaze by narrowing his eyes. Though he embodies the Caliphate of Baghdad, she cannot control her repulsion for the man about to invade her sister's body with the demeanor of ownership. She is careful, however, not to betray in the invader's presence any sign of complicity with her sister, to reveal the plan, lest he imagine them ready to deliver a fatal blow. It would be unwise to alienate the ruler of a reality that supersedes common justice.

Frightened, she wishes she could return to her father's palace. She regrets her promise to her sister, but she cannot shirk her mission of awakening the drowsy Scheherazade after copulation and convincing the sovereign to hear the story her sister plans to tell before he orders her beheaded.

The Caliph moves indolently, with no waste of energy. A rare citrus fragrance hovers around him. His imposing attire bears embroidery of foreign inspiration, whose meticulous details recount the progress of a deer hunt. He avoids meeting the gaze of the intruder, Dinazarda. When he approaches Scheherazade, who is reclining on the cushions of the bed, he shows no emotion as he lies down beside her.

Disciplined in matters of the flesh, the Caliph does not alter his conduct in bed. For a long time his concubines, accustomed to his conventions, have abandoned the chambers immediately after coitus. He disapproves of any outward show of admiration, such as sending him amorous signs in the form of messages, embroidered cloths, or dried flowers. Female whims leave him unmoved.

The Caliph's lack of affection impels Dinazarda to withdraw in search of a hiding place. She hastily passes through the rooms that constitute the royal chambers until she finds a nook in which to spend the night. The screen separating the narrow recess from the rest of the chamber isolates her from what's happening. She is distracted by the walls, decorated with floral motifs and calligraphic designs, and by the lacquered drawings, made from countless leaves, exalting the Abbasid dynasty.

On her way to the far side of the chambers, her eyes burn with an image of the lovers that she strives to extinguish and with an anguish that she tries to combat with straightforward reasoning. What could happen between the Caliph and her sister that Scheherazade had failed to foresee? Before leaving their father's palace she had learned from one of the Vizier's attendants that there had never been in the sovereign's life an instance of conduct against Islamic law. His behavior was guided by the practices of his lineage, save for the recent decree that ordered the execution of his young wives following the wedding night.

But how can Dinazarda find relief when she has reason to believe that upon the Caliph's arrival Scheherazade had said goodbye to her forever? And that when morning comes, her sister will meet the same fate as her predecessors, making her sacrifice in vain?

No sound reaches her ears. Protected by the screen, Dinazarda makes every effort not to look toward the bed. But her imagination, out of control, engenders on all sides small, misshapen phalluses, some with wings, others with fins, all of them erect, poised to shatter the brides' hymen with their illicit desire. Imagining the Caliph's pursuing member, her vulva throbs in anticipation of a painful penetration. She attributes to him attitudes that precede copulation, irritated that he neglects the female anatomy, the now turgid inner lips. At the same time, prey to fantasy, she envisions the Caliph at the other end of the chambers tearing off her sister's clothes as he whispers sordid words that arouse him, the lovers losing all caution, openly enjoying the same sex practiced by the poor of Baghdad.

Dinazarda laments Scheherazade's fate. She doubts that the Caliph, upon opening the portals of love, will transport her to paradise, bringing her to forgive his cruel acts. She hopes he will at least be patient with Scheherazade, for she cannot presume her sister to be skilled in the erotic arts.

In the midst of these reveries, without seeing what is happening in the imperial couple's bed, Dinazarda thinks about her sister's reaction to the Caliph's rigid member forcing itself into her, ignoring the dryness of her sex and violating in his haste the religious precept that grants entry to the female organ only after it shows itself ready for coitus by the welcoming lubricant of desire.

Perhaps the Caliph, driven by this temporary vexation, will refrain from entering Scheherazade's sex, consoling himself with bringing the maiden's hand to his chest, with the command to lightly touch his unruly hairs, then slide past them to his phallus, susceptible in recent times to failure to perform, until it hardens and brings him happiness.

3

While still in her father's house, on the eve of her departure, Scheherazade had imagined herself in bed with the panting sovereign mounted over her body. Anticipating the horror that the scene inspired, she had closed her eyes to impede the conclusion of that copulation that went forward in her dream, despite her plans to combat the intemperate sex of the dictator into whose presence she would be led the following morning. But even once she was living in the imperial palace, she would not assume the role of some celebrated Baghdad prostitute prepared to resuscitate the lover's spent body with magic recipes and age-old potions. She would not have done so even if she had known the formulas and rituals capable of lavishing sex with exceptional skill, and the balms, liniments, and delicacies ingested at twilight, or the prescription made of tail hairs and pieces of the brain of portentous animals like the tiger, the bear, even the ass, that was rubbed into the folds of the uncooperative phallus.

Her destiny was not to conquer him in bed but to triumph by beginning the first story. Scheherazade watches as the Caliph undresses her from the waist down, with obvious disdain for the breasts, a scene whose unfolding, as she remains cold despite the Caliph's scratching her stomach with his nails, makes her think of Dinazarda, at the other end of the chambers. She tries to guess how her sister, bold in matters of sex, would react to the appeals now emanating from the Caliph's bed. For, even though her sister had covered her ears with beeswax from the bazaar in order not to take part in that sexual interlude, all that precaution did not protect her body, now burning with desire. In these circumstances, then, it was natural that Dinazarda's thighs were damp with the secretion running from her vulva, that inexhaustible fount of pleasure, and that she would stroke her sex with the expectation of arousing quivers, electric discharges. And that, racked with anxiety, dreading frustration, she would clamor for someone to rub her sex, stroke the delicate region, tear out the hairs, chew her flesh, all to effect orgasm.

Although the ecstasy she attributes to Dinazarda interests her, Scheherazade's attention returns to the Caliph at the very instant that he, ripping away her undergarment, exposes her dark pubis to the lamplight, and into its closed breech, with a single thrust, introduces his authoritarian member.

The Caliph fears succumbing to the rhythmic movement, threatening to bring to an end a performance watched from a distance by the women who slept at the other end of the chambers. Their presence doesn't bother him, for he long since lost any feeling of intimacy, choosing instead to embrace the notion that his body was his alone and no one else's. Since adolescence, as the court became aware of his every act, he had been the subject of Baghdad's evil tongues. Any action of his immediately swept through the halls, taking on contradictory versions.

While still a boy, he had only to summon a favorite to his bed for word to spread concerning how many times he had impatiently entered the woman and even the instant when, after orgasm, he had tumbled spent at his partner's side.

The obstinate monitoring by the courtiers had awakened an instinct of defense, giving him a reason for never revealing his emotions to anyone. It was with that decision in mind that he mounted the body of the concubine, hastening to climax in order to free himself of her company and then returning the woman to the harem without a single sign of affection. He would take no account of whether she had an owner, and he once usurped his uncle's favorite without asking permission or later apologizing. The theft had occasioned no problems for him, as his uncle had no wish to criticize the heir to the Abbasid throne, whose predatory

acts were visibly hardening his sensitivity, offending the susceptible ties of love.

Over the years, these practices brought about changes in his
behavior. Under the yoke of disillusionment, the spontaneity of
sex had slowly waned, and a sadness for which there was no anti-
dote began to poison him. The process of aging had alarmed him.
He attempted to conceal his body's decline until the day when,
defeated by undeniable evidence, he began to ignore the details,
perhaps because he knew that despite his weaknesses, he had the
power of ordering the death of his enemies.

It no longer mattered to him that the women were perplexed by
his virile stumbles, his continual reserve. With them in his arms,
he insisted on instantaneous pleasure, although there now passed
through his mind the desire to breathe into the ear of Scheherazade, nude and motionless, as a way of orientation, to reawaken
his genitalia, sensitizing his skin with her nails, preparing him for
the battle of love before his wand lost its vigor.

Behind the screen, Dinazarda is not sleepy. Her body tingles
when she thinks of Scheherazade engulfed in a powerful experience. She too, pierced by pinpricks, feels a strange mouth tearing
from her both pieces and delights, while her injured flesh seems to
exude secretions, sperm, amid her lamentations and those of her
imaginary lover, blending chaotically. Surprises weaken her, sap
her will. The taste of blood, springing from her swollen vulva,
comes to her in gushes. In the midst of her delirium, she hurls this
placenta into the witch's cauldron, heated by wood and coal,
under the fire of imagination. Suddenly, she thinks herself the
woman chosen by the Caliph to crucify with his enemy member.

She hears nothing from Scheherazade, whether she is still alive
or has fainted. The sounds she can distinguish correspond to the
arrhythmic panting of the Caliph. Scheherazade herself emits neither sound nor lamentation. She acts in the certainty that it is necessary to survive. But her body burns. Discreetly, she touches her
sex, the breech made by the Caliph, silent at her side, both their
genitals in tatters. She is aware that the passion did nothing to link
them, nor did voluptuousness forge any commitment.

Scheherazade prays for her sister not to tarry, fearful that the sovereign will reject the sisters' proposal. Dinazarda now approaches without a sound. The Caliph first notices her shadow, then her presence, but who would disturb them at that hour by bringing news of the realm? Observed by the young woman, whose face he scarcely recognizes, the Caliph covers himself and sits on the cushion.

In her effort to save her sister, Dinazarda is risking her own life. On gilded slippers she glides, terrified, to the royal bed. She weighs the risks, her head at stake. At the mercy of a ruler who disdains the lyrical will of love, however, she has no one to whom she can appeal. She fears she will distort the instructions she has received, fail to play the part for which Scheherazade has so carefully prepared her, thereby proving herself incapable of demonstrating to the Caliph her sister's storytelling talent. If so, instead of saving her, she will be precipitating her death.

The silence grows in the depths of the night. Despite the penumbra, Dinazarda can see her sister lying exhausted on the bed. Precipitously, she leans over her and in a compassionate impulse licks the blood coagulated between her thighs. She quickly rises, regretting the act and her attempt to remedy a situation beyond her control. Still, she does not become disheartened but bows in deep reverence. She murmurs sounds that the Caliph barely hears, but her courageous words awaken in him the inclination to listen to her. Dinazarda alters the tone of her voice, falling silent only after wresting from the Caliph the promise of giving ear to Scheherazade. Only then does she help her sister tell the first story.

4

Annoyed at Dinazarda's intrusion, the sovereign, still drowsy, decides to listen to Scheherazade before handing her over to the executioner. He is unaware of his wife's intention to use Dinazarda as part of a plan that can save her. He accepted the timid petition without being able to explain to himself why he yielded. Perhaps it was because Dinazarda assured him that her sister's word was a kind of cocoon from which one day, when the time was right, a silkworm would emerge.

Without hiding his impatience, he makes himself comfortable on the cushion. He is surprised by the shy young woman whom he has just slept with, changing positions as she speaks to him, each movement responding to a secret instruction dictated by her story.

Scheherazade is blessed with the gift of fluent speech. Her words, forming an unbreakable amalgam, begin to serve as a shield for the characters parading before him. And though some are friendly among themselves, these creatures do not always come from the same family. They seem united by lust for gold and adventure instead of blood. Scheherazade's stories center on adventurers who risk their lives in hopes of cheating time and poverty.

As she describes how they scale the walls of Baghdad from the west, aiming to reach the banks of the Tigris, the Caliph strokes his beard, incredulous at what he is hearing. But because they seem so real to him, he doubts they could have been born from such an inexperienced young woman, doubts that Scheherazade could have learned to describe fugitives, vagabonds, lovers, people who would unsheathe their swords merely for the privilege of resting their gaze on the naked breasts of the merchant's wife as she bathed in the patio in the heat of the morning sun, and the woman willing to grant them what they were ready to pay for with an arm severed by a jealous husband.

Sometimes playful, Scheherazade smiles in defense of these beings. She delivers them from unexpected places, knowing she will return with them to experience other adventures. But as the night advances and injects into the Caliph a passion he had long ago abandoned, he sees in her neither weariness nor excessive effort. With each word, it is as if she were sipping the sovereign's blood under the pretext of bringing him relief.

Suddenly, he reacts to the possibility that the young woman is abusing his hospitality. The solution would be to hand her over to the executioner, cutting short her aspirations to become a purveyor of an art practiced by the lower classes. As he is about to make the gesture that will signal her end, he decides to hear a bit more from her, eager to know the fate of young Hassaum, who dared steal the crown of a king who, his fortune lost, now lives in poverty, with that adornment his only patrimony.

Before sending her to the executioner, he needs to find out about that other band of criminals, led by a proud young woman dressed as a man, and about the remnants of a tribe that had intercepted a caravan en route to a foreign potentate's summer palace believing they would find jewels in the trunks and wicker baskets—but were surprised at the sight of women, some of advanced age, members of the potentate's harem, traveling through the desert without proper escort.

When Scheherazade tells of criminals who are permitted to possess women belonging to a monarch, the sovereign is shocked. He criticizes her for the bad example, but he does not interrupt the flow of the story, which is already well along. Neither does he suggest that she rest, though she has been talking for many hours.

He notes that Scheherazade makes no effort to endow the plot with features that might prevent him from decreeing her death if he in fact wishes to follow the development of the love between the bandit and the princess. And he fails to notice that she purposely leaves her tale at loose ends, in order to bind them up the following night. To save herself, she foresees the weighing of each word in the sentence, without forgetting to add bones, flesh, and passion to the characters who are the fruit of her imagination. To them she entrusts the burden of softening that man's stony heart.

Morning has come, and the Caliph must leave for the audience room, where he is being awaited. But because Scheherazade has yet to finish the story whose conclusion he is eager to hear, he decides to grant her an extra day of life. Upon his return that night to the chambers, Dinazarda emphasizes to him that among her sister's virtues is that of making a heart pulsate in another's chest. So, after fornicating with Scheherazade, he complies with the request, allowing the young woman to continue her unfinished story, without suspecting that through such a concession she is depriving him of the attention of his subjects. Unwittingly, he is granting her the machinery to manufacture dreams, admitting publicly that a story, told with liturgical solemnity, can save someone from the scaffold. And worse yet, he is running the risk of handing over to the woman a power in open contest with his own.

Light of skin, Scheherazade takes after her mother, whom the Caliph never knew. Despite her diminutive body, her tales contain colossal figures with the mission of shaking the equilibrium of the caliphate. For this, she promises the ambitious and the poor a certain black pearl that possesses the power to heal the dying and impart wondrous benefits to its owners. These facts occur in such a way that the Caliph does not interrupt the narrative flow. Attentive to this kind of masquerade, he trusts in Dinazarda's gaze to assure him that he should enjoy the art through which her sister, at his expense, avoids the nightly sentence of death.

After each copulation, Scheherazade sits upright and demonstrates to him the enchantment that the poor exercise over the imagination. What can his courtiers do that the tramps of Baghdad have not already done in alleyways or in their journeys through the desert? With the voice of flute and lute, she creates verbal spirals that destabilize the reality over which the Caliph rules.

During the nights, despite suffering the same fear that assails the other young women of the realm, she is fierce in her defense of the ancient hunger that motivates each story. Actually, it is in the name of all that devours her from the inside that she goes in search of phrases, themes, and narrative artifices that will preserve her life till the next morning.

5

Under the lure of diaphanous veils, Scheherazade's gaze wanders past the face of the Caliph to consult the stars. Through the arched windows, the starry path constitutes a map in which to read stories to add to her repertoire.

In the care of Dinazarda, who delegates to the slave Jasmine the task of adorning her body, Scheherazade resists losing herself in the indecipherable outward appearance of the Caliph, who has laid tiny traps with the intent of making his way through the woman's labyrinth.

His presence is disquieting. She does not love the man. She is struggling for her life, obeying the instinct of narrative adventure and passion for justice. When terror had spread through the kingdom with the sacrifice of young women delivered first to the Caliph's lust and later to the scaffold, Scheherazade had decided to oppose such cruelty. To do so, she had first confronted her father, the powerful Vizier, ready to embark on a journey from which there was no return.

Now, in the light from the oil lamps, she examines the Caliph, attempting to fathom the man's acts, which compromise even the precepts of the Qur'an. Whatever the pretext, there is no justification for the slaughter of the maidens. What right does he have to determine the life of his subjects, causing families to grieve in the name of his wounded honor?

Determined to save herself, Scheherazade perfects the details, which she uses as a weapon. To lend her words credibility, she thinks, organizes, discerns the world. She allows others to choose her food and garments. All that is missing is for Dinazarda to add her own touch to the tales that Scheherazade recounts. It is her sister, in fact, who in recent weeks, under the pretext of pouring honey on the figs, already sweet in themselves, has hinted to Scheherazade that an artist cannot do without the original touches of an anonymous observer, thanks to whom there come to her ears fragments that, although disjointed, may in the future be merged into a story.

With studied nonchalance, Dinazarda, with Jasmine at her side, entertains herself by draping Scheherazade in veils and cloths from various parts of the world. The two women amuse themselves by experimenting with ways of fitting the fabrics to Scheherazade's body. They take special pains in the use of veils that conceal her face from the sight of others.

Like all Muslims, the Vizier's daughters do not resist the imposition of veils, first adopted by Fatima, wife of the Prophet, following the revelation that Allah had vouchsafed her husband. She was so grateful for the magnitude of the news brought by Muhammad that she quickly cut pieces of cloth found in the house and at once covered herself with them. From that day on, no outsider could see parts of her body or observe the degree of faith that surrounded her like a halo.

From a young age, both of the Vizier's daughters had access to the Qur'an and were impressed by the verses relating to the episode that, by preaching circumspection, prevented female emotion from showing on the face and being observed by anyone outside the family.

Transparent and delicate, the veils immediately became part of the sisters' sphere of imagination. Persuasive by nature, they both protected and exhibited what was at the center of male attention. And they safeguarded uncertainty about female feelings, the unexpected imbalance of reason, the moments when the spirit, tempted by melancholy, could not be restrained. But at the same time that the veils concealed, they also permitted the sisters, behind their protection, to take refuge, even in thought, in the grotto of sin in order to delight in secret pleasures, in the cavern where desire glows and moistens dreams.

They inherited from their mother and their nursemaids the

meaning of veils. The seamless fabric—tulle, satin, silk—hugs the body and serves as stimulus in the erotic game. The language of gestures that arises from veiling propagates ambiguities, lust, discord, disillusion, discernment. Wearing the veils, they are assured of not being recognized and are empowered to flee the tyranny of their father and the Caliph. It is as if, anchored in exotic lands, the danger no longer exists of their being returned to the seraglio, while they trust that their eyes, however expressive, confound the observer by saying the opposite of what they feel.

As a servant, Jasmine naturally does not make use of veils. Without the protection of that shield, she is vulnerable, her feelings exposed to the mercy of male covetousness. She is accustomed to sensing when a man is watching her and wants to take her home, and she wanders freely through the environs of the chambers, going as far as the kitchen, bringing and taking messages and food. She notes the Caliph's esteem for veils. As part of a culture that has consecrated them, he applauds what arises from their fascinating code, which, above all, enhances sexual pleasure. Like the Prophet, whose fingers had unveiled the face of his wife, he too craves a grace that, born from such a mystery, can make him transcend himself.

Before Scheherazade installed herself in the palace, the Caliph, plunged in recent years into prolonged melancholy, would visit his harem, preferably as night fell. Thirsting for erotic attraction, he would cross the threshold of the chambers in silence, always settling into the same chair. Surrounded by his concubines, who greeted his presence with a disorderly clamor, he never reciprocated the feigned joy. He had nothing to add to what he had been told, especially because the women's jubilation reminded him of the Prophet's admonition about signs of feminine wiles. After lingering for a long time at the gates of hell, Muhammad had stated that the majority who made their way there were women, thus insinuating that the female was more inclined toward sin. Confronted with the tumult around him, the Caliph also remembered a certain voice that, intent on showing the cunning nature of women, had spitefully proclaimed, "Oh, vulva, for how many men's deaths art thou responsible?" And he would evoke the metaphor created by Arabian poets who in their fervor to describe woman's sexual organ likened its shape to the head of a ravenous and insatiable lion.

Of late, the Caliph had remained in the seraglio without having sex with his favorites. Allowing them to dance in the hope of arousing his desire, he watched closely the belly dance, which afforded the woman an opportunity for sinuous contortions as she moved her hips. What held his attention was that the woman, as she dropped each veil from her waist, was slowly divesting herself of that protection. Floating in the air for seconds in defiance of gravity, the veils remained in that rarefied region until descending and brushing against parts of the body as they fell.

As the women lasciviously offered themselves, the Caliph felt swallowed up by the violence of a vulva that would drag him into its depths, where he would vanish without a trace. Governed by the demon, he sensed that there was no salvation for the phallus, despite nursing the illusion, however momentarily, of capturing the poetry of evil and of the flesh, of approaching a mystery hidden behind those fluttering veils, waiting to condemn him forever.

6

Night after night, Scheherazade envelops the Caliph in her subtle web. She calms his nerves as her narrative rhythms display a dance of emotions. Her stories, seeded with heroic and imprudent acts, sate his hungry ears, maintaining his curiosity until dawn. Any failure means death.

Her heart is not always bound to the tales she relates. Her desire is to one day resume life outside the palace walls, to be free of the burden of storytelling. Sometimes, in her imagination, she exits the chambers, leaving her body behind, and returns to her father's house, rejoicing upon being received at the gate by the servants bowing in her path. The table, covered with delicacies from her childhood, is proof that she is still in the Vizier's home. Sheltered by so many memories, reconstituted in her mind within the walls of her father's house, she feels protected, no longer sentenced to die. But how can she leave if her father must die in her place?

The illusion of having returned home quickly vanishes. She has nowhere to go if she leaves the Caliph's palace, where the creatures of her imagination are prospering. Driven, however, by a melancholy that is consonant with the gray days of far-off lands having nothing to do with the desert that occupies her heart, she quickens her storytelling and in so doing, brings close to her bed the people of Baghdad.

Longing oppresses her heart. It is suffocating to know her existence will last only so long as she can maintain the sovereign as the prey of her verbal weapon. She takes a deep breath, tightens the strangely fleshy lips framed by her delicate face. She opens them, releasing the phrases and sighs imprisoned in her throat.

The veil over her face intensifies the enigma. Practically clinging to her skin, it is part of her countenance. She resents it when

Dinazarda abruptly rips it away to ascertain whether her sister is still among the living. Perhaps, commanding her adventures, she has embarked on a foreign vessel, never to return to Baghdad.

Even when her face is exposed, it retains a delicate film that prevents others from knowing what she is feeling, something that protects her from the Caliph, especially at the moment he is entering her. But, watched by Dinazarda, she is defiant, almost translucent. The aura of storytelling hovers over her, perhaps a reason for prudently slicing up the stories, keeping the bread crumbs on the table for the later hunger of that day. At times she is aware of success, of momentarily reaching the zenith of narrative, the rare instant in which, upon hitting the sensitive chord of the plot, she cannot turn back.

Fatima herself, who had held her in her arms since birth, used to speak in a bold defense, which Jasmine would later repeat, of Scheherazade's ability to weave with words. With loom and cotton between her fingers, she could twist the fibers and make a shawl capable of protecting the listeners from the cold of desert nights.

Scheherazade, however, felt distressed by the pressure of her talent. She didn't care about praise, and refused to be the weaver that Fatima thought her to be. This did not stop her on certain occasions from swelling with pride, only to regret at once the arrogance that could poison her. On a gloomy Sunday, she punished herself by running through the rooms, the secret passageways, the cellars of her father's palace, until she fell, panting, in the courtyard amid a thousand flowers, begging the demons to punish her. After her exertion, she calmed herself by the ancient practice of hiding lightly scented messages beneath the colorful pillows scattered about the house. Messages that in their unmistakable calligraphy frustrated any who might be tempted to decipher them. These small rolls of papyrus, simple short notes with words sprinkled here and there, squeezed among scattered drawings, were not readily accessible.

Mounted on a steed of the imagination, Scheherazade would

gallop through the house, pursued by conspiring adversaries. Fleeing from Dinazarda, who, searching for her notes, hoped to discover why her sister's calligraphy, seen from a distance, merged into the outline of a camel, an animal that Scheherazade praised given the slightest pretext.

As a whole, the notes, because of their cryptic nature, meant nothing. They were but papyrus, useful only for Scheherazade to elaborate some story ready to blossom under her wit.

Her ability to weave together stories, which perplexed her family, had come from the cradle, inherited from her mother, a woman of fertile imagination. Dinazarda, two years her elder, had learned from their father that their mother, shortly before her death, had spoken to him of how stubbornly the young Scheherazade attributed life to inanimate objects and of her precocious devotion to giving voice to the daily life of the poor who made Baghdad the radiant center of Arab civilization.

The young girl demanded that family members test her on any topic. Sitting in the middle of the room like a sphinx, she would wait for outlandish questions to prove her knowledge. Even when she failed, in no way could they ignore her answers, for everything she said was backed by her memory of Islam. If they truly wished to examine the past of the family, or to trace the path of the Prophet, they could entrust to her, despite her age, the task of binding together legends and uncollected records scattered about the caliphate.

Her mother, on the verge of drawing her last breath, with Fatima at her side, had willed herself to smile. She was moved by the fact that her daughter's fledgling tales encompassed legendary figures of the desert, the mosques, the Islamic marketplaces. As if it were not enough for her to rely on the members of the household for the weaving of her plots, she was precociously preparing herself to deal with the flesh beyond those walls, which suffered, dreamed, forged lies, and had no name.

She had barely learned to walk when it became clear that her memory was infallible and that she had a gift for describing the indescribable. Under the care of Fatima, she would nimbly unearth emblematic figures as well as the dead, pairing adversaries and lovers, translating the heart of love. Even at a young age, she rescued boats from the storm, through the labor of words bringing safely to shore the merchandise from their hold and the stuff of earlier shipwrecks.

The sovereign's rare admonishments, though unconnected to her stories, constitute a warning. She immediately recalculates the time of the account and tests its richness to see if it will entertain the Caliph till morning. To keep him entranced, she makes use of unexpected resources such as leaving false trails and feigning that she has lost her bearing from too much exaggeration.

As she narrates, she brings forth personalities that although lacking any apparent purpose whet the sovereign's curiosity, so that, subject to the young woman's cunning, he will grant her the right to live, so long as she proceeds. But even this, repeated every morning, does not dispose the Caliph to free her from the fault of being a woman.

Her face clouded, she confronts the struggle to restore the fabric of life, using her characters as example. She suffers to think that her value consists of serving the sovereign like a dungeon slave, her existence legitimated only by him.

Dinazarda tries to help her by slowing the daily flow of her stories, perhaps by suspending the Caliph's visit so her sister can finally stroll through the palace gardens. To this end, she might threaten the sovereign with the arrival of a scribe from the north to take Scheherazade's place. This veiled threat might force the ruler to confess that, thanks to Scheherazade's talent, he has frequented the caravans that cross the desert, lived among mariners who sail the Indian Ocean, shared the intimacy of thieves who specialize in stealing treasures. Because of this art, so ancient and neglected, of speaking without stopping, the world has entered his door without his ever having left the palace.

Dinazarda's effort to save her life stimulates Scheherazade to repay the sisterly devotion by small acts of madness, to expose to the light of day the tales stored in her memory. At the risk of over-reaching, she confides that she is capable of trimming away any incongruence in timely fashion. At a frenetic pace, she offers asymmetrical events that make the Caliph, Dinazarda, and Jasmine smile with pure pleasure. And to maintain this effect, she obeys the principle that each plot, ambiguous by nature, originates from a single source, lost in the darkness of time, a matrix to which she adds her own embellishments, decorations, and variations.

7

Dinazarda cannot hear the lovers' words. The sighs she imagines as she passes through the garden are the invention of her own fantasy.

Her upbringing does not allow her to ask her sister whether she murmurs and shouts when the Caliph penetrates her. Whether she climaxes, following the instructions of the Caliph, who maintains his sex erect only through curses and wriggles.

Behind the screen, with Jasmine at her side, Dinazarda hears no sound to make her blush. She is aware that the Caliph disapproves of noisy demonstrations in bed designed to please him. Heart-rending cries and exaggerated contortions remind him of the Sultana copulating with the African slave. Hers was a lust that, according to the Caliph, was part of the tissue of lies and failures that reflect the deceitful character of woman.

Dinazarda doesn't know whether Scheherazade, because of the cunning emanating from a craft that obliges her to pretend at all times, evinces a passion for the Caliph that she does not feel. For even with her, her older sister, she dislikes confidences. Forced, however, to yield to the sovereign's sexual game, Scheherazade uses the bedroom to imprint eroticism on her plots, experiences that make her stories intensely carnal, capable of shaking the senses and exciting the young women listening to her. Scheherazade learned with Fatima that if the imagination constructs intrigues of love, the body inevitably suffers its effects. She is attracted by the realism originating in the body. However, she does not want to be the heroine of her stories, preferring to confer upon princes and plebeians the impassioned words that inflame the desire of Zoneida and Sinbad.

What is certain is that she does not plan to foment her narrative ardor with bitter feelings or to make her characters replicas of herself. She controls her pain and does not express it. She would consider it equally perverse to insert the Caliph into her tales, as either hero or villain. She spares him from being contemptible. And to lend credibility to her task, she tries to free herself of the signs of her individuality. Her deeper being is not at issue. Above all she remembers the words of the royal chamberlain upon her arrival at the palace as he informed her of the Caliph's habits, expecting her to conform to the norms, however brief her stay in the royal chambers. She should keep in mind that her predecessors, brides like her, confident of their beauty, had expected consideration from the monarch and as a consequence were unable to bear hearing the stony voice of the herald, who had been waiting at the door, after the Caliph had discreetly disappeared from the chambers, announce their impending death.

In words that seemed sincere, the functionary feigned lamentations at the sacrifice of those beautiful princesses from the Vizier's line, without, nonetheless, failing to stress that none of the young women who had come to the palace had created a scandal. They limited themselves to stifled tears and prayers to Allah and his Prophet, despite deploring their early demise.

The Caliph's cruelty shines before Scheherazade's eyes. Even so, she pays no heed to Dinazarda, who counsels her to act so that he will fall in love with her. Her goal is to dissipate his calm by means of conflicting emotions, to shift him from sex to words, to inflict upon him the slow agony arising from her clever narrative.

The Caliph considers the sacrifices that Scheherazade's craft imposes on him. But even so, he does not relieve her of the tributes she must pay to hold his interest. He feels it reward enough to please him, to see in the faces of the sister and Jasmine that excitement that would prompt them to follow her in case he should condemn them to banishment from the court.

But his perception of her is obfuscated by an interior light, in the exact instant when she baptizes her characters, shows him their lives, takes them through Baghdad, Karbala, Najaf, to the source of the Tigris and the Euphrates. He has never experienced such emotion with his subjects, perhaps because he has refrained from looking at them, from listening to their woes and their pleas. He has always been indifferent to collective fate, has never raised his head in curiosity as they bowed in his path, not even to see their painful expressions. But what could he say to them if he inquired about their dreams? Would they confess to the sovereign their fear of poverty and decline?

When he saw that the roles had been inverted, momentarily leaving him as supplicant instead of lord of the caliphate, he resisted. Why was he to blame if they all owed him their lives, if he was the one who, with the power to raise the scimitar against them, daily postponed the fatal sentence? He trusts Scheherazade's moral integrity as she tells him a story, the care with which the young woman structures the tale and preserves those whom, having created bonds of familiarity, she has no intention of sacrificing in the name of a banal adventure. Of course she is also treacherous, making use of spurious resources in order to impart to her characters dreams, loves, misfortunes, and impossible hopes. The sovereign meditates on the woman's fate. What does she aspire to that he has not already given her? Does she, as he spares her life at morning, perchance wish in exchange to torture him by offering a new story, one he cannot evade hearing, whose outcome, in the middle of the night, immediately leads into another, and another, in a nervous succession that plunges him into misfortune?

He is angered at such behavior, at the women who, like Scheherazade and the Sultana, by draining his energy and will, deserve no pity. He raises his hand to call for the executioner. But, looking at the three women, he stays the gesture. Discontented with his own weakness, as if repenting, he leaves the chambers.

In the throne room where his grandfather and father, Abbasids of strong character, had exercised power surrounded by profound loneliness, the Caliph dismisses the courtiers with a feeling that he is similarly fated to die. He accepts, resigned, the apricot that comes to him on a copper tray. Slowly, he chews the fleshy fruit, savoring its sweetness.

8

The Caliph's pain, which afflicts him around noontime when the sun scorches Baghdad, does not come from wounded love. He had long ago stopped loving the wife who so miserably betrayed him in the past. In truth, he never loved her. Divided among so many women, he had become accustomed to the heat of desire that never lasted beyond a week. Time enough only to become excited, to weave fantasies that led to the bedchamber and faded there. But so long as the shadow of attraction for any of the concubines lasted, he would practice sexual variations with the goal of achieving the perfect copulation, always in search of a rapture whose prize was attaining paradise, where he would offer thanks to Allah for the riches of the flesh.

In the beginning, despite his youth, he had evinced signs of resisting this type of cannibalism, devouring his favorites without considering their anguish or showing them kindness in the form of a lingering gaze, or a caress to feed their illusions. But over the years, not having loved any of the women, he had not made of any of them a unicorn, according to myth a being invisible to the impure, a source of consolation, a gift for the man on whose shoulders rested the weight of the caliphate.

In general, he looked upon the female body with apprehension. When he ventured into the mystery of the vulva, he felt neither love nor any unusual emotion. And even if he waited for some form of hope to emerge from sex and convince him of love, this fire coming from his body and the woman's did not rise to his perpetually cold heart.

He felt he was practicing a demonic act, without the saving grace of coming to know a restorative feeling capable of establishing new forms of companionship. This in turn led him to conclude that it was not in him to change a situation with which his unfeeling heart had no wish to cooperate.

One day, returning from the desert's infinite horizon, he noticed as he fornicated with a beautiful woman that his actions in bed, though convulsive and fleeting, suddenly seemed automatic to him, as if performed by a stranger who, despite having lent him his phallus, had taken no part in the revel—someone who plunged into female flesh only to immediately withdraw, apathetic and spent. Such indifference forced him to investigate the reason that sex, celebrated by peddlers and artists alike, leads men to madness and blinds them, cleaving them in two. He discovered that since he had never succumbed to love, the natural corollary of sex, life had spared him from insanity but in return had drained him of expectation, of emotion, of perplexity, and of all else about which he had no knowledge.

As a result, when he attempted to revive the erotic variations practiced in earlier years, they inspired in him no excitement. His disinterest in these initiatives coincided with a daily life filled with overly familiar, depleted routines. There was nothing to discover in his kingdom to transport him to rapture, to make him salivate with pleasure, to allow him to forget for a few moments the signs of aging that occupied his days.

Before the arrival of Scheherazade, when he summoned a favorite he would quickly repent. He felt obligated to perform a demonic act that dragged him to the depths of the female body, to ask why he yielded to a desire that in exchange failed to give him the longed-for epiphany. The result, in fact, was just the opposite: frequently he would arrive at the epilogue feeling like a cadaver.

He was so self-absorbed that there was no way to modify a drama that had as its purpose attending to his body's need to reach a spasm resembling death. At the time, he banished his bitter thoughts about love by developing predictions about the topic. As if human love, absent from him but present among his subjects, made everyone equal through its repetition of the desire that any maiden provoked.

The Caliph's loneliness persisted despite the procession of virgins who filled his bed and were sacrificed each day. And because he never had anyone with whom to share his unhappiness, he kept his disillusionments secret. Unlike other mortals, he protected himself from adversity by sending his subjects to the scaffold.

After his decision to sacrifice the young women of the kingdom in order to satisfy his hatred of the Sultana, the Caliph had felt safe. He had found a means of assuring the court that he was immune to woman, to that being with a body as sinuous as the lines of the Tigris and Euphrates, in whose veins he had found milk, honey, poison. But despite protecting himself, he had weakened before females and continued taking them into his bed as a necessary evil. That entity, full of meanings and ambivalence, at once beautiful and wicked, remained to him an indecipherable mystery, to which he had access only in the shadow of night, when, bewildered, he touched the smooth skin that evoked exudations in his body.

In the hands of the slaves for the morning ablutions, his skin, despite the essences sprinkled on it, betrayed the female presence. He had not resisted sex. It had been futile to create subterfuges to free him from the yoke of woman.

Back on the throne, he sipped his mint tea. Melancholy arising from power protected him from outside attacks. The waters of his recent bath, which still warmed him, helped him face the demands of the realm. And to his relief, surrounded by the Vizier and his other counselors, he would not see Scheherazade and Dinazarda again until nightfall.

9

The female slaves gather round the sisters in a flurry of beetles, murmuring opaque monotone messages. No one pays attention to them or understands their whispered imprecations. Natives of Nubia, the region where the gold in mines makes men's eyes glow, they dream of the metal that may one day free them from the Caliph's palace. Impatiently, they await the orders given them.

Upon granting Scheherazade another day, the Caliph withdraws. After the magnanimous gesture, Dinazarda reorganizes the quotidian tasks, as if her sister were immortal. She exacts vows of obedience from the slaves, tells them to prepare Scheherazade's bath before she rests. Jasmine exerts her best efforts, babbling a prayer to a god with whom she seems on intimate terms.

Supported by Jasmine, Scheherazade enters the pool. After the painful nocturnal ordeal, she almost faints from tension. She struggles to put together the pieces of life that remain, to preserve intact the hidden feelings of the vanquished night.

The scent of clove and lemon, wrapped in tulle, impregnates the room, transporting the young woman far away. The tepid water comforts her body and raises her spirits. She slaps her hands on the surface, creating waves as if she were sailing on the Mediterranean, perhaps on the Indian Ocean, accompanied by Sinbad, who has come for her. The sailor and she entwine tenderly, in a prolonged embrace that serves as a sail that unfurls and propels the boat. On the whitecap of the waves, the two are swept far away. The violence of the currents is the work of an evil genie recently released from a bottle found at the mouth of the Tigris and Euphrates. It is this freed entity who tries to lure Scheherazade and Sinbad to the deep of the waters, whose salt immortalizes the sunken caravels.

The princess's gaze hints at unending adventures. Jasmine predicts that it will not be soon that she interrupts the journey. She too aspires to become part of a fantasy that may bring her to know the path of the story. Scheherazade, however, unaware of the slave girl's dreams, splashes the bathwater, advancing to the high seas under the protection of Sinbad. The direction of this adventure disturbs the slave. Where will the young woman head after leaving the anchorage? The game of illusion that so seduces the princess may nevertheless lead Jasmine and Sinbad to shipwreck. In the face of danger, Jasmine fears sinking before reaching shore. Distressed by the sinister prophecy, she strikes the water of the pool where Scheherazade is soaking, forcing her to return to the surface.

Back on earth, her skin lacerated by shellfish and having lost sight of Sinbad, Scheherazade is saddened to find herself once again in the chambers. At her side, Jasmine plays with the foam that splashes over the edge of the pool, bathing the young woman with holy oils intended only for prophets and priests. Their use is forbidden to the profane such as she, for it incites in them lust and envy.

Now, with wedges of lemon in the palm of her hand, she strokes the skin of the princess. And as the rhythm imprints itself on the surface of her body, it affirms in Scheherazade an almost winged lightness. The lukewarm water, again replenished, intensifies the pleasure spreading through her body, helping her to elaborate that night's story. She plans to continue a story line that calls on improbable resources but pleases the Caliph.

Many characters navigate through the interior of her imaginary vessel. Doubtlessly Sinbad, now returned, is among the most persistent. He never tires of asking for opportunities to appear in her stories and gain the sovereign's applause. Other creatures, however, less drawn to life on the sea, hope that Scheherazade, through her power of narration, will one day take them to the celebrated isle of love, where, amid voluptuous embraces, they hope to find the promise of immortality.

Scheherazade feels sorry for these ambitious characters. Docking the boat at the pier, she receives them with victuals and liqueurs. She reactivates their illusions with promises. In exchange, she demands that they save her from the grasp of the Caliph, a victory that will allow her to return to her father's house, or to search for Fatima, who lives near Karbala, not far from the Euphrates.

The sound of the lute's ballad reaches her ears and interrupts her reveries. She must seek out other adventures that will help her survive. Each journey she takes inside the chambers leads her into error. Before coming to the palace, she was a storyteller concerned with laying the preliminary groundwork for a tale and carrying it to a successful conclusion, with the Baghdad marketplace as the setting. Her mission required eloquence and a certain preciosity. But beginning with her decision to save the young women of the kingdom, she has had to exercise caution, coordinate apparently irreconcilable details. She can no longer neglect to gather parts of the soul of the people, which had never been united, and shape them into a character of rare solidity to present to the Caliph.

In the course of the arduous battle, in which the slightest mistake could put her life at risk, Scheherazade enjoys the approval of Dinazarda, who recognizes her merits, and of the Caliph, who, despite being miserly in his praise, looks upon her with admiration. She treads a dangerous path, however, prey to the miscalculations that threaten storytellers like her. In spite of the wisdom she displays, she is often unsure which direction to take, for while she has mastered certain aspects of history, the question of how to construct a narrative is sometimes beyond her. The imagination of which she is so proud often lacks detailed vision. She has difficulty managing the material in her hands—for example, how to trim the excesses that serve only to distract the Caliph from the essential core of the account.

Jasmine walks around the marble pool in search of Scheherazade, who has withdrawn. When she finds her, she caresses her back, then moves to other equally sensitive parts, without neglecting the soft lines that bring her near the forbidden area of the pubis. As she perfumes Scheherazade's body anchored in the waters of the Caspian Sea, or the Persian Gulf, ready to sail in the direction of the mare nostrum, Jasmine notices her contractions, perhaps from pleasure. Instantly, she feels pity for Scheherazade's solitude. As a slave, she knows about compassion more than anyone. She identifies with the wayward and sensitive talent of Scheherazade, who, having begun her mission, cannot stop it.

Immersed in the tub, Scheherazade is relieved; the story she's now conceiving strikes her as effective, even though it contains abundant ramifications. She questions her fate, of knowing more than the common mortal, afflicted by secrets, codes, restraints engendered by human beings as a way of creating a civilization that would fit entirely within the walls of Baghdad.

Once more she founders. Nearly lost, she clings to the metaphors that pursue her. They are both stubborn and beautiful. This poetic vein, with the mouth of a dragon, demands as payment its proliferation among men. But why, in this case, has she, the Vizier's daughter, taken on the task of absorbing the delirious poetry born in Baghdad?

Scheherazade is pained by the encumbrance of the world. She knows nothing of Jasmine, recognizing in her only the condition of exile, a person adrift. She doesn't know whether she was born in Smyrna or was a simple creature of the desert, who swallowed sandstorms, white snakes, loose carpet threads. She could be a descendant of the Prophet, though without the right to sit beside the throne of the caliphate. Her tribe, perhaps at one time related to the Fatimids, had opposed a severe theology that deprived them of certain carnal pleasures. Had the name Jasmine been given her by her parents in a rapture of love, unaware that in the future a tie would arise between the slave and the Vizier's daughters that made them sisters?

Listening to Scheherazade's tales, Jasmine represses her bitterness, resigning herself to her life. She admires the pride with which the storyteller, by playing the game of death, challenges the Caliph's notions of property, accustomed as he is to keeping all goods for himself.

Out of habit, Dinazarda indicates to Jasmine the attire her sister is to wear that night. A sari from India adorned with sapphires. Jasmine envelops Scheherazade in the cloth, which on the young woman's body transforms into folds resembling a shroud. Jasmine becomes excited by the fabric that binds her with the princess, the two forming a single being. Everything inside her throbs as if she had been granted her own freedom. Life, for that instant, becomes a source of delight.

Remote from Jasmine's thoughts, Scheherazade is immersed in a forbidden zone that she has long frequented. Distant from commonplace concerns, she nurtures words and activates her imagination.

10

She had arrived at the palace devoid of belongings, without the pomp befitting the daughter of the Vizier. Like a young woman emerging from the desert who, after losing her language, her tent, her camels, her songs, her track of the clan, had come to depend on the mercy of the Caliph.

Scheherazade's humbleness, bringing nothing of her own, arriving escorted by the Vizier's guards, had surprised the Caliph. He was unable to imagine that beneath her austere caftan, with Dinazarda beside her, the young woman concealed the hope of overcoming the cruel ruler.

Confident from the beginning that her baggage consisted of a persuasive story, she had sacrificed family heirlooms inherited from her mother, marvels like the ivory chest, the golden bowl, the African drum, the diamond-studded ass, pieces that shaped her sensitivity and soon plunged her into a memory so real that she could almost touch it with her fingers and see it contract, revealing signs of pain.

On the morning she was to go to the Caliph's palace, she had awakened early to say her good-byes. The slaves, in tears, brought her the animals, her favorite delicacies, other things dear to her heart, so she would never forget her home. In particular it had hurt her to leave behind the Qur'anic tablets and their sinuous calligraphy from which she had learned to read and write. From so much careful perusing of the verses of the Qur'an, she could repeat them by heart, which she often did on Fridays. She had addressed her relatives and servants with the certainty that she would never see them again. The journey, barely begun, would demand sacrifices of her, the renouncing of reality and familiar values, offering in return only the right to fight to save her life.

Concerned about the poverty of the princesses, the Caliph has ordered garments and gifts, even though Scheherazade must die at dawn. Dinazarda is to examine the apparel at once and choose that whose fabric displays the details of expert embroiderers and artisans.

The gifts, arrayed before the young women's eyes, include engraved bone flasks, containers of ebony, silver, and copper, faceted jewels, filigree bracelets, jade necklaces, chains of heavy metal, even manuscripts, some originating in the earliest religious schools of Baghdad.

At the first hour of day, Scheherazade admires the stained-glass windows behind her bed that filter the strong brilliance from the heat. She tries to see from the window the reflections from the green dome of the palace built by the Abbasid Mansur, while she is brought, in the name of the Caliph, a basket of pomegranates and dates picked at a distant oasis some hours from Baghdad. These are courtesies the Caliph extends to other female visitors, in addition to his favorites, as he is concerned with entertaining them with trivialities and adornments, without relaxing his vigilance over the harem.

The Caliph's extravagance, in contrast to his notorious cruelty, often led caravans from abroad to arrive at the palace entrance in expectation of being received. The wait, which could last days, provoked tumult in the palace surroundings, drawing the curious to the tents erected nearby with the acquiescence of the Vizier. The spectacle of the profusion of men and merchandise radiated intrigue, rapture, surprises. The excitement mounted with the unloading of baskets, trunks, carpets, silks, jewels, dromedaries, thoroughbred horses, lambs, ewes, and animals sprung from a startling mixture of breeds. Casks of oil, wine, and foodstuffs still bearing the odor of infidel realms would be taken to the Caliph.

Dinazarda examines the coolness of Egyptian cotton, runs her hand over Chinese silk, before selecting. She knows what she is looking for. She searches intently for qualities that will emphasize her sister's charms. On these occasions she teaches Jasmine the sense of adventure, affirms that some of the fabrics from the Far East came over the dangerous Silk Road, having faced looting, raids, battles before arriving in Baghdad. As the result of these trials, the magnificent colors of the cloths, often several in a single garment, shone before their eyes.

Dinazarda proceeds with her selection. She avoids the areas of shadow and light that shine pitilessly in certain garments. She serves her sister by thinking about satiating the lust of the Caliph, who delights in the magic of the ensemble, including the jewels. She is unaware that the sovereign, not always inclined toward chimeras, has at that moment, thanks to the clothing, converted Scheherazade from a princess into a mere stranger recently arrived in Baghdad, still bearing on her sandals the dust from the long journey.

The Caliph, endlessly bored, dissatisfied with the women in his bed, had become accustomed to thinking about one woman, born of his illusion, when he was with another. It seemed practical and efficient to do so, at least so long as the fantasy lasted. So far, he had spared Scheherazade that ruse. Now, however, as he asks with his eyes to borrow her body to house a woman who isn't she, he promises not to keep her there for long. In general, they fade quickly, as he has no way of holding them in memory beyond a few minutes.

Still, he had found that these daring tricks intensified his pleasure. Especially when, weaving bitter intrigues, he made the imaginary women cross seas, ravines, deserts, always in hopes of proving a love he did not requite. Fated to adventure, these fabricated creatures glided along the polished floor of the palace, seeing themselves reflected in the surface that retained the footsteps of other equally distressed visitors, ready to be received by the Caliph. Such women did not know that the Caliph, in his long and arduous process of inventing other faces, would soon reject them.

As he groups these fictitious women around Scheherazade, they seem so real to him that they suddenly demand an attention that he isn't inclined to grant. But because he wants to ascertain whether they still live inside the storyteller's body as a product of his imagination, the Caliph, with the expectation that one of the women will answer, addresses Scheherazade in a foreign language.

As the result of his ingenuity, the sovereign is learning that he possesses the ability to reproduce women who display not only disinterested temperaments but also autonomy. This fictional procedure affords him, for the first time, entrance into Scheherazade's world, enabling him to compete with her on an equal footing. By becoming the storyteller's equal, he can exhibit inventive traits not always inherent in the art of governing well.

Fate seems to buffet him. The steam from the mint tea creates new illusions. He concentrates on the incipient signs of the first story about to be told. As such, it temporarily darkens the surrounding reality, just as Scheherazade has come to do with her characters, so that, relying on her, they whisper confidences, make mention of their distress, recount in detail the genealogy to which they belong, helping the storyteller to fortify the social fabric of her plot.

In light of the technique of the Vizier's daughter, the Caliph's imaginary women cannot flee from the fate of providing him with intrigues that, with the appropriate framework, will later blossom. Waiting to hear what these women will murmur to him through Scheherazade's body, the Caliph approaches the window. A sandstorm, so common at the time, is forming, threatening to invade the chambers and stick to the skin. For him it's an indication that life arrives to him through the sounds coming from the bazaar.

With the expectation that his talent will emerge at any moment, he resigns himself to waiting, but the breath of mystery is slow to reveal itself. The intrigue coming from the imagined women fails to echo in him. Irritated at the sand entering his clothing, he moves away from the hastily closed windows. Not a single idea comes to him about how to begin the desired story. He returns to the middle of the chambers and realizes that the women previously occupying Scheherazade's place have vanished without a trace. Disillusioned, the Caliph passes by Scheherazade, pretending not to see her.

Beset by a fantasy that ended before it began, he comes to

understand that he lacks the talent for weaving emotions, for creating characters, for developing a story waiting to be told. Unlike Scheherazade, he doesn't swoop over the desert or take shelter in tents lashed by the fury of the wind.

Debilitated by his limitations, the Caliph walks toward the audience room. The exercise of false creation scourges him. He regrets having left the chambers through the fantasy, without giving any sign of his intent to return. At the same time, he is touched by the dignity that guides the behavior of the Vizier's daughters. That is why he does not dare undress Scheherazade and offend her modesty. After all, she has never been within his reach. Her personal plot is enclosed in poetic mystery. Guarded and zealous, she resents her captivity in the palace. This is the reason her insolent imagination sows illusions, lies. But from this prison she also sows false hopes, giving him daily motive for threatening her with death.

11

The amorous revel unfolds almost before the eyes of Dinazarda, who has nowhere to go besides those rooms. As evening falls, she is happy to know that Scheherazade, comforted by her presence, demands that she and Jasmine, recently brought into the intimate circle of the Caliph's wife, witness her nightly immolation. And that the Caliph, a man not easy to deal with, accepts her company, as if he is fearful of being alone with Scheherazade.

At the beginning, seeing her sister handed over to the ruler, Dinazarda harbored fears about her fate, but she quickly regained her calm. It was murmured at the court that the Caliph, despite his recent cruelty, had never abused the female body, not even to satisfy his lust or on some unexpected whim. According to a confidence Jasmine had heard from a eunuch unburdening himself, the sovereign was held by his favorites to be a clumsy and indolent man in bed. Despite having had an incalculable number of women, he harbored such apathy about the female body that he hurriedly dispensed with any sexual practices that might demand extra effort from him. His ideal was to achieve orgastic completeness without moving too much inside the woman. That was a wearying journey from which he returned bearing memories that the duties of the realm quickly erased.

Wisely, he had never inflicted corporal punishment on his favorites, not even when overcome with rage. His behavior had been transformed after the severe pain inflicted on him by the Sultana's betrayal, and anything might be expected of him, including the indiscriminate application of the death penalty against innocent young women. And in fact, since the sacrifice of the first victim he had stopped trimming the irregular edges of his beard, as a sign of mourning. To attenuate his distress, he had resorted to charging the herald with announcing the sentence to the victims, a decision that appeared to reduce his responsibility.

Scheherazade, however, not wanting Dinazarda to suffer, had forbidden her to watch while they copulated. She had imposed on her the basic rule of withdrawing at the first sign of the Caliph's desire. And despite having been brought to the palace for the purpose of helping to overcome the sovereign, Dinazarda could not violate her sister's rule. She had to obey it, even circumscribed by the limits placed on her by the screen at the far end of the chambers.

In asking her sister to follow her to the palace, Scheherazade had trusted that Dinazarda's wise intercession would prevent her from donning a shroud instead of wedding garments. Thanks to Dinazarda's talent, without which she would never defeat the Caliph, Scheherazade would put into motion her plan to save herself. With abundant reason she had trusted that Dinazarda, that first night, would arouse the Caliph's dormant curiosity to hear the first story. She, more than anyone, would be capable of transforming a detrimental circumstance into a favorable plan, for Dinazarda at an early age had learned from her father to persuade the innocent to declare their guilt if need be. From him she had assimilated the technique of pitting one servant against another, of weaving intrigues that had the potential to sweep through the palace.

It had been as difficult to persuade Dinazarda to come with her as it had been to win their father's consent. Though promised the credit for any victory, Dinazarda had remained unconvinced and refused to discuss the matter. She had doubtlessly harbored ambition of a different kind, about which she said nothing. Unlike Scheherazade, who acted with discretion, everything about Dinazarda called attention to itself. Tall and dark, her silhouette well adapted to the dimensions of the spacious rooms, she had a loud, unrestrained laugh and would issue several orders at the same time, sure of being obeyed. She had not been born for eternal glory, but she suspected that Scheherazade could bring benefits or ruin, a dangerous but stimulating game. At the same time, she felt resentment that her homey tales had never spread through the quarters of the palace as Scheherazade's had. Devoid of creative grandeur, her words engendered no belief, for she lacked the capacity to adulterate reality and enchant her listeners. None of her accounts had acquired the status of magic and taken hold in the chaotic streets of Baghdad.

Aware of Dinazarda's vanity, Jasmine carried out her every command, without distorting her words with false interpretations. She would bring to her the plots that circulated in the kitchen and the stables, with the hope of consolidating her presence in the chambers. Jasmine dreamed of rising in the hierarchy of the court and, in recompense for the favors she performed, not being resold to some other caliph less fortunate than this one. She aspired to become associated in the near future with Scheherazade's stories and augment them with her adulterated messages. All this she would undertake in order that her intrigues, emerging from the kitchen and the stables, might arrive at the insensitive ears of the courtiers when, in a bath of tepid water replenished by slaves, they asked from whom such fascinating accounts came.

It had been established between the sisters that, when the amorous interlude began, Dinazarda would take refuge behind the screen or would visit the gardens, where amid blossoming pomegranate trees, myrtle hedgerows, palms, orange trees, lemon trees, jasmines, and a thousand other species of flowers, all of them requiring water, she would feel safe. On a moonlit night, she could observe from the belvedere the rounded walls that protected the city, the four gigantic gates, the stones of the palace brought from the ruins of Ctesiphon, the tomb of Imam Abu Hanifa. She strolled through the gardens designed by the Caliph's grandfather. The narrow circular lanes, labyrinthine, confused walkers and caused them to lose their way, perhaps to oblige visitors to experience, however fleetingly, the torment of uncertainty and loss. Servants would have to be dispatched to look for the distressed foreigners.

Scheherazade was confident that her sister would not disappoint her trust. She did not imagine that Dinazarda could be surprised seeing her body being devoured by the Caliph, repeating with her the same acts practiced with his favorites, destroying any illusion that she represented to him an amorous ideal to which he would ultimately surrender.

Under the weight of the Caliph's massive body, which heedlessly crushes her, Scheherazade refrains from emitting any cry of involuntary pleasure. Because the flesh is after all a thankless substance that answers to no moral imperative, she might well come suddenly, enjoying the privileges of an enemy's body.

In depriving herself of such pleasure, she explores in her accounts sexual practices vaguely inspired by the Caliph and, above all, examples provided by Arabic rogues. Confronted with characters who lie, Scheherazade describes with painstaking gusto the exhausted landscape that follows coitus, the haste with which the servants expunge the evidence of sex left on the wrinkled sheets or on the streets of Baghdad.

She approaches these themes as if, having frequented the brothel reserved for the exclusive use of the kingdom's officials, she could discuss it. The truth, however, is that she understands little about the carnal tissue that, in contact with the skin of another, tends to fray under the impact of successive quivers. It disturbs her to note the damage that lovemaking produces. Given the delirium of the body, she can do nothing but withdraw from the amorous drama, unable to control the conduct of beings dominated by passion. She fears participating in a spectacle composed of falsely symmetrical spasms and fused, desperate bodies.

This does not deter Scheherazade from confronting the good and evil that surrounds her and her characters. Nevertheless, the human contagion that her stories impose exhausts her. Such a craft, judging from what she knows, has uncertain rules, and at any misstep the Caliph will send her to her death.

12

She eats slowly. She welcomes the food with the aid of bread, accommodating it in the palm of her hand as she thinks. Already, at this first meal, Scheherazade commands the words she utters. In the midst of the ablutions, her body imbued with essences, she establishes to her satisfaction the direction of the story. And though revered like a queen by the many slaves under Jasmine's command, Scheherazade is not the mistress of daily life, much less of the immediate future.

In her anxiety to free herself from the death sentence hovering over her, she must halt the narrative at first light, after taking care to reveal the fragility of narrative passion. In so doing, she will cast the hook that will spear the Caliph's heart with the latent intrigue of the plot so that the sovereign suffers the asphyxiating agony of a truth to be revealed only the following night.

In the service of her craft, man's time, marked by a hypothetical hourglass, is fragile. The minutes she foresees, before sunrise, are based on misunderstanding. As soon as Scheherazade determines the path and the oscillations of the story, she fears that life will flee her control. Her nights, always sleepless, block the immediate perception of fate. Under a threat whose graveness surpasses her ingenuity, she must make a plan, however subject to strategic interruptions.

Jasmine brings her infusions, teas, liquids that mitigate anxiety. She glides across the marble, supple as the snow-white snake that slithers through the desert sands leaving sinuous trails. But despite her pains and the watchfulness of Dinazarda, Scheherazade hesitates to decree the epilogue of the tale or rigorously mark the extent of a story with only scant minutes before dawn.

The onrushing reality of time terrifies her. Her efficiency in creating the characters hints, however, that the horizon line is fleeting. So she is forced to endow the heroes with further resources, filigrees, spirals just to keep them on the scene, visible to the Caliph. But if, on the one hand, such arabesques indicate skill, what will happen if they fail to achieve the desired effect?

The fear of death makes her tremble. But she forges ahead undaunted, for there is still much to relate. Her imagination, subject to the ebb and flow of the tide, presses her ceaselessly. Subjugated to the volatile character of the Caliph, she folds and multiplies the mesh of the plot, envelops her characters in the tunic of humanity woven in the streets of Baghdad.

Spared once again in the sparkling morning, Scheherazade refuses to celebrate the life so indifferently conferred on her. She accepts the delicacies because she is hungry. The lamb on the tray is served with a garland of herbs around its head, reminding her of her own, which may soon be severed by the executioner. At times her life, far from the pomp of nobility, strikes her as miserable. She welcomes the salted olives, come from trees that nearly witnessed the birth of the Islamic empire. Their meat and their oil feed the poor of the caliphate. As a princess, Scheherazade is an arduous daughter of the desert, a scion of the medina. Why not try, before death, the cookies known as gazelle's horns, which enhance young people's evenings?

Scheherazade resists. Unprotected before the sovereign, with whom she shares only a bed, she yearns for her words to awaken in him the notion of adventure, akin to the very act of living. She recognizes that her plan is a failure in the hands of the Caliph. She thinks of her father, who circulates around the kingdom and the rooms of the palace, forever baiting traps, seeking out the guilty. In the eyes of the public, he is a contradictory figure engaged in hateful defense of the caliphate.

For years he has kept the position of vizier at the cost of an oft-tested talent that brings him endless humiliation. In a place unknown to his daughter he awaits the confirmation of that death, a silent distress that hastens his old age and dishonor.

Wherever he is now, who will hear the sound of his ragged breathing? In the solitude of the palace, safe from the Caliph, her father pants, a cornered animal searching for the air that eludes him, unresigned to the tragedy poised to descend upon his house.

13

Nor does the Caliph dispose of the mysteries ratified in the shadow of the throne, of a power that cannot shield him from distress. Neither can it shield him from the memory of the Sultana who, by sating her lust with slaves and sullying the royal bed with alien seed, was indifferent to their depositing in her womb a spurious substance and thus attributing to the Caliph an improper paternity.

Despite his ruling the Caliphate of Baghdad, dishonor, which pursues him even today, inflicts distorted ideas of reality. How to trust the female who, even under surveillance, shames him before his subjects? He has vowed that no woman will ever again betray him, but to uphold his word he must condemn to death each wife who shares his bed. Leaving his arms, she must go immediately to the headsman's blade.

He grants no future to these young women and shows them no gratitude for their having known copulation through him. Though painful, his decision prevents any vile act against him in the future. Having no intention of rescinding an unpopular decree, he rebuffed the appeal from a neighboring leader who, fearful of rebellion, invoked religious precepts and the need to absolve those who were presumably innocent. The insidious apologia to conjugal love from the respected bey had no effect on the Caliph's decision.

To confront the reactions calling for him to cancel the measure, the Caliph has forbidden any discussion of it, even promising to apply the same punishment to anyone who acts against his interests. And let none dare consider his decision the weakness of a deeply wounded heart incapable of overcoming the embitterment of betrayal.

Long immune to feelings, he has denied women the key to love. Especially now, when the twilight of life, by acquainting him slowly with the ritual of death itself, has granted him the prerogatives of solitude.

Scheherazade, however, a voluntary victim in this endless chain of murdered young women, remains watchful. The Caliph's narrowed eyes, almost a horizontal line, render him inscrutable. The disguised cunning with which he rubs the back of his hand against his lips, as if to rid himself of an irksome speck in the corner of his mouth, reveals the deliberate effort to contemplate the enemy without being seen. Scheherazade's tentative impression of him first fades, safeguarded behind the imperial seat, then surges tensely, when he notices that others would divine his inner traits.

Under Scheherazade's vigilance, the Caliph softens his expression. He denies her the right to discern which of his gestures stem from favor or disfavor. He longs for a description befitting his lineage, one that would proclaim him an agreeable man whose moderation is the sign of a just ruler. An image, framed by his beard, that exudes a scent of sandalwood and when reproduced in the popular imagination becomes the inspiring iconography of his legend, becomes—whether in the bazaar, in the desert, or in homes by the kettle—the protagonist of the tales that circulate among Bedouins and merchants. The object of a cult, like Harun ar-Rashid.

Although he yearns for popularity, he dislikes contact with the people. Near a crowd, generally kept at a distance, he never knows whether to smile at them or wave his right hand, whose fingers hold rings as symbols of his authority. An Abbasid like Harun, he cannot easily duplicate the deeds of the ruler who more than any other enjoyed the babble of the marketplace for the mere pleasure of experiencing human emotions.

His temperament, incompatible with mundane life, isolates him from anyone who is not of use for administering the caliphate. At the slightest pretext, in a sudden outburst, he might abruptly abandon the audience room and wander through the halls, followed by his guards. Such a measure might last until nightfall, in total disregard for the visitors waiting for him in the audience room. A stroll might be interrupted to sip the tea provided him wherever he was. At such times no one can address him or consult him about pending matters. With his turban low on his head, practically covering his eyes, his anxieties go unnoticed.

The Caliph's behavior intimidates the courtiers, and his intransigence has become more accentuated since the betrayal by the licentious Sultana and with the series of innocent deaths, which have engendered absurd tales, with each courtier reflecting upon the peculiarity of his methods of inflicting punishment. It was said that once, bellowing terrible cries, perhaps in repentance of his crimes, he had tried to throw himself from the palace balcony into the inner courtyard, after first having bathed in the blood of a young woman he had murdered with his own hands, careful to smear the already viscous liquid on his genitalia as a belated orgasm.

Enclosed in his cocoon, the Caliph provokes an opposite action from Scheherazade. After defeating death for another day, she vigorously exercises the masterful art of seduction. It is all a pretext for unveiling the future, wherever it might be, even when she polishes a copper tray in the hope that the images of Sinbad and Zoneida will appear on its surface.

The Caliph wishes to see her bowed by fear, defeated. He looks in her eyes for signs of anguish over his verdict, which he fails to find. Even so, he persists in intimidating her so that the accounts, arising from that fright, will be replenished and make him happy. He has overlooked, however, that there has perhaps developed among his subjects a romantic rebellion aimed at stimulating the imagination, thanks to Scheherazade's stories.

The Caliph's silence worries Scheherazade. Instinct suggests that she should reconcile with the sovereign, concern herself with the strength of his rancor by conceding a narrative that penetrates his unfathomable enigma and pleases him. But her prospects are less than auspicious. The Caliph becomes haughty, speaking to her of death as a pleasurable fact. He admonishes her to take care, saying that if she doesn't offer continuing proof of ingenuity he will rip out her heart, as he has done with the others.

These scenes, witnessed by Jasmine, prompt the slave to assuage Scheherazade's suffering with modest initiatives. She observes that as each night approaches the princess sighs as if it were a battle cry. This is the way she perfects resources, overcomes obstacles, looking for the pearl that Sinbad promised could be found at the bottom of the sea.

Dinazarda too, seeing her sister so close to being sacrificed, rebels. But unable to poison the Caliph and escape unscathed, she feigns resignation. She shows indifference to the drama of a Scheherazade who transmits to the sovereign the keys of human imagination. She resorts to the flourishing and singular archive of memory to discourse on the narrative universe that men, once slaves of darkness and fear, have constructed since the days of the caves, which not even the light of fires could later vanquish.

Ever since Scheherazade had enunciated her first sentence, under the watchful eye of Fatima, who, staff in hand, drove away ghosts and evil genies, the young woman had evolved vertiginously. To this end she orchestrates phrases, shaping them sumptuously, capturing the adventures that hypnotize the Caliph.

He notes that the woman stimulates emotions, the insidiousness with which she shamelessly moves among the hidden spaces of the lives of people like Sinbad and Zoneida, with no respect for limits. Scheherazade does not allow these creatures to elude her persuasive power. Although dazzled by these characters that she maintains intact within the bell glass of the story, the Caliph resists, at times wanting to cast them into the dungeon, tie their feet, their fingers, just to cancel out the commotion in Scheherazade's brain.

Subject to the sovereign's will, she allows nothing to hold her back. Fragile and alone, Scheherazade proceeds with adventures whose outcome foresees the distribution of bread and fantasy in the square in Baghdad. It is her ruin and her good fortune to grieve and be moved by characters that have sprung from her heart. For, like them, she too has suffered from the agony of improvising.

14

Insolent in her storytelling, Scheherazade is circumspect in bed. Wrapped in silk sheets, she yields parts of her body to the Caliph. After copulation, Jasmine covers her with delicate fabrics that shield her discreet panting.

The Caliph obeys her rules, respecting her modesty. Upon gaining access to the young woman's soft, snow-white flesh, he places his hand over her womb, where life is born, probes it as if visiting sheltered viscera. With a gesture devoid of rapture, he accommodates himself to the shape of her body, finally sliding down to her pubis. In pursuit of swift pleasure, for he is in a hurry, he penetrates the hidden area of her vulva with his phallus.

At the end of this copulation, like the others, from which the Caliph removes himself efficiently, Dinazarda and Jasmine, behind the screen, reclaim the territory from which they were expelled, where Scheherazade awaits them. Still on the bed, her eyes closed, she allows them to cover her with silks and affection. Dressed again, the Vizier's daughter enhances the details of the story she is about to begin.

The Caliph accepts some fruit and slices of cold lamb. As he eats, he prepares to listen, avoiding looking at her. He doesn't explain why, following coitus, he is ill at ease with the young woman, as if he needs to erase the memory of the recent intimacy. Perhaps it is because he has executed a mechanical act in bed, an act whose realism, compared to Scheherazade's accounts, lacks grandeur.

The young woman, however, a disciple of the Caliph in the art of hiding feelings, excludes from her gaze the figure of the sovereign, as if he doesn't exist for her and the reasons for his embarrassment cease to be. Without intent to offend him, she returns to Baghdad, once again the center of her story. Amin is concerned about her inconstancy. He is a character who, falling in love with exaggerated frequency, relishes his own frivolity as part of the amorous battle. He revels in leaving behind, wherever he goes, traces of the sins he commits.

As Scheherazade proceeds with Amin, whose way of life she no doubt finds dangerous, Dinazarda, by coughing insistently, sends warning signs. She signals that she considers her sister unmotivated in her work, barely covering aspects of Amin's temperament that should be appealing to the Caliph, precisely because the ruler is so different from that young adventurer. Schehcrazade has overlooked perilous voids, which she must fill while there is still time. Dinazarda reacts, therefore, to her sister's obscure eclipses, which give the impression that Scheherazade, eager to accompany Amin, has distanced herself from the chambers, at the risk of not soon returning.

Perhaps Dinazarda exaggerates in judging Scheherazade inept in the development of that segment of the story, not giving her a few minutes to present details of the plot in accordance with what had been planned during the afternoon. She is expressing her growing displeasure at not being consulted by Scheherazade as has been the custom in the past.

She resents the fact that Scheherazade has excluded her from her decisions, as if she lacks the prestige to affect the fulcrum of her stories. Angered by this absence of consideration, she yanks from Jasmine's hands the basin of hot water to which the slave had added essences, intended for the storyteller. She plunges her feet into it in search of the relief her own sister has denied her. The heat, rising from her soles, evokes the illusion of roaming through Scheherazade's imagination, still busying itself with Amin. Calmer now, she finds joy in reaping the benefits of her sister's imagination, as if it were hers as well, inherited from the mother who had bequeathed this gift to her daughters.

Scheherazade adds new characteristics to Amin's latest fiancée, whom he is about to abandon after swearing eternal love. While she attracts the Caliph's attention, she forgives the resentment of Dinazarda, who did not hesitate to follow her to the palace despite the grave risks. They loved each other and cherished an intense memory of family. At the sight of certain objects, they would weep at the same time, looking for a relationship to the treasures they had inherited from their mother. And sometimes, in the afternoon when the sun illuminated the chambers, they would speak of the family life they had left behind and the memories each of them had of their mother.

Dinazarda, as firstborn, retained more information about the mother who seemed never to abandon them. The image of their mother, so clear at times, stood out amid the shadows. She moved toward it, but the figure faded, after promising to return at another time. She felt then the urgency to tell Scheherazade that she alone had inherited from the woman who bore them the harmonious face framed by dark hair. For, slight and fair like her mother, with an intense gaze, Scheherazade was beyond doubt the living image of her mother. But was it really as everyone said? Or was Dinazarda merely imagining this similarity to assuage her longing for her mother? To comply with the desires of the dead to see themselves falsely reconstituted by those who survived them?

The dry season is accentuated by the heat. The slave women replenish the water in the jars, prepare baths, and wave gigantic fans about them. Summer steals their air, which is returned at night by the breeze or by the strong rains of the season. Scheherazade takes numerous baths, pushing aside the base thoughts that asphyxiate her. Dinazarda and Jasmine struggle to clear the atmosphere, wishing to save her. Any cry from the storyteller, even as an exercise to give vent to her anguish, might help her. After all, Scheherazade hasn't yet been assured that her life will once more be spared at dawn.

And as proof that life is smiling on them daily, the Caliph sends them gifts, garments of blue satin, of scarlet and ochre silk, of purple cotton, offered by merchants who, aware of his prodigality, vie to merit his favor. Dinazarda runs her fingers over the bejeweled cloths, raises them to her cheek, at the risk of the stones' scratching her. She delivers the silk to Scheherazade, curious to know the route of the caravan, what the fabric tells her of the fearful journey to Baghdad after having faced storms of snow and sand. She brings it to her ear, enraptured that such fineness, coming from a cocoon, should at the end be exuded by the worm and transformed into material of such indescribable texture.

Under any pretext, Scheherazade's imagination makes the world speak. She emanates such veracity as to leave her listeners pale. It is her intention to make the Caliph suffer whenever she introduces him to her creatures and he becomes a participant in the pain of others. And could it be otherwise? How could she spare him the confessions whose purpose is to both broaden and narrow his heart?

Scheherazade caresses the cloths, listening to what they tell her. Coming from the suffering hands of women, experts in the art of embroidery, some of them show landscapes, domestic scenes, signs of happiness—in short, all that is dear to the burning fantasy of men.

Fatima used to tell her that some cloths displayed an unhappy fate. An example well known in Baghdad had happened to a Hindu slave woman. Fascinated by a formal gown, she had put it on in the dark of night, not thinking that in so doing she was usurping the fortune of the princess for whom the garment was intended. Caught in the act, the young woman was immediately dislodged from her dream and despite her repentance was dragged pitilessly to the scaffold.

Scheherazade discerns in her garments the footsteps of women. She struggles to locate the secrets of the artisans, of tormented souls, each in its domestic exile. She fears going too far, thrusting herself too deeply into the life of another, and worries that the weeping of Amin's fiancée, whom he abandoned without a word of consolation, will steal her humanity. But what to do in such cases? After all, she bears the burden of speaking for the pariahs of Baghdad, the pirates of the Indian Ocean, the victorious and the vanquished. She cannot be unfaithful to them or expel them from the hell and paradise of her stories. She cannot fail to offer them the only dwelling where they breathe and shine.

15

Jasmine is beautiful and a slave. She serves the two sisters with the illusion of having been born into the powerful family of the Vizier. In her dreams, adrift and hopeless, she craves belonging to the people of Scheherazade and Dinazarda.

Raised in the desert amid sheep, even today, years later, she rubs her skin with pumice stone from the sea to rid herself of the smell of the animals that nestle in her soul. And as she sighs listening to Scheherazade's stories, she sees her life and that of her ancestors. She is intrigued that the princess, who is not part of her race, knows better than she the spirit of her clan and transmits the plots as if speaking with the voice of the Bedouins.

By agreement, the sisters allow Jasmine to share the intimacy of their chambers, practically living there even when the Caliph returns from the throne room. They consent to Jasmine's benefiting from the alliance that Scheherazade establishes between the aristocracy of Baghdad and the world of the marketplace. In her simple view, the Vizier's daughters imagine themselves in the medina buying pistachios and goat cheese, swept up in the smell of sandalwood mixed with ambergris, the essence from the whale that Sinbad had captured for them.

From the beginning, Jasmine had distinguished herself from the other slaves. When the young women were installed in the chambers, Jasmine had shown perseverance in serving them, through kindnesses that demonstrated her feelings. Incorporated into the small court, she would extend her stay among them beyond the necessary hours, doing so by appearing during the night with small services. As this sometimes made it late for her to return to the servants' quarters, Dinazarda, taking pity on her, would insist she stay on the bed beside her, behind the screen.

Jasmine's devotion, expressed in every detail, moved the sisters, who no longer knew how to inhibit her excesses or reduce the time she spent among them. But when they ordered her back to the slave quarters, they missed her when she was slow to return. Used to her company, they came more and more to value the small comforts that Jasmine, unlike anyone else, bestowed on them and that they now could not do without. After her daily duties, they assigned her tasks that required her full-time presence.

Unlike Jasmine, who lived in poverty, Scheherazade had been born in a golden cradle in her father's house. After the premature death of his wife, he had handed his younger daughter over to Fatima, whom he ordered to do whatever was necessary with her, but he recommended that she never leave the palace, even if she were in the future to insist on visiting the old bazaar. It was as if the Vizier foresaw that his daughter, drawn by adventure, would thrust herself into the abysms of Baghdad, promptly establishing an alliance with the city's sinners. He did not take into account that when the moment arrived for Scheherazade to emerge from the cocoon, the paternal interdiction would hasten her curiosity and steal his sleep.

Through the years, curious to know the territory her father disdained and therefore designated as a zone of danger, Scheherazade bombarded Fatima with questions. She insisted she tell her about the market, which for her was becoming a world that, although unknown, represented the people of her city.

Fatima tried to resist. Recalling the Vizier's warnings, she emphasized the dangers present in that part of Baghdad. But the more she talked about a city populated with the cant of thieves, assassins, merchants, and the evil-natured, the more Scheherazade, crying plaintively or in anger, demanded to see for herself the unexpected curves of the alleyways, the marketplace itself, where it seemed to her that her imagination had been born. She longed to cross the boundaries of the forbidden geography that occupied her fantasy.

The influence of the marketplace quickly became a presence in her first stories. She would describe Baghdad with such acuity that Fatima, her only listener, was impressed. The scenes that took place there, told in her still evolving voice, showed such unrestricted fidelity to the medina that Fatima wondered whether some magician, in the name of good and evil, was dictating the details to her. Or whether her mother, from the kingdom of death, whispered precious information to her. That girl, despite the jewels, the veils, from a fine family, did not seem to be of the nobility. Beyond a shadow of a doubt, she had a soul polished on the stone of the Arab imagination.

As witness to the happenings in the palace, Jasmine refuses to describe to the other slaves, who lack access to the chambers, the nature of the drama in which she participates thanks to the Vizier's daughters. And she also avoids, in all circumstances, evoking the sisters' pity by showing any desire to one day return to her family, who are surely now dead or scattered in the desert, though at an earlier time they had all lived in tents frayed by the wind. She thinks of them frequently, wishing to tell them that she serves Princess Scheherazade, wife to the Caliph of Baghdad. She lives at her side, at the cost of her narratives. For she does nothing but tell stories to the sovereign. They too, such incredulous nomads, would be enchanted with her, despite their precarious knowledge of the Islamic world. But let them know, from this moment on, that this princess, a true herald of the imagination typical of the desert, can utilize like no other the rupestrine and guttural sounds of the language, the typical speech of the caravans, the scattered tribes, the forlorn Bedouins.

The Caliph barely looks at Jasmine, ascribing no importance to her. He doesn't know that she bears in her bosom mysteries typical of the nation he governs. Accustomed to infinite horizons where human significance is reduced to a grain of sand, Jasmine resigns herself to the Caliph's indifference. She takes refuge behind the screen, next to Dinazarda. When she is able to sleep, she is grateful for blessings received. And on her own initiative, as an exercise, she adds to certain parts of Scheherazade's account a cunning originating from the entangled genealogy of Semites, Hindus, Aramaeans—wandering peoples who were everywhere at the same time.

Returning to Scheherazade's side, she is enchanted once more with the storyteller's depth, which remains undeterred in the face of obstacles. When she recounts, she all but drinks Jasmine's blood whenever she needs to extract the secrets of her tribe. Unceremoniously, Scheherazade takes possession of the plots housed in that captive heart, or of whoever comes in her path. It is in this manner that Scheherazade roams among the water vendors, the snake charmers, the dentists who exhibit like trophies the teeth pulled from heroes and famous assassins.

Scheherazade had not always depended on reinforcement brought her by one or another slave. Her febrile imagination, by itself, without the help of anyone, formed its own judgment about things. How often Fatima and she would go resolutely to the market, at once claiming a spot near the rhapsodists, who wore amulets and exhibited chests tattooed with elements to ward off evildoers and whose occupation was telling lies with an honest face.

They also met an old man, a ragged Tuareg who because of his advanced age bumped into objects, making it more difficult to cut fine shavings of watermelon with the same knife he once used to slice open the heads of bitter enemies. Always talking to himself, he attracted buyers to his stall while he repeated extolling catchphrases, all evoking Harun ar-Rashid.

Despite his neglected appearance, the result of poverty and adversity, the old man became impassioned at the memory of the legendary Abbasid caliph. At the same time, driven by inexplicable vanity, he would mention his own talent, thanks to which he stayed alive. In telling his stories, he demonstrated a clear preference for the adulterers who, merely from the sin of confusing the symptoms of lust with love, easily fell into misfortune. And, his vocal cords nearly broken from exertion, he convinced himself that in paradise there was a place for those who, having been victims of the passions that obscured the senses, dared bravely to venture along the edges of the abyss of evil.

Impressed by stories like those of the melon vendor, Scheherazade had kept the memories like relics. Plots that had blossomed far from the family nucleus were to her as transparent as any other. For her, there was no excellence in an account merely because it boasted noble provenance. Her merit as storyteller consisted of adding to each of her tales allusions, raptures, images—everything that had crystallized in the manuscripts and minds of Baghdad.

She had always demanded the right to recount whatever she pleased, and the art of narration had only matured by her moving fearlessly amid the bog of improvised words. Thus her insistence on imprecise planning susceptible to sudden changes, as if each sentence imposed by any means at hand had a law of its own. It was a unique wisdom, with which she imprinted direction on the story that, precisely that night, would evoke disquietude in the Caliph.

In the afternoon, sensitive to the sounds of Dinazarda and Jasmine, she finds it difficult to concentrate. She has much to do, such as untying certain knots that prevent her from taking flight. Not to mention that, especially in the scene when Zoneida, maddened by her lover's ingratitude, turns her back on him, Scheherazade must create conditions so that the listeners will weep over the woman's misfortunes, while at no time forgetting the emotions common to all human beings.

But as the Caliph will soon be returning to the chambers, Scheherazade has other urgencies to which she must attend as well: how to balance, in the correct dosage, the despair and hope of certain characters inclined toward exaggeration without compromising the naturalness that should flow among them all.

Contrary to what is said about the Vizier's younger daughter, her imagination, fed by the incunabula and scrolls brought to her home by the sages of Baghdad, depends greatly on the words that come from her gut. It is as if in the hot and airless hollow of her insides lies a manuscript from which she reads as she speaks.

In the whirlwind of so many plots still to weave, Scheherazade behaves before the Caliph like a false prophetess who, though able to divine the world, is incapable of understanding her own life. She seems to be someone who, amid the pain, forces herself to form a collage of real events in order to graft them onto the psyche of Aladdin in doses that do not affect her life.

Chained also to Sinbad's ship, now anchored beside the dock of the Caliph's chambers, she wonders whether she can boast of the same freedom that she attributes to the impassioned mariner. Is giving rein to imagination enough to redeem her?

She feels unprotected, without means of entering the dark mouth of the mystery to light in this desolate and barren land the fire to illuminate a soul now in shadow.

16

In her thoughts she journeys through Baghdad. In the same way, she transports herself about the world, with no one reining in her flight of imagination. Back in the chambers, she obeys the basic rule of not distancing herself for a single moment from her stories.

Going to the market with Fatima, she had learned that in order to seduce the listener it was advisable to introduce pauses for breath, to give one's words a touch of sinfulness. Even when selling a pomegranate with its golden splendor, it was necessary to dramatize the mundane, to make the buyer see that the fruit, because it came from Asia, had the attribute of enlarging the meager breasts of the Caliph's favorites.

Quite early she had created expectations around any theme, from the lamps of Aladdin to the masts of Sinbad's ship. She wandered easily among the beehives in her father's orchard, which provided the ideal architecture in which to find the honey-coated keys to open a story.

Scheherazade has accepted Jasmine at her feet like a mastiff that disguises its ferocity in exchange for devotion. She offers no admonitions when Jasmine distracts her from her work. The slave doesn't suppress her desire to replace the memory of Fatima in the princess's soul and to take part in Scheherazade's rapture, especially when the princess, tripping on the words that gush from her lips, suddenly reins them in to maintain the coveted harmony of the whole.

Dinazarda interrupts Jasmine's reverie. She enters and leaves the chambers, concealing from her sister something that reduces her to tears and contributes to the revelation of a cruel reality about to descend on them. At best she represents, always in reduced scale, a poor copy of the drama. It is already enough to live under the constant threat of death decreed by a caliph who, embroiled in ruses and betrayals, remains indifferent to Scheherazade's efforts to lend veracity to the diverse voices of her creatures and impart cunning to her stories.

Exhausted, Scheherazade motions Jasmine away. The effort to confront dilemmas and conflicts coming from all sides drains her, and to that are added private pains. Leaning against the pillows, at last alone, she searches for meaning in what she had related the night before. It seems to her that she will only cause Aladdin to scintillate tonight if she has him assume a different role, beyond that of lamp vendor. Perhaps she should make him into a prince, despite the contrast with his rustic ways. Under her tutelage, teaching him how to blink his eyes, hold the muscles of his face, he learns to convey convincing shrewdness.

Scheherazade recognizes that her role as storyteller is not productive. It is, after all, a craft long since relegated to obscurity, earning its practitioners little pay. And for that reason it is exercised in the bazaar by the luckless, those touched by indomitable melancholy. Nothing more than a mere storyteller, she carries in her saddlebags a handful of plots that emanate an aroma of the people. She is anonymous and, had she not been born a princess, would today live in poverty.

She sees, over the years, that she is part of a race that, though disdained by the learned masters of the Qur'an schools, dares to locate its stories in the alleyways of the medina, drawn by the smells of cooking, by sweaty bodies, by the promise of immortality. She wins in exchange, thanks to her fidelity, the privilege of being a woman, a man, a rock, lamb, mint, the genie in the bottle, all conditions at the same time, feeling each of them with the same intensity.

She has always loved the undying silence of those beings of the desert who, when praising the Prophet, hold their breath because it is easy for them to give up their lives if necessary. Scheherazade, however, does not live in the sphere of faith. To her restive nature, religion does not constitute a vocation. On the contrary, focused on the banality of daily life, she long ago turned away from the divine plane to cast herself into the fury of the characters who ravage her imagination. Smiling at the idea of anything other than her creatures pacifying her soul, she allows Jasmine to approach and once again keep her company.

17

Scheherazade's voice echoes through the palace, arriving at the kitchen and mingling with the herbs vigorously rubbed against the flesh of the sheep rotating over the coals. Each servant of the empire tears off chunks from the meat and the half-heard words, unable to foresee the conclusion of the stories.

The art that she exercises at bedside owes part of its fiction to the life of the Baghdad marketplace and to the accounts conceived in the seraglios of Arab palaces, where the favorites recorded their frustrations in symbolic words, hidden from their masters—words that, transmitted from mother to daughter, established basic parameters among their successors in the Caliph's harem. Many of these stories, sad and repetitive despite originating from an individual sacrifice, lent weight to a universe that, well exploited, had afforded Scheherazade an unlimited repertoire.

Sensitive to the morning gestures that come to her after the Caliph spares her life, Scheherazade sips with relief the mint tea brought by Jasmine. The slave, as she places the copper tray with the teapot and glasses on the low table near the storyteller, is unaware of the emblematic meaning of each object. But Scheherazade, who watches her closely, doesn't reveal to her that the tray, which Jasmine caresses as if preserving the memory of her tribe, represents the earth, while the teapot, for some unfathomable reason, is the sky. And the glasses, perhaps because they contain the liquid, are the rain that for anyone living in the desert is a gift from Allah.

Jasmine moves about, wanting to be appreciated. She sates her morning thirst with the hope of saving Scheherazade in the days that follow. She alternates with the other slave women in serving the sisters, but she is the only one who is close to them. It has not always been that way, however. In the beginning, neither of the

Vizier's daughters paid her any mind or distinguished her face from those of the other slaves. Undiscouraged, Jasmine had hovered around, performing small favors, bringing them whatever they requested. Within a few days the sisters had come to demand her company, a dispute even arising between them over the slave with tawny skin and long legs. Dinazarda, especially, demanded continuous attention. Perhaps her observant temperament was due to not having had in childhood a tutor as devoted as Fatima— or to not having understood from an early age that Scheherazade's brilliance shaded everyone around her, not allowing them to shine. In the palace, Dinazarda uses having to live under the constant threat of losing her sister as justification for her outbursts.

The poison inflicted on Dinazarda in these circumstances affects Scheherazade as well. To compensate her sister for the suffering for which she feels responsible, Scheherazade wraps her arms around Dinazarda's shoulders, brings her head to her breast, and frees Jasmine to serve her. The struggle she is waging with the Caliph provokes in her a pessimism that surges against her will. She concentrates solely on the taciturn man with whom she goes to bed and who, at night, obliges her to invent fables for no reason at all—and who, despite demanding from her an extravagant fantasy, shows disdain for anything that contradicts the logic and coherence with which he rules over his caliphate.

Dinazarda recovers from her jealousy. Strolling through the palace, she renews her vows of love to her sister without neglecting her defense. In the mornings, awaiting the Caliph's announcement of Scheherazade's fate, she kisses her with abstracted tenderness. She wishes to rob the kiss of its tragic immanence. It is futile to warn her of the dangers that surround her discourse, for Scheherazade acts at times as if saving herself were not a priority. But the confidence she expresses in her skill moves Dinazarda. That storyteller knows better than anyone how to brandish before the immutable face of the Caliph the commotions and the reveries that assail her characters, making him see that he too is at risk of perishing with the death of each being she invents.

As the result of a temporary dispute, Jasmine is intimidated. She fears being sacrificed in the middle of an unjust decision. She reads in Dinazarda's face her anxiety about Scheherazade's future, the fragility that surrounds that life. She trusts, however, that by avoiding the lacunae of memory, the princess will bypass the dangers that emerge in the course of the story. But how could a storyteller, despite the diabolical resources of her talent, deprive herself of the surprises of art? How could she seduce the Caliph if she lacks the autonomy that only material forged in lies can assure her?

Alongside these domestic disagreements, Scheherazade shuffles feelings that, inside or outside the story, brush against the sovereign's troubled heart. With fierce instinct she uses discretion, evading the chaos that springs from her uncertainty. As challenging as her characters, Scheherazade insists that Aladdin and Zoneida, being mere mortals, bow under the weight of individual destiny.

Scheherazade zealously respects the rituals of the craft. Though skirting the cruelty emanating from the Caliph, she acknowledges the blow that he may inflict upon her for any reason. Despite the kind hearts of her sister and the slave woman at her side, she suddenly weakens, feeling she is drowning, unsafe. But she notes the effort with which Jasmine defends her life. Everything about the slave allies itself to forces alien to the human drama, as if it were easy for her to visit her tribe, even in exile, and return from the spectacle of poverty beautiful and revitalized, pretending to belong to an opulent people.

In Scheherazade's shadow, Jasmine watches the hours slip away. Often, in a desire to encourage the sisters, she attributes to them a power that belongs to the Caliph. Her role is merely to transmit to the Vizier's daughters what they need to know, such as the smell of the stables, of the cellars. To retrieve to the royal chambers the odor of an impious and suffering humanity.

Wherever she goes, the voices of Scheherazade's people pursue Jasmine. While she transports objects, clothes, food, from the kitchen, which had been her home, to the chambers, from whose elegance she had been mercilessly excluded since birth, she finds it difficult to resist encirclement by the world. On the other hand, through the force of the princess's imagination she once again hears the bleating of goats, the Bedouins, nomads like her. She sees herself back in the family tent, whose details she recomposes in memory. Inside the tent, accompanied by sweating shepherds who pant and groan as one, Jasmine contemplates the ceiling, drawn by the delicate balance of the framework, a work done with fine strips woven from the wool and hair of animals and stitched from one edge to the other, and the canopy, whose weight is supported on the roof ridge by broad and taut straps, attached by ropes to stakes, to resist the wind.

She remembers the briefness of the days, of the life that was dismantled, and soon they were moving through the desert erecting the itinerant dwelling according to their needs. The family tent reflected poverty, unlike those of rich tribes with their splendid cushions, ringed by gilded spheres symbolizing the chief's authority and power. The oil lamps, poorly lighting her mother's wrinkled face, could not hide the threadbare carpets that, hanging from the roof ridge, separated the members of the tribe by sex.

Now suffocated by the luxury of the Caliph's palace, Jasmine exalts the footstool, the embroidery frame, the folding bed, items brought by her mother when she married her father. The simple remembrance brings the past flooding back, pursuing her with the intense smell of the newborn goats that slept among them so they wouldn't stray.

Prior to being sold under circumstances never revealed, Jasmine would yield furiously to reveries before succumbing to sleep. Upon waking, she would leave the tent and go in search of cities buried under the dunes. She hoped to discover, peeking from some crater, a palace with a facade carved from stone, whose long-opaque vault would open by a magical mechanism to allow her to contemplate the heavens.

Jasmine confides in no one. However, the madness that flits through her soul attracts Scheherazade, who observes how she reconstitutes a universe from which she had been cruelly cast out. And she, the Vizier's daughter, sees herself incapable of dealing with Jasmine's losses, even as she feels compassion for her sorrows.

Although excluded from the intrigue, Dinazarda hurriedly puts her arm around Jasmine, breathing the perfume that the slave woman emanates, leaving a scent that might bother the Caliph, who at that instant crosses the threshold of the chambers, distant from the women's anguish. He looks at them, and makes no gesture that favors Scheherazade's daily struggle to save herself. He demands only that the young woman accommodate in her internal landscape the greatest possible number of creatures, animals, and minerals—and above all that she not forget to shape the soul of her characters in order to better adapt them to the tales she is to relate. This fact alone interests him. Because of this he has left the audience room early, ceasing to decree the fate of his subjects, ignoring the concubines in his harem, renouncing the hunt and the hawk perched on his shoulder. In the face of what he has given up, let Scheherazade begin, wasting no time, telling what has finally happened to Sinbad, imperiled with shipwreck on his seventh voyage.

18

The Caliph showers attention on Dinazarda, confident that the young woman, despite her passionate defense of Scheherazade, will not turn against him. He appreciates, therefore, how at his first advance, leading Scheherazade to the bed, she averts her gaze and heads toward the screen.

Even though she retires from the scene, into the far reaches of the chambers, Dinazarda participates in the amorous frolics that ignite her fantasy. At her side, Jasmine, indefatigably diligent, invents pretexts to remain in those quarters formed by rooms united by arches, all of them integrated into the central nucleus, which has the bed as its axis.

Designated to serve the sisters, Jasmine has from the beginning made an effort to be noticed, fetching delicacies and accounts from the kitchen. She brings Scheherazade, who never abandons that wing of the palace, samples from the garden in the form of petals floating on the surface of the water in the large wooden vessel. And because of vivid memories of punishments and humiliations suffered, she does everything possible not to be reprimanded. To this end, she has assimilated the habits of the court, wishing to pass for an Ethiopian princess who had lived amid the dunes. She began with the elegant walk, in which her feet barely rise from the floor as she glances about, attentive to every detail. But, although she is familiar with palace life, what stands out in the slave is pride at having belonged in the past to an opposite reality, whose rules were dictated by the breath of scarcity and hope.

After a few minutes, Dinazarda loses interest in Jasmine's allusions to her family history. It matters little to her whether the slave, prior to captivity, came from desert nobility and had therefore entertained some sultan whom she planned to marry, or whether he was a prosperous gentleman who, because of ambition, had sold her to slave traders in exchange for magnificent sorrels.

From Jasmine she expects reports of the happenings in Baghdad, that the slave discover, without Scheherazade's knowledge, the degree of truth in the intrigues that make their way to them, generally fomented by the people, with the goal of driving away poverty. Thanks to the good relations the slave woman has with the stablemen, guards, and cooks, she can easily recount to Dinazarda details of a day-to-day life that appears seductive to the sisters.

Urged to contribute a daily dose of slander, Jasmine does not shy from prolonging the conversation time she has, especially with Dinazarda, always focusing on stories originating in the cellars of the palace. And when she wishes to shine in the princesses' eyes and move them, Jasmine combines aspects of life with the use of popular catchphrases.

Suddenly elevated to the category of modest narrator, Jasmine is touched. She is grateful that Dinazarda doesn't interrupt her ramblings by demanding cultured words. Even if she so desired, she would have no way of renouncing the dimension the desert has imprinted on her spirit. For despite the young women's approval, she must never violate the rules that govern the princesses. She has also learned, since her nomadic life, that it is not good to trust human beings who employ ruses as a means of defending themselves. Each of them, protecting the secret tracks of their respective hearts, nurtures contradictory feelings that are the source of profound disquiet.

In the course of a single day, the three young women would suffer various turnarounds. They would go from harsh moments that occasioned tears to overflowing happiness—to the point that Dinazarda, in her anxiety to dissolve the tension, would order from the bazaar a valuable Chinese ware: cream of tortoise, which promised miracles when rubbed on the feet. Beyond doubt a disturbing game, to which Scheherazade submitted in the hope of warding off the imminent threat of the scaffold.

Scheherazade resents that the closeness imposed by the small chambers denies them ceremony. Distressed, she closes her eyes even to the light of day, in order to think and resolve certain questions. Their proximity in the space becomes evident when the Caliph, calling upon his feminine side, lies down languidly in front of all the women. Ready to copulate, he rids himself of part of his clothing, exposing only his dark genitalia and leaving the rest of his garments to shield his feelings.

The sovereign prefers to fornicate in the dark. He guides himself by the lamp that distracts Scheherazade from her lovemaking role. Imprisoned by the tenuous flame whose shadow, projected onto objects and the Caliph's face, changes the shapes of what she sees, she convinces herself that the small bronze lamp is a present that the astute maidservant of Ali Baba sent when her master asked for her hand in marriage, as thanks for Scheherazade's efforts on her behalf.

Before listening to Scheherazade, the Caliph orders a pause. In the last months weariness has aged him and stolen the illusion of pleasure. Scheherazade's gaze, as if she guesses his discouragement, pierces him, defeats his manliness. She too pretends in his presence. To tolerate him, she uses facial disguises, calls forth courage. She protests, in silence, his threats of death. Her consolation, then, is not to love. The germ of love that exists in her neither speaks nor complains. It merely asks to whom it is to address this love that it needs. To whom to offer it in the future?

19

Scheherazade incites the Caliph's imagination, never his desire. Despite the finery chosen by her sister, she becomes paler every day, glowing only in the words with which she tells stories.

Since the time when they lived in their father's house, Dinazarda had taken charge of selecting the garments that both would wear at family ceremonies. Her selections ignored the taste of the Vizier, who constantly accused her of adopting pernicious habits. A few years older than Scheherazade, Dinazarda took pleasure in defying parental authority. She saw no reason for yielding to his will when her father, though he continued to complain, would regularly show signs of forgetting an incident that had taken place days before.

Thanks to simple insubordination, Dinazarda dared to mount the magic carpet furnished by her sister's fantasy and seat herself in front, pretending to visit places her sister had described earlier, imaginary regions where both of the Vizier's daughters felt safe.

The expressions Dinazarda would introduce at home, under the guise of following the path of modernity, bothered their father. He did not intend to submit to the imperative of the fantasy that his two daughters were spreading around the palace. A man of few words at home, where he would often arrive late at night and exhausted, the Vizier combated habits that might undermine the morals of Islam. When he admonished them, already on his way back to the Caliph's audience room, where in actuality his life seemed to take place, his hastily delivered sermons emphasized that his daughters must never violate a single rule of the Qur'an or give themselves over to practices offensive to the religion they professed, stressing those that prescribed modesty and obedience on the part of the woman.

After some discussion, the following night he admitted to

understanding how his daughters, merely from curiosity, might take refuge in a foreign taste in flagrant conflict with that which ruled Baghdad. Now in a conciliatory tone, he told them he saw no reason for both the young women to esteem daring colors and styles that the Caliph's court had surely not yet approved. So he should refresh their memory, in case they had forgotten certain fundamental precepts, that in pursuance of revelations made by Allah to the prophet Muhammad the women of his family, acting under emotional fervor, had covered their faces with pieces of cloth available in the house, in order to prevent such a revealing part of their bodies' being exposed to male concupiscence.

He was, however, attentive with his daughters. Upon seeing them, the Vizier smiled slightly, and as ongoing proof of love allowed them to speak with him, even at the risk of their contradicting his arguments. He accepted that Dinazarda saw nothing to reproach in the new expressions of beauty that were making their way into the interiors of princely domiciles in Baghdad, each of them demonstrating prerogatives originating in other kingdoms. Wherever it was, Islamic civilization, of which the Vizier and his daughters so proudly were part, soon erected magnificent monuments, always in keeping with the knowledge that the beautiful flowed from Allah and into the hearts of the devout.

The Abbasid rulers, descendants of Abbas, uncle of Muhammad, who conceived Baghdad in the eighth century, on the banks of the Tigris to the north of Ctesiphon, when they built mosques, minarets, round walls, had in mind miracles that would please Allah and astound human eyes. And it came to pass, to the point that the period was designated the golden age of Islamic culture. Why, Father? asked Dinazarda, or might both daughters have asked in unison. He replied that it was because they had the courage to manifest nostalgia for the greatness that emanates from the divine, while declaring themselves products of the grandeur of the Almighty who had given them life. Besides which, had it not been the Vizier who had so generously conceded to Scheherazade resources with which she impressed teachers and listeners?

As a result of these privileges, the formerly peaceful daughters began to rebel against the Vizier's way of thinking. They saw nothing improper in both serving Allah and proving to their father that the world itself held diverse manifestations of art. For all purposes, one could renounce traditional forms without falling into moral iniquity.

Such an impasse, instead of displeasing the Vizier, evoked in him pride in his daughters. He had done well to allow them an excellent education, bringing into the palace teachers who conveyed the basic fundamentals of human intelligence. Sages, circumspect in appearance, entered and left the rooms of the palace bearing every kind of knowledge, at the time concentrated in Baghdad, a knowledge so heavy on them that they seemed to be dragging through the quarters of the house a camel carrying on its hump a basket filled with manuscripts and calligraphic tablets.

The Vizier, who collected exorbitant taxes in the Caliph's name and gagged the people, obstructing any gust of liberalism, had conceded prerogatives to his daughters. Perhaps because of his early widowerhood, and the assistance from Fatima, he refused to punish them or deprive them of the benefits befitting their class. And contrary to the practices of the court, which were punitive toward women, the daughters displayed their own ideas in front of him, and fought for them. The privileges, of course, were enjoyed only intramurally and would last only so long as he lived. Afterward, the daughters would marry and their husbands would do away with such prerogatives.

He had loved the young women's mother gently and persistently. He had given her everything he could, without fear of her betraying him. The complicity between the spouses brought about an uncommon happiness that had lasted till his wife's death, from a fever impossible to overcome. Sheltered in his arms, breathing her last, she begged him to care for their daughters, to see that they received a fine education, taking advantage of Baghdad as a metropolis propitious for wisdom. Besides the study rooms frequented by teachers from the Middle East, this type of university attracted to its public readings crowds calculated at forty thousand, including women disguised in men's clothing.

Continuing with her final requests, the dying woman asked her husband to take into account the abilities and temperament of each daughter. Dinazarda, the firstborn, would have succeeded her father in his functions as Vizier had she been born a man. When his wife spoke of Scheherazade, her voice, which had been barely audible, took on new strength to tell him how the glow in Scheherazade's gaze, ever since birth, had engendered mysteries. She would not err in prophesying that this daughter's memory retained the knowledge of the world, meriting that they open the doors of erudition to her. And how else could her husband fulfill the designs of Allah?

Though absorbed in his tasks, the Vizier had bountiful feelings for his daughters, who, amid the frolicking, laughed and seemed happy. He did not shy from asking Allah to spare them bitter disillusionment in the future.

In this phase of development, Scheherazade passed her days with Fatima exclusively at her service, while Dinazarda followed her father, when he would come back from the Caliph's palace, generally exhausted. But despite their mutual affection, father and daughter often came into conflict, especially when the Vizier showed her the art of negotiation. It was a rare moment, in which, in an insistent tone, he demanded of Dinazarda consistency in defending her point of view. She must learn to what extent to compromise in order to reach a satisfactory accord with her adversary that held the possibility of later favoring her.

His daughter entertained herself equally with the mundane universe of which her father spoke. Aware of the idiosyncrasy of his followers and his courtiers, upon his return at the end of day Dinazarda would extract from him administrative details relating to the caliphate, information that her father gave her without suspecting that his daughter was committing it to memory. While he parceled out one piece of information or another, she would kiss him and move on to questions about other matters, still unknown.

Removed from these family altercations that so pleased the Vizier and Dinazarda, Scheherazade would receive her father with discreet effusion and quickly seek her place of retreat. But she was grateful to a father who allowed her to concentrate on the embattled and precious stuff of imagination. Her method was to avoid direct disagreement with him, having long since learned that it wasn't in her interest to leave traces of her mischief.

Always reclusive, Scheherazade loved silence. Without the least effort, she could remove herself from reality. With a few minutes of meditation she would plunge into imagined human conflicts, forgetting daily duties. She asked for neither food nor water, taking pleasure in stealing hours from sleep to dedicate them to adventures of a certain genie of the lamp who in those days pursued her to the point of endangering her health. It was a genie who, alternating between good and evil, spoke loudly to hush the chorus of voices that from the other side of the ravine was drowning out the telling of Scheherazade's story.

At such moments, which Scheherazade fought to prolong, it did no good to speak to her. At most she would concede a monosyllable. Nor would Dinazarda knock at the door or insist. For the princess's heart, having journeyed afar, would be beyond reach for several hours.

20

Scheherazade had not taken after her father. The Vizier had not been granted the imagination his daughter had inherited from her mother. By way of compensation, the pertinacious and astute nature of the man enabled him to exploit the intense family disputes among the Abbasids, especially the intrigues at court, which in his hands became an instrument of rare persuasion.

This was how the Caliph thought of the Vizier, as an unyielding servant whose devotion to the crown foresaw and punished any advance by enemies, even without consulting him. He kept the Vizier close to the throne, confident of his obsessive loyalty to power, which bent only in the face of his love for his daughters.

Long a widower, the Vizier remained faithful to the memory of his wife, resisting any new marriage, even at the Caliph's encouragement. At home, bewildered by Scheherazade's talent, he afforded her an excellent education. The teachers of Baghdad, called for this mission, would come to the palace every morning and leave Scheherazade only when night fell. Armed with knowledge of every kind, even of the Greek classics, some of the sages came from the school for translators, while others, associated with the madrassas, perfected their exegetic studies of the Qur'an. As theologians they held a power far surpassing that of their colleagues dedicated to philosophy, thus proving that to attend to the transcendence of Allah constituted a greater stimulus than speculating about man in his earthly wandering.

While Dinazarda was negligent in her studies, Scheherazade demanded from the teachers keys with which to open the doors of perception and wisdom. Nothing sated her intellectual ambition, to the perplexity of her mentors.

Aware of how demanding his daughter was, the Vizier thanked

Allah for the privilege of having a child who was no stranger to
the world. When, years later, Scheherazade voiced her intention
to join the Caliph, thinking by such an act to forestall the death of
so many young women, he rent his turban and fasted for several
days, prostrate from the pain consuming him but which he hid
from others. And in the Caliph's palace, as he rigorously followed
the daily schedule, without losing courage in his audiences with
the ruler, it was as if his daughter didn't exist. He discouraged
people from speaking to him about her, as if death, poised at the
threshold of the house, had not threatened any member of his
group. To the contrary, over his daughter's head hovered the
crown of queen and not the blade of the executioner.

The Vizier's fragile situation, put to the test between loyalty to
the throne and torment because of the temporary loss of his
daughters, made the Caliph ill at ease. In his audiences with the
Vizier the sovereign limited himself to matters pertinent to the
caliphate, never mentioning the daughters or even suggesting that
the Vizier visit the royal chambers where they lived in seclusion.

Submissive to the hierarchy of the court, the Vizier reacted
without comment to the news that found its way to him, even if
his eyes gleamed at the mention of their names, or when he
learned that Scheherazade had once more been spared from death.

He didn't know how to persuade the Caliph to lose interest in
Scheherazade. In the beginning, the Vizier intensified the ruler's
tasks, hoping to get him away from the palace. But not obtaining
the desired results, he then advised him to travel through the kingdom, so needful of his presence. This would take him away from
Baghdad in the coming months.

The ruler firmly refused. He did not plan to live so close to the
conflicts of the kingdom, which already weighed heavily on him
from a distance. That was when the Vizier, in excellent Arabic,
urged him to go to faraway Egypt, with the expectation of meeting
sages who would add wealth to his wisdom. It was said of them that
their untrimmed beards dragged on the ground and raised dust,
shedding hairs that were then gathered up by disciples as relics.

The Caliph saw no reason to go so far away if in Baghdad there were men of equal capacity, without the inconvenience of being confounded by beards of such length. The Vizier's arguments, however, were not without foundation. Between sips of tea from herbs in the garden, those old men, perpetually vigilant, offered visitors a structured view of the universe never heard before, a synthesis so perfect that it caused perplexity in listeners eager to unveil secrets trusted to only a small circle. In compensation, perhaps nowhere else would the Caliph's valuable intelligence be more appreciated than in those sacred locales. He deserved to hear them discourse on the science of warfare, translated into expansion of territory and winning of spoils, on the art of apprehending the demonic aspects of human nature, on the blessed use of unlimited imagination.

The Caliph's gaze seemed to assent, as if the chancellor's tactic was about to yield results. The Vizier assured him that other sultans, beys, sheikhs, beyond Mecca and Medina, with caravans of their own, were venturing along the banks of the Nile, crossing the desert in the direction of the Dakhla Oasis, in search of those wise men. Under the shade of date palms they meditated, preparing for the mystic encounter. Then, after taking lodging at the foot of the high, steep slope, they headed toward Qasr, confident that despite the sketchy descriptions afforded them, the intuition so esteemed by the holy men of the desert would help them find the hideaway they sought.

The Vizier narrowed his eyes and, with a gesture like Scheherazade's when she was facing some enigma, wondered aloud, as if there were no need for reply, whether such a sacrifice wouldn't be worthwhile to hear stories whose intriguing plots surpassed what Scheherazade, a mere apprentice, had been telling the Caliph. And, probing the ruler's interest, he persisted with the matter, not realizing that the sovereign, unmindful of his deliberation, was now concentrating on plans for building the new mosque whose design had been delivered to him that morning. He seemed to hear once again the voice of the architect assuring him of the magnitude of an edifice conceived by a dreamer who erected minarets in the belief of their flying by themselves, unbound from the creative impulse of the artist.

Kneeling before the throne, the architect, with a mixture of timidity and pride, had promised the Caliph that the shining gilded domes of the future mosque, in contrast to the green dome of the palace, would be equally esteemed by those along the banks of the Tigris or navigating its waters and by those who entered Baghdad on foot through its four gates after circling its round walls.

His eyes almost popping from their sockets, the architect foresaw airy, translucent minarets, poised to blossom from the central courtyard, drawn upward by the firmament—a miracle that would give believers the sensation of rising into the paradise promised by Muhammad.

Perceiving the Caliph's indifference, the Vizier regretted the move. Lately, perhaps because of the abusive frequency with which he took advantage of palace intrigues, his missteps were beginning to surface. It was becoming difficult to persuade the Caliph of anything, even a matter of a relative desirous of usurping the Abbasid throne—an accusation that the Caliph pretended not to heed, even though weeks later, before the treason could be consummated, he would strike without mercy.

The truth was that the Caliph's disenchantment with court intrigue had become accentuated after Scheherazade submitted him to the voluptuous effects of her tales. His adviser's words, though pertinent, vanished before his eyes. Attracted by the young woman's nocturnal accounts, he thought for the first time of a day when he might be capable of preserving the burdens of tradition and simultaneously modernizing the dream of a posterity made up of anarchy and dangerous freedom.

The Caliph had inherited from his father an appreciation for laudatory speeches. But the Vizier's flattery, albeit well intentioned, now seemed insipid compared to the legends brought to their bed by Scheherazade, legends that surpassed the arrogant affirmations of the courtiers preaching the immutability of the imperial daily life of the Abbasids.

But what the Caliph demanded in those moments was a reality that constituted a source of surprise and entertainment. For in him was growing the ambition of one day stealing Scheherazade's zeal and thrilling his subjects gathered in the bazaar by presenting himself to them as a character of universal dimension at the level of Harun ar-Rashid, like him an Abbasid.

Fortunately, these deliriums abated, and he resumed his haughty character, resistant to change and demanding that the acolytes, attendants, and courtiers revere his majesty, symbolized in the turban encrusted with pearls and diamonds that, seated on his head, covered part of his brow and emphasized his aquiline nose.

He hurriedly took leave of the Vizier, following a route opposite to that of the chambers. He wandered about, tracing the path of a laborious labyrinth that mirrored some of Scheherazade's plots, tending to turn back to the starting point and from there to proceed to a place where he had never been before.

As he advanced down the endless corridors, oblivious to the marvelous calligraphy painted on the walls in the form of murals, Scheherazade's words blossomed in profusion from the stories. The breeze of twilight brought the Caliph the voluptuousness of sylvan fragrances wafting from the gardens, prompting a strange languor. His steps, slowed by the years, forced him to reduce his pace. But so that none would notice his weariness, he hurried toward the chambers. Perhaps the young woman's words would lubricate the erotic imagination, rekindle the fire of the genitalia. At the mere idea he blushed like an apprentice in the artifices of the flesh. Within a few steps he would face the material that Scheherazade had drafted with the goal of tormenting him.

At the entrance, Jasmine announces his arrival before the herald, to whom this task belongs. The violation of protocol disturbs Dinazarda. The Caliph, however, feigning not to have noticed an

act deserving punishment, smooths his beard. The aromas emanating from the scene free him from judging details, from asking
which world conforms to his sensitivities. He is concerned with
following Scheherazade to the places to which she introduces him
in her stories. To India, Damascus, the banks of the Bosporus,
transported always by the gift of traveling through these settings.
When he is certain of having grown fins, granted him by
Scheherazade the night before, he feels himself swimming, conquering the seas.

21

The hours snatched from death impart tension to the account and a brevity that Scheherazade fears she cannot restrain until morning. Each night it becomes more painful to defend her life and the story. However, she disguises the vicissitudes she faces, as if, free of the constraints imposed by the Caliph, she enjoys privileged conditions.

Though she is drowsy and distressed, her tale takes on substance as she prods the Caliph's memory in an effort to activate his mind and prepare him for her narrative.

The pair copulate out of obligation. The feigned performance of love that they practice on the princely divan is grotesque. She cannot admire the ruler who cruelly saddles her with his weight. But she recognizes his talent in assimilating the facts linked together in the stories, and the swiftness with which he visualizes the material that she instinctively exaggerates with the goal of saving herself.

Confined to the palace, the sisters, with Jasmine's help, often amuse themselves by imitating the courtiers, the merchants of Baghdad, one or another visitor observed from afar. Under this irresistible playful impulse, which helps to dispel their fear, they imagine they are daughters of a sultan who, because of his libertarian spirit, has allowed them to settle in Baghdad, in a sumptuous palace outside the city walls, on the other bank of the Tigris, in the direction of Karbala. They pretend they have just returned to the city after a prolonged stay in the Gobi Desert, on whose sands they had pitched tents in hopes of enjoying a restless sojourn in the wilderness. Accustomed to comfort, they had chosen this desert as a place to discover what it would be like to travel, to live at the whim of the elements, and to experience the simple joy of returning home when they felt bored. Therefore these princesses, surely frustrated after a few nights in that inhospitable region, had concluded that the pleasure of travel lay in going home, in bringing back the wagons, the trunks packed with souvenirs.

Scheherazade reduced her daily agony by engendering stories, while Dinazarda, dependent on the fantasy lent by her sister, concealed her secret desire to climb on a magic carpet and soar over unknown places, to venture as far as the Persian Gulf, merely to see a fish with silvery scales, and then to return to Baghdad, where she would experience for the first time the harsh realities of the bazaar. But eager for the tenuous fantasy the three young women experienced in those chambers not to dissipate, Dinazarda, in coded language, demanded of her sister information that seemed absent from daily life.

Scheherazade divided herself between her sister, who despite loving her showed signs of ambivalence, and the Caliph, who frequently vented his cruelty. In fearful moments she would repeat aloud the names of her characters to keep them close to her. She needed their protection. Summoned, they would approach: Sinbad, Ali Baba, Zoneida, all of them upset by the most recent carnality and ready to rebel against the original scenario of a story that often left them idle.

Scheherazade felt compassion for a rebelliousness that sprang from the courage with which she herself had imbued them. She understood that these characters would no longer accept a decree of death, even if it came from her. As genuine actors in the drama, they would not countenance, even to benefit her, being condemned to silence by Scheherazade, for only by fighting for their humanity and their survival could Sinbad and Zoneida embody a relevant role in the story destined for them.

They experienced anguish like ordinary mortals. These creatures, in their anxiety to truly become people, aspired to mingle with the Caliph and with the others in the palace. And perhaps, by forming a single family, they could help these beings of flesh and blood to free themselves from stifling norms and become coura-geous characters like them.

Scheherazade hesitated. How to give dimensions of character to the Caliph, to Dinazarda and Jasmine, if so far only the people of Baghdad had filled her tales? Since childhood, urged by Fatima to experience all kinds of adventures, she had strengthened her belief that over the centuries there had spread through the caliphate a people of scintillating imagination and that, though unhappy, ill-fed victims of the Caliph's despotism, they knew bet-ter than anyone how to weave irresistible and emotional plots.

Scheherazade trusted that in the future these very people would sit at her side solely to hear the stories in which they would be restored to their original beauty. Surprised, perhaps, by a princess who had perfected the art of pretending, whose cleverness, as she proceeded with the adventures, exposed to the light of the sun, in view of all, the true desires hidden in each of them.

22

At first, cursed by fate, Ali Baba did not dare draw in the sand a future that favored him. Thus Scheherazade speaks of her hero so the Caliph will accept that poverty may be linked to adventure.

She describes this character, a paradigm of typical Baghdad virtues, wishing that she herself could be in the cave where the forty thieves were piling up treasures stolen from caravans that had crossed the desert for centuries.

Scheherazade entices the Caliph by describing gems stuffed in linseed sacks, and she pretends to hold up to the light rubies, emeralds, and sapphires and trace the veins whose brilliance dazzles the eye.

The story of Ali Baba both excites and frightens her, especially when the thieves rapidly approach the cave on Arabian steeds whose powerful hooves raise the desert sand as they pass. Scheherazade's body shivers, roused by the rubies.

The zeal with which she tells the stories leads her to exaggeration. She describes certain precious stones with excessive detail, pointing out the blazing character of the jeweler's art. And with the intent of leading the Caliph to trust his imagination, she opens her hand so he can see, amid the fate lines, the most brilliant stone of the thieves' collection: the rare ruby that she has sculpted with cupidity.

Scheherazade parades before the Caliph the treasures accumulated in the cave, so that he can appreciate those chosen by Ali Baba, already on his way back to Baghdad with the jewels on the back of his mule. He had made his selection at random, driven by anguish and the eagerness to enjoy the fortune unexpectedly bestowed on him by fate.

With her imagination inspired, Scheherazade continues to

embellish her tale. Her listeners, eagerly awaiting news, accompany Ali Baba as he crosses the city, not far from his native village, where he plans to spend the night. The lateness of the hour suits him because he has no desire for the animal's burden to awaken suspicion among the neighbors, whose idle talk might make its way to the ears of the unlucky thieves.

As repeated by Scheherazade, Ali Baba's words expressing happiness with his newfound riches drive the Caliph into fear—this despite the muleteer having hired a female servant (the next to command the scene) whom he has had the good fortune to meet. A woman who, combining shrewdness and devotion to her master, would come to please the Caliph in his slow process of humanization.

Jasmine is excited about the role of the servant in the tale. Though a member of the inner circle, she cannot ask the princess for additional information about the new character, who is loyal and courageous. She observes sadly that here, unlike in her other stories, Scheherazade has not given the servant a name, even a simple one, or mentioned any of her physical characteristics—which would, after all, play a role in captivating Ali Baba in the future.

Born in the desert, Jasmine loved the stories that exalted those of humble origin, as she herself was one of them. She wept along with characters forced to forget happier days in order to save themselves. How willingly she would have fought openly for the glory of one day becoming part of the gallery of heroes to whom Scheherazade sometimes credited acts of renunciation. Having suffered so many humiliations, Jasmine would think it a punishment if in the future Scheherazade did not see in her sufficient merit to play a role in one of the stories. She would be content if they merely gave her name to the servant, thus associating her with a tale begun precisely when Ali Baba, shuffling among the rocks of the plateau, chanced upon the entrance to a cave where the forty thieves were shouting in unison, "Open, Sesame."

Scheherazade herself is moved in the course of the tale. As she

repeats to the Caliph the words "Open, Sesame," the key to opening and closing the cave and allowing entrance to the thieves, her
voice resounds gravely through the palace. And the more she
issues the miraculous roar, the more the timbre grows, as if by
saying "Open, Sesame" so often, through some strange magic she
might add density to a plot already thick with intrigue. The trick is
enhanced by the fact that the Caliph, confronted with the mischievousness of Ali Baba, suffers and marvels at his fate.

In fact, the Caliph himself, helpless to assist Ali or to prevent
his falling into the trap set by the forty thieves, suspects that the
death of that subject will cause him injury and unthinkable hurt.
Experiencing such a feeling is disturbing for someone who has
become accustomed to issuing sentences of death without pangs
of remorse, and he looks at Scheherazade almost as if to ask her
for mercy, while warning her that, despite her authority as narrator, she dare not strike Ali Baba a mortal blow.

It surprises the Caliph that such a popular plot should cause him
suffering, that the fate of the protagonist has anything to do with
him. But he stifles the impulse and says nothing. Nevertheless, he
hopes for the triumph of the man and his servant, whose features
are gradually taking shape in his mind.

At Scheherazade's mercy, the sovereign tests a theory that in
these circumstances comes to naught. It is not in his power to save
the unthinking subject from the trials of the narrative. Both he and
Ali Baba are dependent on the paths the young woman chooses to
show them.

Until tonight he has been interested only in matters concerning
the Abbasids, long seated on the throne of Baghdad. That dynasty,
like no other, had been able to amass many victories, guaranteeing
them invincibility and a permanent place in Islamic history. For an
Abbasid ruler, a neighbor's success would only go against the
foundations of the crown, reducing his degree of command.

So the hope that Ali Baba and his vivacious servant girl will
emerge victorious, besides striking the Caliph as unprecedented,
impels him for the first time to take on the burden of solidarity. A

feeling that, if not actually enveloping his soul, impresses on it certain signs of gentleness—especially because Scheherazade, after telling this story, immediately introduces him to others equally feverish and delightful.

On that strange night, which seems endless to the ruler, he doesn't realize that Scheherazade's words are a blade pressing against his aquiline nose, threatening to mutilate it. Nor that, despite being resigned to the subordinate position of listener, he has the right to insinuate with his gaze his desire to decide Ali Baba's future.

Scheherazade in turn, for fear of that same look, lets him see that she agrees for brief moments to share with the contrite Caliph the reins of the story. But before he can conceive of an ending for Ali Baba, he learns that the cunning servant was slowly pouring boiling oil into the ears of the men, hidden in barrels at the entrance to the house, who were waiting to kill Ali Baba in revenge for the outrage they had suffered.

As Scheherazade unfolds the story of the man and his future wife, expecting the sovereign to contribute some essential detail, he begs her, paralyzed with emotion, to continue, not to interrupt for any reason the enchantment with which she is carpeting everyday life.

23

Scheherazade is a carnal being. She will soon be twenty and fears she will never reach old age. Her body commingles fright and excitement as she imparts life to the stories she narrates.

The material of imagination that rocks her senses has her voice as its conduit. Each night her age-old timbre echoes the fantasy and the words that give body to her plots. Her vocal register changes, especially when she plays the roles of disconsolate heroines, as she asserts the existence of Aladdin, Zoneida, or Ali Baba, whose cunning servant saves her master with remarkable tricks. With exemplary impartiality, Scheherazade bestows upon them a modulation that, according to circumstances, ranges from opaque and dark to scratchy and nervous. Her vocal cords, now emitting sharp timbres, now forging a guttural utterance, take on the patina of a lost time, a coloratura that confounds even Dinazarda and enchants the Caliph.

While Scheherazade is careful not to let her characters immediately satiate her listeners' curiosity, at the same time she shields her feelings. She resists the offers of affection and admiration that might reduce her to the condition of ordinary. And when Jasmine quenches her thirst, or refreshes her heated skin with slices of melon left overnight in the coolness of the courtyard, she thanks her without sharing her thoughts. She is there to instill a degree of perplexity in the Caliph, not to make it possible for him to relax in comfort on the pillows, lost in the distant dreams of her accounts.

With Dinazarda and Jasmine as witnesses, before the Caliph's nightly arrival she assumes the role of imitator. She easily takes on the personality of a baritone, recently come to Baghdad, boasting a voluminous paunch—a gentleman who spreads musical notes and curses in the same phrase, introducing villainy into the plot that she has chosen to defend amid high-pitched chords.

To the other women's applause, she doesn't persist in the portrayal of an exhibitionist who once served at court. She now describes a woman, equally opulent, said to have the voice of a soprano, whose life, as intense as Zoneida's, merits inclusion in one of her stories, perhaps by becoming the attendant of the voluble Amin. This singer, by using her voice, shares the stage with a man full of romantic gestures, despite the woman's body not being the kind to inspire passion. For both, however, in each other's arms as they sing, a tragic fate awaits.

Concentrating, Scheherazade copies their nervous tics, their successive dissonances, ignoring Dinazarda's and Jasmine's laughter and requests for more. Especially when the female singer, amid falsettos and swaying, now in a turban or burnoose, brandishing a scimitar, passes herself off as a man, even passionately kissing her own hand, like the lips of her partner. She and the tenor, each in character, portray a love affair on the eve of extinction.

And so fleeting is the actors' duel that the tenor, attempting to seduce a humble date seller in her stall in the medina, is startled when she asks with morbid curiosity how women in the royal harem are usually treated. She wants to know whether the Caliph, when he takes them to bed, presents them with gifts befitting a night of pleasure. But as the tenor moves toward the young woman, seeking to trade information for copulation, the ungrateful vendor demands more. She wants to know if eunuchs make use of lascivious glances, agile fingers, and flexible tongues, and whether they are masters of practices that drive the favorites wild, to the point that they resort to woven cotton from the banks of the Nile to muffle the women's cries.

Scheherazade's voice, which neither flags nor breaks, expands its range, assumes new narrative prerogatives. She lends to each role an indispensable comprehension. As man and woman, she laughs and weeps, with unparalleled emotional range. She tells fables of legendary figures of the Arabian world who radiate voluptuousness, exude odors, distill secretions, challenge giants and monarchs, all with magical dimensions. At her coaxing they take flight, cross the tunnel of time until they come to the Prophet, in the period in which Muhammad and his followers, suffering hostility at the hands of the inhabitants of Mecca, take refuge in Medina, where they will live in exile. A dolorous hegira that, enriched by the word of Allah, marks the beginning of the Muslim era.

The roles that Scheherazade plays do not always suggest an ill-fated outcome. Some, offering a happy change, make the women smile. As proof of this, she returns to the scene of Baghdad after her imagination has taken her far away. This return indicates that she has wearied of visiting the other end of the world, a great distance beyond that foreseen by any mortal, and following the indefatigable Sinbad, now on his seventh voyage by sea, which could well prove to be his last.

But though Dinazarda delights in such fantasy, she rebukes her sister, who should not waste this revel on them. Scheherazade must reserve the best of her talents for the Caliph, soon to arrive at the chambers. Only when he is listening will it be wise to resume the cycle of human drama.

24

The Caliph's heart is devoid of hope. He does not love Scheherazade or any other woman. The cold in his heart, which shuns emotion, radiates in his impenetrable gaze. The cruelty born of his thirst for vengeance threatens to age him.

Confident in his oath to do away with the young women after copulating with them, he returns to the throne room in the morning without freeing Scheherazade of his vow. The certainty that he will soon administer his daily dose of justice hovers over his subjects.

Despite this proposition, he delays ordering the death of Scheherazade. It disturbs him how he uses the young woman's stories as a pretext for keeping her at his side. He admits, to be sure, that the storyteller's fantasy anoints his body, and that her words, sometimes cultured, almost always from popular roots, threaten the way he once viewed the world. Without his needing to leave the palace or visit the kingdom, the Vizier's daughter brings to him in the chambers, in the audience room, in his heart, wherever he goes, the vision of grotesque beings, unknown lands, adventures that he has yearned to experience since adolescence. But he has lacked the courage to abandon the kingdom in exchange for human misery and the instability of fate.

He half closes his lips, sighs, contracts his chest as he follows Scheherazade's words. Even though he doesn't speak, he mentally links one word to another. Some, on his own initiative, he leaves hanging in the air, saving them for an emergency or for the moment when he feels needy. Through these exercises, which excite him, the Caliph forgets the wife who betrayed him with the black slave. A humiliation made public on a visit to Baghdad by his brother, a sultan like him, who through unhappy fate had fallen victim to the same infamy.

As soon as he leaves the chambers and the young woman's magic, the sovereign succumbs to the vision of that wife, dead only a few years. Thanks to the fascination of conjugal betrayal, she emerges forcefully, looking deep into his eyes. In the course of these evocations, the Sultana's ghost, arrogant as always, offers no sign of repentance, doesn't throw herself to the floor, pulling her hair, rending her garments, asking his forgiveness. Just the opposite—through these vague memories she wishes to remove his turban, vilify him with obscene acts and words. She insults him, cursing the day she met him in Karbala, the holy city where she was born.

That asphyxiating shadow grows brutal and eloquent. It wrenches the ruler from the throne and hurls him to the ground, to make him feel human terror firsthand, life without the bribery of power. The Sultana's abundant breasts, once the source of milk and honey in immense doses, heave under the delicate silk of her garments.

She shows her disdain for the Abbasid crown, unworthy in her eyes. She blasphemes in protest against the inexorable sentence that meant her death. By what power did the Caliph arrogate to himself the right to punish her merely for enjoying pleasure in the sweaty, exuberant arms of her slaves?

In the throne room, protected from human frailties, the Caliph's movements display his uncertainty. He wants to blot out the image of his wife fornicating in his own house, in broad daylight. In the courtyard, to be exact, which is graced with trees whose crowns cool the air. There she was, naked, fierce, splendid, her legs spread, dishonored, ready to give birth. Entrusted to the care of the servant girl who ushered the other slaves and attendants from the scene, the Sultana moaned like a cow, gasped like a sheep, an animal in heat.

Small in stature but possessing surprising energy, the servant was herself from the holy city, to which she had once returned to pay homage to Hussein, grandson of the Prophet, before his golden tomb. Almost touching the Sultana's body, she directed her movements, preventing her outcries from shaking the trees and knocking the ripe fruit to the ground. Or from crossing the walls and corridors and arriving at the Caliph's chambers, to the ancient medina, to the gates of the walls of Baghdad.

He remembers the woman being speared by the slave's phallus and the caution with which, almost in agony, she pushes away her lover's head. She doesn't wish to drink the sweat dripping from his brow. Impelled by so much desire, the copulating lovers collide with the stone fountain, whose waters splash onto their bodies without cooling their inextinguishable ardor.

The woman's form, as the Caliph evokes it, shows fury, lust, demanding from the slave uninterrupted thrusting. At the service of the Sultana, it is the man's role to exhibit unflaggingly the required virility. And though the African is forbidden by ceremony to address her, his ragged and savage breathing utters obscenities as if he were speaking.

The servant girl, a constant presence on the scene, who has been with the Sultana since her time in Karbala, keeps a strict watch on the slave. Kneeling beside the lovers, ready to intervene, she disengages herself from the convulsions that threaten to engulf her. And, untiringly, in an effort to prevent the African's copious secretions from staining the royal flesh, she dries the Sultana's body.

The delicacies brought to the side of the throne, where the Caliph meditates and suffers, are barely touched. He strokes his beard with his ring-adorned fingers. Nothing erases the memory of the Sultana motioning to her servant, who immediately interprets her desire. Unceremoniously, the servant pulls the slave off her mistress's body. Her act roughly and harshly detaches the man's tumescent member from the woman's vulva, with the secretions produced by both emerging together. And the faithful servant, wasting no time, cleans the woman's lethargic body on the grass, using a sponge scented with musk from the Indian Ocean.

The sight of the orgy, which even now seems fresh in his mind, engenders blind rage in the Caliph. He wants to kill them, but his brother, his companion in misfortune, intervenes, telling him to control his righteous anger. It would be better for the Caliph, like his brother in the past, to learn the limits of pain. To observe how the slave's outsized member, as erect as an obelisk, acting with a will of its own, subdued his wife's body, penetrated its depths, almost coming out of her grimacing mouth.

This same African, with synchronized movements in obedience to his mistress, glides an oil-soaked cotton cloth along her body. He traverses her breasts, circulates among the shapes, noting the voluminous details. And because he has left semen between her thighs, with the same cloth he rubs the woman's open sex. It is imperative to erase any trace, smell, mark, sign that he has left behind in the Sultana.

The impersonality of the scene impresses but does not console the Caliph. Nothing expunges the betrayal or mitigates his anxiety to put right the offense with the scimitar inherited from his father, but his brother dissuades him in time. The task of flogging his wife's impure flesh belongs to the executioner, who can wait. The two brothers will take a trip, leaving Baghdad behind.

Upon returning from this odyssey, the Caliph orders the death of his wife, not forgetting the servant girl, the slave, and all other participants in the orgy. But once condemned, the Sultana begs to be heard, for she has a secret to reveal to him. The Caliph allows the woman, led by the executioner, to see him before the sentence is carried out. The Sultana, in the face of the indifference of the Caliph who also condemned her to be silent, rages, hurling imprecations, in a language learned with the slaves. Even provoked, he does not react. Nothing moves him. Not even the terrified face begging him for clemency, at least a few more days of life, while the executioner, deciding to silence her before death could, gags her without any sign of compassion.

The mercilessness of the scene, as he relived it, shook the Caliph. That woman, who had usurped his honor and cast him into unrest, after all that time still held him in subjugation, to the point that he repented of having granted her such a quick death. If it were in his power, he would bring her back to life, whatever the cost, merely for the pleasure of having her confess, of hearing the sordid details. So that, finally burying her in his memory, he would retain not the smallest recollection of her vileness.

But what would have been her last words? What could she have said to him that might have placated his anger, removed the nail driven into his chest? Did words exist in the language of men to justify such betrayal, such breach of trust? Or did the woman, plunged into the area of shadow, where she had been queen and slave at the same time, lack the ability to choose between good and evil, the nefarious and the sacred? At the threshold of death, would the woman's final word have expunged forever her silhouette so that at the end of her dramatic discourse there remained only a faded shadow?

25

The Caliph imposes his tyranny on Scheherazade in the days that follow. The weight of time ages her, every second transforming her into a different being. She looks at herself in the mirror that Jasmine brings her and confirms her desolate gaze. Subject to the unrelenting temporal mystery that rules her brain, she faces, alongside Dinazarda, the eloquence of the hourglass, the grains of sand that afflict her heart.

In the brilliance of the valuable objects around her, which gleam with the first rays of sunlight, Scheherazade feels like crying but resists the loss of her illusion. A prisoner in that mausoleum, she perceives the tragic dimension of the minutes that flow away without commiseration or deliverance and in a matter of seconds can take her to her death. Her sole salvation consists of engendering pauses, intervals, interruptions, breaks, in defense of a story that must survive until morning.

To control the frequency with which the minutes throb in her forehead, she looks at her sister and the slave, both of whom believe in her plan. Scheherazade asks little of them, longing only for a focal point radiating comfort, warning her of her weaknesses, telling her what to do with the cursed plot now at hand.

Her sister's impending death presents a conflict for Dinazarda, who avoids looking at her, simulating indifference. By this gesture she hopes the Caliph will take pity on Scheherazade by thinking her unprotected by her own family, which she alone represents in those chambers. But to her displeasure, the ruler doesn't notice her disaffection for Scheherazade. The Caliph holds no key to happiness, absorbed as he is in his own tiresome reality.

Dinazarda's strategy fails. She was ingenuous to count on solidarity from the Caliph, whose indifference is legendary. While

Jasmine outdoes herself in diligence, her focus at the moment is to make sure that Scheherazade doesn't weaken from fatigue as she narrates, exhausted by the lateness of the hour. By sipping the warm lemon tea where two symbolic petals float, served by the slave, might not Scheherazade regain her energy and be encouraged? Or will she continue to demand that they whisper ardently in her ear their belief in her talent and proclaim that through the grace of Allah, they today once again have at their disposal fervent words and a harmonious body?

Scheherazade transforms her grimace into a smile. Nothing protects her from the imminent sacrifice. She has always known of the risks of the undertaking, that to save herself she would have to entertain the Caliph with episodes full of surprises, imprinted with the insignia of her imagination. She knows herself to be master of an impetuous, unbridled fantasy that must be held in check to better reconcile the conflicting interests of the story. Any imprudence in overemphasizing scenes censured beforehand by the Caliph will result in her condemnation.

Between the walls of the chambers, which she never leaves, Scheherazade suffers the conflict of serving both life and death. In intransigent combat, they reach the paroxysm of respective splendor at the first signs of dawn.

Upon emerging victorious each morning, she experiences the truce of rare hours won from death amid a whirlwind of emotions. It is a reprieve owing to the cunning of her narrative, but one that, by way of compensation, comes at the cost of sacrificing the initial plan.

Suddenly forced to revive details buried in her memory, her goal always to seduce her implacable lover, Scheherazade enriches the vein of tales with unyielding zeal. To this end, she tosses one character into another's bed, in the absence of love or even passion. She knows that somewhere in Sinbad's body lies a memory that will soon respond to desire and make him a perfect lover. He feigns love as if he knew what it meant.

26

By chance does this illustrious Abbasid yearn for a dish of lentils with floating bits of sheep that, prior to slaughter, had seen the brilliance of light on the scalding desert sand? Or seek the indulgent gaze of a woman who, instead of poisoning him with resentment, would nourish him with mother's milk?

The Caliph has never asked about Scheherazade's motives for coming to him, for exposing herself to his cruelty. He dispenses with explanations that reveal his own weaknesses. He acts differently than Harun ar-Rashid, his noble ancestor who, desperate to know truth from lie, would go to the marketplace disguised as a potter, a beggar, a merchant, obliging his subjects to disclose to him his despotism and his errors.

The sovereign had learned from an early age the corrosive power of men and beasts. In the case of a caliph, any concession of intimacy, to anyone, undermines the essence of power, which he believes lies in the absolute reclusion of his soul.

The chambers offer Scheherazade her only refuge. More than anyone, she understands the interstices of that imperial clan, erected in the shadow of the Prophet, how they consolidated their irresistible ambition for the throne through various rulers. And as the day flees and she tensely carries out the quotidian details represented there by Dinazarda and Jasmine, she calls upon the sagacity of the Caliph, the monosyllabic ponderings of a man who knows no other concept of life than that coming from power.

As the Caliph's prisoner, she feels that the garden is inaccessible to her. When she regrets losing sight of Baghdad, she invents it in order to have it back again, as if Fatima were leading her through the narrow streets lit by the setting sun. Despite the adverse conditions that prevent her flight and make her feel she's a bird with pinned wings, there is vibrant life around her. The slave women laugh, forgetting that the princess observes them, and thanks to these young women, Scheherazade experiences the pulse of life. It helps her beat back the odor of death that glides along the carpets.

As night falls, the Caliph appears. He is never late, and is unforgiving to those who give no thought to the value of time. He appears at the curve of the corridor, preceded by the diligent phalanx of warriors. By protocol, the herald is responsible for his movements. A meaningful figure in the court, he announces the monarch's approach from a distance, giving time for the Vizier's daughters, who are not exempt from the duty, to prostrate themselves on the marble floor as the ruler crosses the threshold.

From this position, the sisters cannot gauge the Caliph's mood. They cannot see whether he is still upset from that morning, when something unknown challenged his steely power, robbing him of the illusion of immortality.

Often he forgets to release them from their prostration. This prolongs the sisters' ritual, begun the day Scheherazade, mustering her courage, told her father of her desire to sacrifice herself for the salvation of the young women of the caliphate. From their curved posture, which delays the staging of Scheherazade's stories, the women wait for the Caliph to free them.

A foreigner to the group, Jasmine imitates the princesses. But she is humble, and her reverence lasts longer than that of the others. As the sisters scrutinize her, she quickly brings delicacies, careful not to offend the Caliph's palate. But he takes no notice of her, accepting absently the treatment that is his due. He has become accustomed to being surrounded by women, for no male is permitted to enter the chambers. Little by little, the Caliph starts to forget the audiences he granted during the day—to officeholders, religious leaders, prominent Bedouins, men of the desert. Coming from far and wide, they proposed to the sovereign negotiations of every kind, from spurious alliances, the territorial expansion so favored by the Abbasids, to personal advantages that would augment his fortunes.

In the ornate audience room, full of rare, gleaming pieces, the Caliph is parsimonious, pretending to meditate on the offers made at the foot of the throne. Frugal with his words, he boasts a highly developed sense of justice. He listens to the complaints, feigning attentiveness, without saying anything. He doesn't take into consideration the difficult governing of individual and collective destiny that is now his responsibility. Though relaxed, he doesn't neglect to display the trappings of the power that extends throughout the caliphate. He absently accepts delicacies, submissions, offers of the female body, the mysterious arsenal that he merits as immortal sovereign.

27

Dinazarda wanders about the palace, and wherever she goes she lauds her sister. She never knows if the kiss she has given on her forehead will be the last of her life.

In the garden, she smells the flowers and wonders about the future. How much longer will she have Scheherazade at her side? In those moments of solitude, which heighten her sensitivity, she laments her sister's having been gifted with such irresistible talent.

She imagines what Scheherazade must be doing now, isolated in the chambers among the slaves who never leave her side. Perhaps she is consulting the future in the mirror that Jasmine insists on showing her so she can be certain of her beauty.

Scheherazade shows signs of fatigue. In the mirror, she resists looking at the features that will soon offer evidence of aging. Fear has left marks that bear the Caliph's name. But what weighs on her most is that she will one day be forgotten, without having had the chance to bring her stories to the people of Baghdad.

She fears that no one except Dinazarda and Jasmine will ever hear her accounts, that one day she will have no friend to demand that she continue with her tales, as if they were the daily bread of a universal family.

Dinazarda strolls insouciantly through the flowered pathways. She carefully pushes aside the bushes, the unexpected thorns. For a long time she has lived her life at her sister's side, defending her interests, sucking away the poison from her adventurous blood. She witnesses Scheherazade's actions as if living them.

She inspects other areas of the palace, and nothing escapes her criticism. Back in the chambers, the sight of Scheherazade asleep torments her. Her sister accepts captivity as if wishing to forget the configurations of the world so that she can create her own realities.

Her level of concentration exhausts Dinazarda. She feels compassion for her sister and hesitates to wake her fragile body, deep in sleep, forgetting for a few moments the daily rounds of the executioner. Perhaps rest is good for the reflection Scheherazade needs to begin her nightly story. On the other hand, she must review the details and not waste precious hours, each one calculated to save her.

Scheherazade is startled by the lateness of the hour. The sun has receded and there is little time left. But the delay will not harm her. She calms her sister, for it is essential that Dinazarda continue to believe in her ability to weave a carpet from the simple threads of her memory, to be able to filter the materials of the world in the service of her skill.

Perhaps Dinazarda is right to point out her excesses, her tendency toward the improbable—though the Caliph has never criticized her. Not once has he told her that her unbridled, limitless fables clash with his interests by contradicting the reality at his command.

Her sister's expression disturbs Dinazarda. She thinks it wise to relieve Scheherazade of the pressure she exerts over her. She caresses her fingers, her cheek, assuring her that she will always be at her side. She mustn't feel unprotected because of carrying out the inexorable laws of her craft. Was it not in fact she, Scheherazade, who confessed that lack of narrative skill is itself the fruit of experience?

After reviving her spirit, Dinazarda speaks proudly of the garden, where by her own initiative she has christened some of the walkways with the names of her sister's characters. Nooks serving as hiding places, propitious for experiencing a forbidden love. Or for confessing to a lover that the time had come to tell him that she no longer loves him, that she yearns for another, a prince whose absence renders life meaningless. But, no artist like Scheherazade, Dinazarda can convey to her sister only the hazy brushstrokes of the Baghdad landscape.

In the expectation that the Caliph is coming to see them, the hours pass quickly. And when he approaches, preceded by swords, pennants, and bugles, he seems to be in a hurry. Despite his subtle gaze, he arrogantly signals the bed, the nightly coupling. The pair remove part of their clothing and he waits for Scheherazade to entice him. But before he can prolong his motions of copulation, a spasm overcomes him, as if death rather than pleasure is visiting him. In consequence, the ablutions are quick. Still furious at the problems of the caliphate, he orders Scheherazade to continue the story she has been telling for three days. He hints that if she falters, at dawn he will hand her over to the executioner. But, to please him, she swears to tell a bold tale, removing some of the characters and replacing them with others, and including all manner of intrigue.

Scheherazade is aware of the sentence with which she suspended her account the evening before. She knows exactly in what circumstance Samira's husband, approached by the Grand Vizier, who hoped to bribe him, expressed his disinterest in material goods. But she knows she must bring the scene to an end if she is to entice the Caliph, now lying apathetic on the bed.

The ruler's disregard, a lassitude stemming not from sex but from boredom, can cost Scheherazade her life. She responds quickly to the danger, using words that create windstorms, whirlwinds. She all but sets herself on fire, for her flames to burn the Caliph's heart. Nothing remains untouched by the furious passage of her story. Can he not see how the characters, leaping from spirit into flesh, finally pant with eagerness?

The sovereign surrenders momentarily to the tragedy she introduces. His voracious gaze doesn't let her falter, demanding completion of the task. She confronts his nervous, unstable game with an ironic smile. She almost proves to him that she is sole master of her imagination, by virtue of her instinct for weaving words together. She prefers, however, to continue the enchantment with which she has seduced the Caliph since her arrival at the palace. There are many rituals she still must perform.

28

She frequently evoked Fatima, her accomplice since childhood, who had accompanied her every step since her mother's death. She enjoyed her company. Her humor had opened the doors of adventure to Scheherazade. Fatima had helped her forge a Baghdad filled with intrigue, populated by nobles, plebeians, and strange animals—some of gigantic size, others pygmies, but all of them allies of the supernatural.

Led by her nursemaid, Scheherazade reacted to what she heard from the teachers of Baghdad, who were daily visitors to her father's palace. Hailing from the school of translators and carrying sacred scrolls and manuscripts, some of Greek origin, perfectly translated into Arabic, they assured her of the rigorous predominance of the rational world in all things.

Fatima took pleasure in occupying the vacated chairs that still retained the smell of their bodies, as if hinting to Scheherazade the existence of humble actions unknown to those wise men. Thus her request that Scheherazade include goblins, genies, beggars, and princes in her accounts. Creatures that, having won space in her imagination, might simultaneously express the sordidness and the magic of daily life.

She had been named Fatima in homage to the daughter of the Prophet. When she spoke her own name, she would beat her chest several times to pay reverence to her ancestor. Discreet in her artifices, she did not fear the Vizier. She was sympathetic to the needs of the lonely girl, and as soon as her father would leave for the palace without setting a time for his return, she would ignite Scheherazade's fantasy. It mattered little to her if the servants, or even Dinazarda, witnessed the scene.

Fatima sensed in the girl a curiosity that radiated from her eyes and nostrils, as if to assure her that despite her tender years she was aware of the existence of other universes beyond the Caliphate of Baghdad. She challenged the nursemaid to read the reactions on her face when she described the circularity of the alleyways of the medina.

Questioned by the girl, Fatima resented the limitations of her knowledge as she looked at the calligraphic tablets and the manuscripts that Scheherazade studied as she submerged herself, perplexed, into that world of dense and intricate beauty. She longed to provide the girl with means that would expand the territory of childhood and take her to places distant from her father's palace, where the spectacle of life, to be found everywhere, reverberated, incongruent and multifaceted.

Encouraged by Fatima, before going to sleep Scheherazade would lull the nursemaid with her accounts, sometimes emphasizing a certain camel brought from the Sahara by Omar, a recently invented character. Or she would speak of Hassid the Sailor, who, ready to board his ship and journey toward the daunting Pillars of Hercules, took leave of his homeland while chewing on pieces of watermelon that dribbled their juices down his solemn chest.

Fatima slept at her side, expecting to awaken restored through the magic of the powers coming from the girl. It was common for Scheherazade, listening to Fatima describe the mythic figures of Baghdad, to burn with fever. It excited her to think that in the future, walking through the bazaar, they might find traces of sand from the desert in the merchandise brought by the caravans.

Scheherazade could wait no longer. The time had come to cut the strings, to visit the marketplace. Nor did Fatima have any way to postpone such a decision. So, before they headed for the center of Baghdad, she took careful measures to prevent the Vizier from discovering the grave offense. To hide Scheherazade's marks of noble origin, she made her pass for a beardless boy with a delicate complexion. She effected such a transformation that in the end Scheherazade, in a disguise that reinforced her ambiguity, no longer knew who she was or to what name she should answer— a dilemma that, though it bothered Scheherazade, amused Fatima. Proud of her handiwork in neutralizing the adolescent girl's body and disguising her sex, she showed her, through concrete examples, the advantages of experiencing the pleasure of being boy and girl at the same time. Scheherazade reacted to her dual status with a wisdom that she would need in the future, in case she remained anchored solely in the female body.

Holding her hand, Fatima dragged Scheherazade through the narrow streets like a blind person, tripping over stones, between angular walls, all sense of direction lost. But she could not stem the tears of the girl, moved by so many revelations. She would alternately blush and pale, experiencing the gamut of emotions that would accompany her on later visits. Then, sure of not being caught by the Vizier's guard, they explored the mysteries of the city, opening closed spaces, secret doors, becoming more and more daring.

With a change of Scheherazade's disguise, supported by a walking stick, it would be difficult to note her delicate features, the snow-white skin that was almost never exposed to the sun, or the traces of sensuality under her appearance of poverty. On these outings they would walk slowly, and Fatima never let her out of her sight. In her chiseled face shone the willingness to raise her fists against any intruder who looked too closely at Scheherazade, shooing him away with a stick or coarse words. Fatima's hostility did not interest Scheherazade, who was intent solely on accumulating experience, storing away the features of the universe of the medina, penetrating its labyrinths, those corridors that, in addition to protecting their dwellers from enemy attack, funneled the breeze and provided shelter from the inclement sun.

When she saw the market for the first time, Scheherazade immediately identified the true setting of her stories. Beset by the imprecations of the masses, permeated with all kinds of unknown aromas, she probed the very heart of the craft of storytelling.

Scheherazade would return from those flights with a sensation of helplessness. Divining her alarm, which the girl had not yet learned to suppress, Fatima held her to her breast, smoothed her hair, assured her that despite the giddiness and the commotion she would not weaken. She asked only that she not let the signs of insubordination show on her face, for all to see.

Following Fatima's orientation, Scheherazade in those days would retreat to her room, where she took her meals under the pretext of not feeling well. Her father, absorbed in the administrative tasks of the caliphate, never perceived the transformations affecting his daughter. Dinazarda herself, usually attentive, when informed of her indisposition, respected her request.

With Fatima's help, she retraced the path of her feelings in the days that followed. The impressions left by what she had experienced were diffusing into her body. She felt no obligation to prove to the Vizier or to her sister the wisdom springing from the visit to lands impregnated with poverty, illusions, plaintive cries. Proud of his lineage, the Vizier would never have pardoned his daughter for being in the midst of rabble, in danger of defilement.

Her apprenticeship in those years had accelerated, with Fatima bringing her flowers, stuffed insects, and sweets, determined to offer her the precious gift of knowing the world. She didn't shrink from secretly taking Scheherazade to the marketplace, whenever the girl asked, even though she might have to pay with her life for such disobedience to the Vizier.

Unselfish by nature, Fatima had accumulated no wealth in those years, and by temperament she would not flatter the Vizier in hopes of gaining rewards. Never had she envisioned herself with the right to a home outside the limits of that palace. Scheherazade had become her only family. For this reason more than any other, she helped to consolidate the repertoire of stories that the girl quickly recorded in her memory.

Beginning with the visits to the medina, Scheherazade had come to understand that the secrets of daily life that were the materials of knowledge and the distant reality of the Arab universe were easy for her to accept. Her spirit, after all, sprang from this people who had deliberately created disorganized labyrinths. This was why she perceived no difference between the group at court, forever arrogant, and the vagrant crowd, hungering for food and fantasy. Both of them, as if by common accord, displayed equal amounts of delirium in their impious carnality.

29

Contrary to his plan to eliminate his young wives each morning, the Caliph spares Scheherazade's life. Although he struggles to decree her death, he continues to frustrate the executioner who awaits his prey at the entrance to the bedroom.

Ever watchful of the sentence menacing her, Scheherazade perfects the art of overlapping stories. The master of meager time, she ties one plot to another while untangling herself from the web of intrigues with the skill of an accomplished narrator.

Buried in the uncertainties that accompany his reign, the Caliph arches his right eyebrow, a sign that he intends to order the death of a foe or an innocent. Such a gesture affirms that, life having offended him deeply, he possesses abundant motive for exacting revenge.

What he feels for the young woman, which translates into pity and admiration, affects his autonomy, his acts of governing, without his grasping the reasons for not directing her death and putting an end to this torture. His distress, however, stemming from these conflicts, smothers him like infamy, taking shadowy root in his heart and banishing any ray of light that signifies happiness. He combats this by reducing Scheherazade's influence, erasing her capacity for creating fables about life, as if it too were the object of her invention.

In his eagerness to forget the princess, he weaves small deliriums. He again imagines a strange woman introducing herself into Scheherazade's body, without even asking permission. A woman whose origin and name he doesn't know but a woman whom he covets. And with whom, after a nervous and imaginary coupling that drains him of emotion and hope, he crosses swords.

The Caliph's fantasy does not go unnoticed. Scheherazade perceives in the ruler the decision to dramatize his encounter with the stranger, as if, protected by the theatrical illusion, he reflects the desire to empty the content of Scheherazade's body, remaining with only the shell, in order to offer it to another woman. He had done this on an earlier occasion, without her having reacted at the time. But now the sovereign's plan is to dislodge her from her chambers, and the herald's trumpets would soon announce his intention.

The urgency to destroy her impresses itself upon him, convincing him that unless he drives away the source of the evil, misfortune will befall his house. But he can prolong the illusion of multiple women, at the same time sapping the young woman's energy, only if Scheherazade cooperates, if she willingly yields to him the envelope of her precious flesh in which to encase the woman of his making.

Scheherazade guesses his trick and what he is inclined to do if she lends him her body and thus becomes a mere pawn for the ruler to move on the chessboard of his lust. After having disguised herself so much in her characters and having taken such pleasure in using the voices and gestures of others, it would be natural if she duped the sovereign into believing she had accepted his magic, even at the risk of losing her soul.

Since childhood, the Caliph has dreamed of creating fables about daily life, and only now, by means of this trick, does he feel capable of transcending the limitations his position has imposed on him. But, confronted with the dilemma of continuing with this playacting and thereby losing the meaning of any reality, he is frightened. He fears experiencing an orgy of prodigality, of using up the coins of imagination that he dreams of handing out for free in the bazaar.

Anticipating the emotions to be exposed to listeners in the next few days, he asks himself what kind of maiden now occupies Scheherazade's body, transformed into a mere carcass. But if she has in fact left, then who was it that he held in his arms? Who was wearing Scheherazade's features behind the veil? Could it be someone from the desert, familiar with tents, which at the coming of the rains close like mollusks to protect their dwellers from the hounding wind?

The gentle acceptance by Scheherazade of such a fantasy disturbs him. He doubts that she supports an imagination acting on its own, vying with her for the scepter of the chimera. But he doesn't know how to analyze the young woman's expressions. Lately, in his daily contact with her, he has grown disdainful of the game of masks that had marked his upbringing. This repudiation does not protect him, for he fears the consequences of a delirium that, in the name of recovering his youth and seeking happiness, has expelled Scheherazade from her quarters.

And why should he care? For a long time she has been doing him injury. But without her at his side the world lacks cohesion, fragments itself, without the advantage at least of the woman's wringing from him the strength he depends on for rejuvenation.

He has gone too far in his whim of implanting different women inside Scheherazade. Perhaps he has prompted her decision to avenge herself, to impose on him the burden of a reality that, by himself, he can no longer bear. Or to disappear from the palace without saying farewell. But if Scheherazade were truly to flee, where would she go? Would she return to her father's house, or undertake a voyage long dreamed of? Was it possible that in those moments she has already set out en route to Damascus? That would explain her tense expression, though she says nothing and never complains of her captivity.

Seeing her before him, the Caliph asks himself where Scheherazade has gone, leaving behind her mortal remains. He wants to follow her and demand her narrative monologue, without which existence is mere suffering. Has she turned sullen, inclined to leave him a trail of hatred, a legacy that Dinazarda and Jasmine would inherit?

Amid such inquietude, he wonders if he has aged to the point of losing any forbearance with himself. And if that has in fact occurred, why has he yielded to a childish impulse that has hurt

Scheherazade, leading her to run away despite her presence before him?

Feeling guilty for yielding to a fantasy whose pernicious flow he cannot stop, everything in him surges uncontrollably, signaling that age is punishing him. He no longer knows how to break free of the gift of imagination, once so yearned for, that now comes to him with no sense of measure, forging stories that imitate a coarse and crude reality.

This talent, so recently acquired, asphyxiates him. Unlike the vagabonds of Baghdad, the Caliph has not prepared himself to be moved by the distressed notes of the lute that he listens to in the throne room, or to accept the contradictory versions of simple day-to-day life. His heart desires only to rest, to be rid of human tribulations.

As a result of these difficulties, which artists manage so well, the Caliph realizes that the imagination never rests. It is onerous, promiscuous, the captive of limitless resources. With its improbable and infinite combinations it moves about a territory occupied by masters of nonsense. Among beings who, by impregnating others with their mental deeds, earn their applause in the public square.

Scheherazade observes this new prodigality in the Caliph's anxious face. She quickly evaluates the gains and losses that might result from the sudden emancipation of the ruler. Generally taciturn, little given to pleasure, the Caliph nonetheless consumes novelistic absurdities and finds them diverting. This other man now emerging in him surprises her. She doesn't know whether it is better for her to perpetuate this state or to incarcerate it once more, to make him renounce the voluptuousness emanating from his newfound imagination, to return him to his habitual apathy. And only this way, resigned as ever, does he listen to Scheherazade narrate, submitting to a mastery that subdues his proverbial cruelty.

30

Scheherazade is living a bold adventure, though her journeys around the room lead nowhere. What transports, loves, corrodes metals and hearts, is the imagination, that intrepid warrior that brings her back to Baghdad whenever she strays too far.

She never tires of yielding to the irreparable voluptuousness of storytelling, as if in this way, whatever direction she takes, she is setting out on a pilgrimage to Mecca or Medina. And which, in the Genesiac vision of these lands, offers her prodigious revelations.

Scheherazade goes alone on these undertakings, leaving everything behind. Obliged to hasty farewells, she quickly forgets everyone. She loses family ties and disdains endearments, staring at Dinazarda as if her sister weren't there. It does no good for Jasmine to gaze at her, disposed to help in her hours of distress. Engulfed in the odyssey of a crossing that threatens to become permanent, Scheherazade doesn't question this fate from which she is unable to flee. In these moments, she has in her favor the aptitude for storytelling, which takes her to a place where the head of an invisible god rests, dispensing false benedictions.

Small in stature, she has grown little since puberty. Her snowy skin, in contrast to Dinazarda's dark complexion, shies from the sun that invades the chambers. Everything about her is sensitive to collapse. But as she paces the marble floors, with the gardens behind her, Scheherazade is determined to bring down the Caliph. To do this, she traverses the veins of her characters, listens to their pulse of life, wanders through an area of danger. It protects her to recognize that the Caliph, although desirous of doing so, is incapable of prying into her secrets, her deepest intent.

Submissive to the world, she seeks in this crusade an uncertain terrain that exists but has no name. Nevertheless, it authorizes her to approach a different center, once dreamed of by prophets and poets, that has imagination as its guide. Though slave to the blade of death at the Caliph's will, she sets out on the heroic journey that holds obstacles of every kind.

At the helm of the boat that floats through her memory, Scheherazade, her hair fluttering, overcomes whitecap waves, attracts the legion of dragons that with fishlike lightness pursue her on the ocean's surface. In the role of heroine, she fulfills gracefully the task that destiny has imposed on her in resisting the wrath of the executioners, never acceding to being a lamb resigned before the sacrificial altar. Her goal continues to be the same: to save the young women of the kingdom caught in the sights of a despot.

During this initiatory voyage, without set destination and with a postponed date as prize, Scheherazade is totally dependent on the monarch's whim. Facing this, she demands the right to confront through her stories an unknown world, one that holds adventures of every kind.

In the service of the Vizier's daughters, the slaves form a circle around the storyteller. Some discreetly babble sounds, while Jasmine, shaking a mosquito net, goes in pursuit of the only insect now bothering Scheherazade. The young woman accepts being cosseted, knowing that she occupies a position of prominence in the Arab imagination. It is as if since childhood, encouraged by Fatima, she had taken on the corporeality of all the heroes whose legends put down roots in the memory of men. And through this conviction she proudly clothes herself with the face of her vagabond characters.

The Orient is dizzying in her soul. Under its attraction, Scheherazade plunges into the archaic memory and the arcana of other lands, relives historical mysteries like the encounter of Priam and Achilles after the death of Hector. And she reproduces it with richness of detail, from feminine solidarity emphasizing the laments of Andromeda and Hecuba, women battered by pain. That singular moment when the king of. Troy, kneeling before the haughty son of Thetis, claims the mortal remains of Prince Hector.

On the horizon of her frequently overflowing narrative mind, engendering multiple versions, the suffering of the venerable old man for his beloved son arouses her sympathy. She supports Achilles, upon returning the prince's remains, offering the downcast king an expression of his compassion and thus gaining stature in the eyes of history.

Imbued with such magic, Scheherazade foresees in the mirror of time other mysteries from beyond the sea. She witnesses the solitary trek of the knight Percival, designated because of his merits to discover the Holy Grail. She examines the faith of Arthur's knight, the spirit governing an adventure that constitutes one of the centers of any narrative.

With this conviction, Scheherazade smiles in contentment. Life appears to favor her in retaining civilizing distances and centuries, in being able to follow the steps of Percival, in heeding his suffering, his perseverance, his failure. But where had the knight hidden the Grail, the object of his search? Had he found in the chalice the ineffable essence?

Perhaps the solitary hero's endless peregrination stimulates her to enrich her own stories. Subject to the illusory game of plot, she may be acting wisely in mixing such legends with those that originate in the fearlessness of Sinbad, Aladdin, and Zoneida, creatures who thirst for adventure. And could not she as well, in giving rein to her secret and ambivalent nature, become the Percival of the desert and go in search of a dream of her own?

31

The Caliph notices her unexpected voluptuousness. Scheherazade perspires, her body dampens. He senses the smell coming from her wet, tumescent flesh. Upon seeing her amorous euphoria, everything in him throbs, surrenders, and his member hardens for several instants.

Transported far away, Scheherazade experiences desire, but not for the ruler. More intrepid than her father, she covets whatever is in the sovereign's presence, with the intention of punishing him. She doesn't disguise her emotion, acting as if he weren't there, an attitude before which the Caliph retreats, cowed. The veins of his phallus cool and weaken.

Free of the Caliph, she disguises her excitement behind an expression as cool as marble. Her thoughts drift again as she remembers the youth passing through the marketplace, his brown eyes staring at her as though not to forget her in the future. Fatima, who forbids anyone to gaze too long at Scheherazade, shoos him away with the staff, whipping him and shouting as she would at a sheep. The youth's smile, however, directed at Scheherazade, announces the seasons of the year, the heat of the desert, from which his swarthy skin surely comes. Scheherazade's body, reacting to the gaze, pulsates as she feels him at her side, his wide hand flattened against her belly, moving in circles, her organs expanding at his touch, stirring her, a disturbing, unceasing emotion.

Fatima has seen the exchange of looks but does nothing, as if she wishes for Scheherazade, upon returning to her father's palace, to preserve the youth's image and never forget it, like a present she gives her in the form of an intangible lover who would never be hers. And as if she should be happy at having been courted in a glance by a humble Baghdad youth.

Although yearning for the burning flesh of the youth she has recently seen, she busies herself with goblins, monsters, creatures in rags, or the king's crown, inspiring her listeners to laughter and tears, forever inseparable—especially for those who, wherever they are, make love without scruples. In the shade of a tree, on the blazing desert floor, or behind fruit stalls, engaged in amorous battle, they moan, rage, murmur, and any nook serves for the shudders that precede orgasm.

Thanks to Scheherazade, the Caliph has the illusion of being a stallion or a unicorn as, fearful of being rejected, he pursues her characters. He suspects that she has created these beings solely to defend herself, in order not to remain unprotected, at the whim of the sovereign. At the same time that she offers proof of not fearing the lash of his cruelty, she seems to be saying that one day she will go far away, never to return. She seems willing to assume any risk, without measuring the consequences. In the end, what could the sovereign expect of one who depends on his temporary pardon for survival? Someone who, under the pretext of telling the lives of others, molds her characters using the gauge of her chimera.

Forgotten in her corner, Dinazarda doesn't let the Caliph out of her sight. His nervousness as he walks, disoriented, almost causes him to slip on the marble floor. He quickly rights himself, however, disguising the weakness, not wanting his aging to be noticed. The blood of the young women, which he had drunk before killing them, had neither regenerated his skin nor deterred the ongoing ruin. As he ages, he loses small joys, all of them precious.

Despite these woes, Dinazarda helps him. All that is lacking is to offer the houris to open the doors of paradise while still alive. While she attends him, he sends signals to Scheherazade's sister to take care, not to trust too much in talent to save her. The sovereign will not long tolerate a submission that humiliates him. Why believe in human glory?

Scheherazade's nimbleness, nevertheless, frees Dinazarda from participating in her distress. Whenever Dinazarda tries to bring her back to practical reality, Scheherazade, driven by fantasy, proceeds unfazed. She crosses cliffs and oceans, uncertain where to spend the coming nights. The Arab world to which she belongs affirms the archaic condition. A cross of itinerants and the inventive, the young woman's body is infused with joy at hearing the bleating of animals, at the sound coming from the six-string guitar, at exalting a camel's supple hump, whose shadow on the desert sands reveals that notable brother of her race. Nature, taking such pity on humans, adapts itself to the rigors of both heat and cold, freezing and warming the blood according to the needs of Berbers, Bedouins, and so many other peoples.

She continually revisits the core of her race, nursing the hope of one day achieving narrative synthesis, and from encompassing its most cherished myths, to gain in return the ability to disguise herself as both man and woman indiscriminately, interpreting each with uncommon patience.

As she chews the unleavened bread, enriched with saffron and butter, Scheherazade crosses the Red Sea on her way to Damascus, eager to claim rights she does not possess. The successive displacements bring to her, from wherever she has been, the fruits of the experience that now she can no longer do without. She also brings back music, dance, poetry, religious feeling, harvested from every era.

Neglectful of the young woman, the Caliph absently fingers the taboret, attentive to the sound of the lute that the musician coaxes from the instrument with an eagle feather, at the entrance to the royal chambers to which he has no access. Each string, as it vibrates the instrument's pear-shaped wooden body, anoints the Caliph's soul.

Vulnerable and shrewd, the sovereign wonders why Scheherazade smiles and he does not. What does he lack to be able to experience that kind of joy? He yearns to probe that happiness, the mystery that flourishes in the young woman and isolates her from him. It is as if the Caliph, compromised by the solitude of power, envies her the pleasure that never wanes, despite the death sentence hanging over her.

Submissive in the tiny details, Scheherazade records the nature of that conflict. Followed closely by Jasmine, whose breast moves with an imperceptible tremor, Scheherazade longs to tell the Caliph that he knows but little of the secret homeland of men. Despite his power, he cannot cross the threshold of the human adventure. He is unlike her, who though sentenced to die at any moment relies on her imagination, to wander through the markets, to chance upon the vernacular, the scatological legends that come from the dirt floors of the people—able to feel compassion for the misery of the thousands of slaves of the caliphate.

Almost everything that she has produced, at the Caliph's expense, is the fruit of invention, of the parchments she has read, the stories she hears, the marvels her memory has accumulated over the years—and of her vocation of making up and living many lives at once. As well as conceiving of buried cities, of deciphering long-vanished inscriptions, of translating the cryptic messages of dreams, not forgetting the perseverance of the teachers of Baghdad, the flights to the bazaar, where she had sometimes gone in men's clothing, giving her voice a raspy, harsh accent. Almost always with her hands inside the pockets of her tunic so none would see her alabaster fingers, long and nimble, and holding her body erect with a boldness denied to women.

Scheherazade knows she is the instrument of her race. Allah has given her the harvesting of words, her wheat.

32

She must come to love. To yield to impassioned flesh and forget momentarily the misfortune of others that has played so prominent a role in her stories. To suspend her indomitable narrative instinct and transform herself into a character of her own destiny.

Scheherazade fears suddenly discovering love in some stranger, in a simple exchange of glances, an arrow shot by a prince or adventurer piercing both the walls of the palace and her heart. He might be a Harun or a Sinbad who, overcoming the imperial guard, would ride off with her through the desert to his tent decorated with precious adornments, the place they had decided earlier would be perfect for uniting their voracious bodies, as yet unknown to each other.

In matters of sex, the Vizier's daughters proclaim inexperience. While Scheherazade had the Caliph as her sole lover, Dinazarda, without her sister's knowledge, had furtively made love with her father's attendant on a visit to the palace. The youth was killed days later, suspicion for the crime falling on a betrayed husband. Dinazarda's tears for him lasted only a day. Although she never loved him, she still remembers the first time they copulated in the bedroom, with the servant girl's complicity.

She had not been moved by the slightest passion but rather by the wish to feel radiating desire being born and dying between her legs. The lover's premature death had left him owing her a bolder type of sex, which Dinazarda knew to exist from the erotic treatises her father kept hidden from his daughters' eyes.

Brought up in a secretive world, she had not told Scheherazade about her lover. She therefore felt she had no right to demand of her sister what she herself did not offer. But then what would she say about her own vulva, the Caliph's phallus, matters of the heart, when she lived ensconced in her stories, keeping sex at a distance?

With little sexual experience, Dinazarda has doubts about her sister's innocence. She suspects that before becoming the Caliph's wife she had removed some clothing so a certain lad from the marketplace could caress her moist sex before spilling on her his incandescent sperm. She scrutinized her sister's pubis, the satin sheet, looking for hairs.

Defenseless before Dinazarda's morbid gaze, Scheherazade retreats. On the alert against her sister's curiosity, she entwines herself with Zoneida and Ali Baba, hoping they will shower her with plots to throw truth off the scent. Her penetrating gaze becomes her shield, affecting Jasmine, who in the bath rubs her with a sponge perhaps brought by Sinbad. But despite the intimacy, the slave doesn't exaggerate her zeal. Putting aside her anguish, she limits herself to detecting sudden movements in the young woman, shudders of desire. Anything there might be between a princess and a slave is superficial and fleeting. Perhaps the brushing of the fingers that sometimes evokes spasms in Scheherazade, a signal that Jasmine has ventured into the concave area below the mount of Venus.

Seduced by Jasmine's caresses, which advance and retreat based on her tremors, Scheherazade notes that the constant expectation of death has quelled her desire. Even when dreaming vaguely of strangers menacing her lonely flesh, she doesn't extol passion or love as beneficent. Reality, originating with the Caliph, blots out the mystery of love, extinguishing its rage.

She has not yet truly loved. Confronted, however, with the breadth of feelings in her stories, Scheherazade flays humankind with ferocious descriptions. Her lexicon becomes scatological, realistic, devoid of lyrical brushstrokes. At times, perceiving the absence of love that leaves a hollow in her soul, she repents, finding consolation in plunging into the heart of the plot, looking for the consciousness of evil and the essential attribute of good.

She assuages her daily nostalgia by observing the firmament.

From the garden seen through the window, her gaze advances to the city that lies wrapped in a reddish sphere. Foretelling an unhurried nightfall, Baghdad emerges like a plan conceived in foreign lands by King David himself, who in a paroxysm of reverence to Jehovah charged Solomon, his son by Bathsheba, with building the temple of which the god of Abraham presents himself as guardian and architect.

During her childhood, Baghdad had been the embodiment of a forbidden illusion, which provided reason enough for Scheherazade to beg Fatima to allow her to walk through the medina, just to hear what her fellow storytellers would relate. From these outings she had reconstructed in her imagination minarets whose skylights opened to let the believer speak to Allah without an intermediary. She had explored the interior of old houses and tiled palaces, had found in alcoves stains pointing to the sins of furtively consummated passion.

It had also been her objective to learn the genesis of Baghdad— the curves, meanderings, circles, wavy lines, vestiges of the people's needs. By consulting manuscripts, she had discovered the first secret passageways through which Harun ar-Rashid, becoming lost on a certain occasion, had been led by a vegetable vendor who supplied cactus and tomatoes to the palace.

On these walks, some imaginary, some real, Fatima refined Scheherazade's taste, her didactic nature calling the girl's attention to relevant details. Now, attuned to her nursemaid's story lines, Scheherazade populates the urban landscape with characters immune to a type of heroism that has always struck her as grotesque. She dislikes the hero who swells his chest to boast of his exploits. In the solitude of her room, attracted by the vagabonds who normally forgo niceties and reverences, Scheherazade brings them, shrewd and cunning, to the center of the stories. She molds them into the type of heroes who, despite their almost mythic dimensions, sell dates, dried fruits, onions, lamb meat, spices.

Under the pressure of death, which the Caliph never allows her to forget, Baghdad fades on the horizon. Looking at the city nevertheless frees her from the bonds of her narrative burden and attenuates her agony.

Sensitive to the princess's feelings, Jasmine kneels at her side, offering her delicacies. Sipping tea, Scheherazade reads her fortune in the leaves at the bottom of the cup. The future is dark and melancholy, affording her no respite. It tells her the narrative soul is an ingrate, formulating its characters' plans without consideration for the fear in the storyteller's body.

Among the small court made up of women she gradually forgets the shadow of the scaffold that spreads along the palace walls and reaches the windows of the royal chambers. She hopes to survive the hour set for her death by telling the Caliph another story as soon as he arrives. Cheered, she anticipates love blossoming in the narrow Baghdad streets. Her body envisions a day when it will open to love.

The Caliph, still seated on his throne and about to head for the chambers, is unaware that from that moment on, he is doomed once more to be betrayed by a woman.

33

Dinazarda bends every effort to saving Scheherazade. She lives in fear of sudden disaster, that her sister's repertoire will be exhausted without warning, or that the Caliph will tire of hearing it. He does not want to live with an interminable mystery that threatens him and never seems to reach its end.

She calls upon Jasmine, who months earlier, inflating her chest and emphasizing the erect nipples under the transparent garment, had confided to Dinazarda her wish to prosper. Dispossessed of belongings, the slave made Dinazarda see that her knowledge exceeded what she had studied. She liked to listen and to imagine about any subject at all. On one occasion she alluded to the deep shame that had long afflicted her, without specifying the reason behind her anguish. She added only that in her previous captivity, before being brought to the Caliph's palace, she had learned some rudiments of the magnificent art of calligraphy, but not enough to display a vanity rarely granted women, much less slaves. Though she exercised this art stealthily and with true tenacity, her lines, convulsive and unsteady, still showed a high level of uncertainty, as they said nothing. There were no words in her randomly drawn calligraphy.

Called to service in the royal chambers, Jasmine had devoted herself passionately to the sisters, kneeling at their feet, her preferred position, eager to please them, on the slightest pretext asking their forgiveness for errors committed, always willing to assume the faults of the world in exchange for a retreat where she might one day find some part of herself.

On the morning when Jasmine first arrived in the chambers, Dinazarda had immediately found favor in her dark-complexioned skin, the black hair tied atop her head that elevated her above the rest of humanity, as if from the heights of that mountain the slave could make out the imagined city. She was of humble extraction, but her regal air motivated Dinazarda to discover her provenance. Though curious, having inherited from the Vizier a commanding mien, Dinazarda had not asked her where she came from, in shackles, to serve in the palace. She had not inquired whether she by chance originated in a northern tribe of absolute integrity, said to be the descendants of King Solomon, who by Jehovah's grace had impregnated countless women come to Jerusalem in search of his proverbial wisdom.

Bonds between them grew quickly, and the sisters could no longer do without her care. While Scheherazade acknowledged her courtesies with absent gentility, Dinazarda, by exercising authority, evinced the distance between them. But she soon repented her despotism and, unable to resist Jasmine's look, a mixture of languor and combativeness, she offered her gifts and proved her confidence in the slave by entrusting her with small missions. She was truly intrigued by the sagacity with which Jasmine, stealing away through the palace, returned with that which would reestablish the equilibrium between them.

Recently Dinazarda has sent her to the bazaar, with the admonition to keep her mission secret even from her companions in misfortune. The language that Dinazarda uses, instructing her to leave and return to the palace at day's end, bringing certain things of value, is clothed in symbolism that disturbs Jasmine. Noticing, however, the princess's embarrassment, she is eager to be put to the test, for them to judge her intelligence, how she becomes involved in palace intrigues. Their asking her for the impossible would allow her to rise on the palace's social ladder.

Like Scheherazade, Dinazarda tends toward minutiae, toward foreseeing the follies of reality. Seated like a Buddha with crossed arms, she gradually raises her voice. Touched by the poverty and the enchantment of the slave woman, she stresses that she must be careful, above all when she makes her way to the last palace gate in the direction of the city. She must watch to see whether some bailiff is following her. No one can know she belongs to the young wife of the Caliph.

In Baghdad there is no such thing as too much caution. Between its walls it can easily happen that a stranger, even begging, can be a prince. By tradition, no one knows who is a visitor, a thief, a noble, each more bellicose than the other, ripping off chunks of life with his teeth. It is no excess of prudence to be on guard against some maiden inclined to seduce her, taking Jasmine for Harun ar-Rashid himself disguised as a woman. And especially, she must keep her ears open for the clamor of cunning vendors of fraudulent merchandise, who wander through the medina. It is they who elaborate extravagant theologies about the fruit of the tree of evil, of the fig and the date, growing in the paradise promised by Muhammad.

According to Scheherazade, who better than the thieves and adventurers of Baghdad to honor the elemental act of story-telling? Despite the fact that, perhaps because of the poverty in which they live, their plots tend to be overblown.

Dinazarda is confident that nothing escapes Jasmine, and that, charged with such a mandate, she will return to the Caliph's palace with her hands full of pomegranates, golden grapes, and love poems—simple details yoked to the humanity of the market, which Scheherazade would, if necessary, know how to bring together to form a story.

Jasmine is impressed by Dinazarda's mission, to offer Scheher-azade the mystery that radiates from the minarets and the square. But how can she act like a princess and return to the palace without such a task damaging her soul? How can she transport popular imaginings to the royal chambers without introducing into them the profound touch of her personal aspirations?

In defense of these notions, the slave remembers that she was born in the desert, warmed by poverty and melancholy songs. And that she has slept among goats and sheep, breathing the per-fume of camels, slaking her thirst from wells whose waters, mea-ger and contested, sustained the nomadic tribe. Did fate now intend to make her a princess, part of that dynasty, to the point of one day being burned on the pyre of hope when the two women go away?

Watchfully, Jasmine wanders about the medina, finding it difficult to choose which tales to hear. But shortly before nightfall she has everything in hand. Her bag full of provisions, she places before Dinazarda sweets, cheese, words, the products of the land in the form of stories. Dinazarda takes her aside, demanding details, demanding that she tell all.

Not far from this dialogue, Scheherazade ignores the whirlwind besieging the two women. Concentrating on what she will say that night, she fears losing the essential rhythm of the sentences now that the Caliph has arrived. Exhausted, he sits down on the divan and makes a gesture dispensing with copulation. But Scheherazade is to proceed, beginning where she had left off the night before.

She resumes at the point where she had introduced Aladdin, the character of the new plot. The theme, large in scope, quickly enthralls those present. With the life of Aladdin at its center, she follows the malevolent recesses of imagination. It is easy for her to expand an adventure that promises to absorb parallel themes without losing sight of the lamp vendor. As she presents the temperament of the youth, however, she is slippery, her words ambiguous, and she surrounds herself with chance events, outsized elements. But with lightness and agility she convinces the sovereign that inside any story is the germ of another. Others will follow in Aladdin's wake, like him eager to become rich. All this from the storytelling that is so much a part of her.

From these humble starting points, which intertwine before the Caliph's eyes, she obeys her calling as a raconteur and postpones death for one more day.

34

The Vizier's tension grows as he watches the hourglass. He has no trust in the future. He suffers for the daughter handed over to the covetousness of the Caliph, who is never sated. And it avails him nothing to swear to serve the ruler for eternity in exchange for the young woman's life.

Wanting to save her, the Vizier struggles to stay away from the chambers where Scheherazade seduces the ruler's imagination. In an effort to distract him, the Vizier reminds him of the duties in governing the Caliphate of Baghdad. Besides being the object of a cult on the part of his subjects, the Caliph also answers to public functions and the art of warfare. It is not in his interest to remain indifferent to his territorial neighbors, especially Samarra, which in the past had usurped the designation of capital. Only decades later, at the cost of a war, had Baghdad recovered the coveted title.

Though he lacks his daughter's gift for fantasy, the Vizier is a tenacious man. And in defense of Scheherazade he must not fail. Softening his speech, he practically whispers in the sovereign's ear like one of his favorites. He mentions the belligerence of Samarra, now considered a friend. But the Caliph nevertheless should not be fooled. As before, Samarra harbors the ambition of stealing back the title of capital of the lands of the Prophet. The coveted Baghdad that at nightfall, bathed in a red glow, projects onto every street and alleyway a trail of light as bright as day.

He refreshes the Caliph's memory with concrete facts about

Samarra. How that kingdom, unresigned to the political degradation suffered by the loss to Baghdad, moves in secret, how its leaders' objective is the undermining of the city. He must never let such enemies out of his sight. And the Persians also warrant attention, because of the warlike spirit shown on earlier occasions. Thus, if the Caliph examines the maps, both he and the Vizier would come to the conclusion that, given the precariousness of the present borders, it would be worthwhile to annex these kingdoms to the caliphate even at the cost of war. Such a strategy was a long-standing practice of the Abbasids, the illustrious clan that, associated with the city since its founding, had won important conquests for Baghdad.

Those headstrong people, claiming a place in Islamic history from the beginning, settled issues of power and faith by the sword. In so doing they faced determined battles that required the stuff of heroes. In this manner the Abbasids, of whom the Caliph is a descendant, had been on guard against the heretical and menacing Ishmaelites, a sect that, according to legend, Abdullah, son of Fatima, had founded near the rivers of the Persian Gulf. The Ishmaelites, having promptly fallen into disagreement with the Caliphate of Baghdad, provoked the ire of the caliphs, who were displeased with a schism that they deemed injurious to the Islamic world.

The Ishmaelites, because of their mystic vocation, were initially austere and seemed convinced that the words of the Qur'an, divine in origin, had a sacred meaning that only they could fathom. With this dogmatic nature, the sect had spread through Islam, thanks to its followers' feigning intense religious activity while actually conspiring against the constituted powers.

What is certain is that Abdullah and his horde of heretics, condemned to wandering, emerged on the Islamic scene with the designation of Fatimids, creators, beyond a doubt, of a prodigious civilization that the Abbasids themselves had absorbed into their daily life.

The Vizier does not lose heart. His persuasive reasoning

returns to the Persians and other adversaries the Caliph has idly driven away. Besides these peoples he mentions others, equally threatening to the grandeur of Baghdad, which among its many centers possesses the notable school of translators, responsible for the dissemination of the timeless wisdom of the Greeks among the inhabitants of far-off Europe.

It is difficult to persuade the Caliph, to make him agree that the moment has come to deplore the behavior of the tribes that, in isolated actions in the desert, have long harassed the caravans making their way to Baghdad, transporting goods essential to the region's commerce.

Concentrating first on Scheherazade and now on the chords from the harp that the musician uses to entertain him, the ruler allows his mind to drift from the reality the Vizier attempts to demonstrate through monotonous argumentation. The musician, wearing an African cap, who tunes the instrument by the beating of his own heart, hints to the sovereign that he abandon the scimitar that the Vizier is urging him to grasp and venture into unknown and disturbing places.

The Vizier is irritated by the sound of the instrument, which prevents him from attending to the affairs of the caliphate. Controlling his anger at the musician, he goes on about the stray Persians who in their incursions into the desert steal water from Bedouin wells.

So avid about the favorable outlook for war, given the political deterioration of their neighbors, the Vizier focuses his entire attention on military maneuvers and neglects to defend his daughter.

Amused by the magnitude of the palace rooms, the Caliph stares at a tapestry hung on the wall, in which the artisans of the kingdom, contrary to the norms against reproducing human faces, had recorded the famous battle fought by a fierce Abbasid ancestor. The artistic depiction of the warriors' convulsed faces at the moment of death awakens in the Caliph's breast the din of combat. The ruler's indulgent gaze at the warriors prompts the Vizier, visibly proud of his administration, to declare that the royal treasury is bulging with coins. With undisguised greed, he lists the kingdom's holdings, citing each detail as if he were dealing with the treasure of the forty thieves recently discovered by Ali Baba, without ever mentioning the name of his daughter.

On hearing of Ali Baba, cited by the Vizier under the guise of curiosity, the Caliph considers the description of the royal treasury, which in many ways coincides with Scheherazade's story. The details emphasized by the Vizier relating to gold, silver, and rubies have caught his attention. He wonders whether Scheherazade, before coming to the palace, had spoken to her father of Ali Baba, or whether she had heard the same descriptions that the Vizier sometimes gave him when stressing the power of the coin.

The concern with goods and jewels doubtless expresses a family obsession, albeit with disparate results. For though the Vizier lacks verbal charm, his daughter, driven by a powerful imagination, transforms any unpolished material into a refined substance. Not to mention that the Vizier, in his task of governance, shows repeated signs of miserliness, while his daughter in her storytelling outdoes herself in profusion and fantasy.

Before immersing himself in the soft musical chords that relaxed him, the Caliph had found the Vizier's insistence unreasonable. It exhausts him to think of mounting his white charger, an animal as tense as a lute string, clutching his dagger and scimitar. To yield once more to the warlike life, celebrated by courtiers and poets, no longer arouses the excitement that Scheherazade's accounts now inspire in him.

After the young woman came to the palace, the Caliph turned against the court, sparing only the Vizier from criticism, in consideration for his devotion to the kingdom. But what is he to do with a servant who, by keeping him in the audience room past the appointed time, deprives him of following Scheherazade's suggestion of closing his eyes, at any time of day, even in the middle of an audience, and envisioning Sinbad's tempest-tossed ship smashing against the rocks, while a certain queen, atop the promontory of the island over which she reigns, eagerly witnesses the spoils from the shipwreck washing ashore, hopeful of converting, that very night, the mariners into beasts and lovers in her thrall?

Under the double imprisonment of Scheherazade's spell and the cruel queen, the Caliph is distracted, as if he has already left the Vizier and is on his way to the chambers.

35

Scheherazade, who thanks to the Caliph has never fallen in love, believes love is like theater. The spectacle of lovemaking, as she now conceives it, requires illusion, artifice, masks adhered to the lovers' faces while they copulate. Masks that, molded in wax, melt and renew themselves during the night as they add and subtract gestures and words to a shared life.

She glides in gilded slippers across the cool marble of the ample chambers toward the royal eagle with an almost six-foot wing-spread, which by order of the Caliph is brought each morning after he spares her life. She is excited by the bird of such proud origin, which after reigning in the heavens and nesting in the inaccessible escarpments of the caliphate's seas, has come to perch in the gardens, where the Caliph keeps it chained.

She is grieved by its presence. The sight of the bird emphasizes the freedom she has lost. She allows it at her side, however, only long enough to enjoy the sense of grandeur the animal emanates in its indifference. She then dismisses it with the same curtness with which, having lain beside the sovereign in bed, she wishes to immediately be rid of him. In fact, it is common during coitus for her to absent herself, it making no difference if another man takes the Caliph's place. The same, to be sure, happens with the ruler, who makes use of her to obtain the orgasm that a stranger could accord him, after which he feels empty and melancholy.

From atop the minaret the distant voice of the muezzin calls the people to prayer. In the chambers, where life flows away, Scheherazade prays but asks nothing of Allah. Wrapped in silks, tulle, and veils, she rehearses a few steps from a choreography dictated by Ishtar, the goddess of love in ancient Babylon. But she quickly loses heart. The night breeze coming through the window clears the atmosphere, breaks the equilibrium of her countenance, dis-arranges the hairs of the Caliph's beard as he sweeps his small eyes around the bedroom. Inside, he harbors a secret life.

She hesitates to apply adjectives to the Caliph. Ugly, haughty, apathetic? Or a man whose aquiline nose, in shadow on the wall, has the shape of a deadly scimitar? Despite the nights she has lived under threat, Scheherazade has survived the ruler's sentence. Intoxicated by the freedom to enjoy another day, she eats each meal with renewed pleasure, breathing in the fragrance of spices recently arrived from India.

Jasmine dreams about unlikely situations. Without neglecting the finer points, she assimilates the gestures of her mistresses: how they behave, sigh, and feed themselves. She refines details in order to later imitate the sisters on the sly. And while the Vizier's daughters savor the meat of parchment-skinned dates, Jasmine parsimoniously copies them.

Even though they are under the same roof, the sisters demon-strate no intimacy with the Caliph. Scheherazade never confuses her lover with the ruler of Baghdad. The hasty ceremony that united them, dispensing with ritual, had prevented Dinazarda from any great show of emotion, seeming more like an execution than a wedding. What attracted attention was that the Caliph, checking any amorous sentiment, did not utter Scheherazade's name. This was a habit he extended to all his favorites, treating them like part of an incorporeal entity from which he must escape.

Jasmine removes the tepid lavender water in which float petals picked in the gardens. It pleases her that after each meal the Caliph and the Vizier's daughters dip their fingers in the alabaster chal-ices, confident of the outcome of the battles that will shortly engage them. Impelled by Scheherazade's imagination and facing ever-growing danger, they all make their way through the desert, through the forest, through the seas—in a word, through the world that she breathes into life anew before each dawn.

36

Scheherazade unravels the colored threads of the story from a spool safe from harm. While he listens impassively, the Caliph rests, restraining any movement. With each word from her he forgets the humiliation inflicted on him by the wife who betrayed him with the lowest of his vassals. The degrading scenes that sometimes rob him of sleep, pursuing him with inexplicable terror, slowly fade away. It is as if fear, shackling his feet, had stolen the pleasure of life and replaced it with civilizing chaos, leaving him unable to comprehend the rules of a world where he had learned both to live and to reign.

He need only return to the audience room for the ghost of the Sultana, dead for some time now, to pursue him. No hiding place any longer affords him protection by barring her presence. At such times, the implacable shade of his wife, in flagrant disrespect for the power of the throne, advances toward him, climbing the steps, licking him with the venom of her saliva, biting him with a mouth baring teeth and tongue.

She points with a voracious gesture to her own vulva, the site of crisis and betrayal, the fiery depository of her sex, from which pour lava, mud, and secretions—exactly where she had lashed him, beating him with the weapon of delirious desire. In this dark and damp retreat, the Sultana had experienced orgasms that the outsized African had brought her from his remote origin.

The memory of the woman's insulting lust strengthens the Caliph's spirit of revenge, as if, having her still by his side, that mournful voice exhorted him never to trust another female, to kill them after possessing them. And each time that he yields to vengeance by sending a young woman to the scaffold, his dead wife's face fades, but never completely disappears. Clinging to the ruler, she watches him closely, claiming her rights.

The Sultana's ghost rails, asking in the name of what principle the Caliph decreed her death. And why he didn't release the women, for whom he had no affection, by a simple writ, thus allowing them to pursue their own fantasies, to experience amorous games. Her arrogant smile confirms that thanks to the art of making reality into fable perfected during those years, she has enjoyed the pleasures of the flesh. When, practically next door to the sovereign's harem, she fled from the prison of living tied to a man who, though he had made her his queen, ignored the impulses of a person like her.

Back in the chambers after the audiences, the Caliph entertains himself with the Vizier's daughters. There is no longer even a trace of the queen's face around him. Watching the young women's gracious movements, he has the illusion of victory, as if the Sultana, having never existed, could not perturb him.

At certain moments, however, he examines the damage done to his heart. He realizes that not even free of her bitter presence does he feel compassion for his subjects or pity for the queen who is responsible for his living under the dominion of Scheherazade's imagination.

At nightfall, the years weigh heavily on him. Resting on the pillows spread along the divan, he casually accepts the dried fruit, gesturing to the Vizier's daughters with movements that affirm his majesty or distance him from the radiant center of his egoism.

When he later joins Scheherazade's body, part of a ritual that threatens to perpetuate itself, he fears the feelings now under way, the path of the story she is beginning to tell him. He realizes that his power, compared with Scheherazade's imperial narrative, is of little value, which leads him once again to threaten her with death at the first sign of dawn.

37

Dinazarda boasts of her sister's merits when in the presence of the Caliph. She doesn't exalt her physical attractions or make him see that Scheherazade's body, discreet in lovemaking, houses silently palpitating life. But she lets him surmise that the narrative seduction that he is subject to exceeds the erotic pleasure with which he amuses himself each night.

She spares no effort to endow her sister with countless virtues, even as she rages, touches Scheherazade, acts as if she belongs to her—to the point that she asks herself why not consider Scheherazade hers, if she has put her own life at risk to save this storyteller? If since their arrival at the Caliph's palace she has sacrificed her hopes in exchange for the well-being of her sister?

Dinazarda makes no attempt to hide her growing frustration. She has reason for regret and for voicing her protest at having linked her existence to Scheherazade, for being the prisoner of the Caliph, who neglects to honor her. In no way does she consider herself compensated for so much effort. After all, her sister and the sovereign owe a great deal to her. Thanks to her, order reigns in that corner of the palace. Under her persistent ability to weave intrigues and command daily life, the reality of the court has calmed.

In alluding to her sister's wisdom, Dinazarda proudly stresses her own. She is tempted to confess to the ruler that Scheherazade, threatened by faulty and fading memory, frequently asks for her help. Then, moved by her sister's imminent misfortune, she restores her confidence through subtle signs that entwine Scheherazade once more in an account ready to yield to an asphyxiating logic.

In recent days, foreseeing dry periods in the young woman's

imagination, Dinazarda has charged Jasmine with going to the bazaar to gather pieces of stories to replenish her sister's stock. Not wanting to convey to Scheherazade the impression of having lost confidence in her plots and thereby wounding her vanity, she has said nothing. She has merely demanded that Jasmine be careful, not wishing to endanger her.

A beautiful slave, Jasmine has a way of walking that attracts attention, leaving behind her a sylvan fragrance wherever she goes. She is of elegant carriage, tidy, with long, slim legs perfectly consonant with a neck adorned with silver rings. The clothes she wears affirm her attitude as princess. Such pomp, incongruent with her status, is because of Scheherazade, who takes pains to make her forget her captivity.

It is this same Jasmine who once declared unconditional fealty to the sisters and her desire to be put to the test in times of distress. This because she experienced, for the first time, the feeling of belonging to the Vizier's daughters, who would claim her body and mourn her in case of her death.

From this perspective, Jasmine was not unsuccessful. In defense of the princesses her valiant temperament saw enemies even in those who spoke with meticulous diction as if to deprive her of her tribal language.

Jasmine leaves the palace walls behind. She appears poor and weary with her head limp on her shoulders, which ages her. She eagerly breathes in the smells of the city. Between the narrow spaces separating the houses, she glimpses the palace walls in the distance, the Caliph's world that stretches out beyond them. Drawn by danger, she strays from the planned route and advances in the direction of the Tigris, on Baghdad's western bank. The waters that zigzag along the city have earlier bathed other lands.

She feels free. By divine design, the environment suggests that she make use of the unexpected time ahead, and she prays to the vision of the monumental mosque that looms over the Baghdad landscape. She thinks of the family from which she was so brutally separated. The memory grieves her, but she continues on her way.

The gabble of the people in the middle of the tumultuous square fascinates her. Moving about at random, no longer obliged to give satisfaction to her mistress, she forgets the tasks that brought her to the medina. Emotion makes her imprudent, and she smiles for no reason, inventing what she desires. She passes through the narrow streets, taking note of the objects for sale. She seems to behold Harun ar-Rashid, who, alive again years after his death, celebrates the adventures and misadventures of his people.

The image of that Abbasid ruler is unclear. She asks herself whether the powerful prince, whose ghost follows her, was handsome or fat. And whether his weight made it difficult for him, in this return to life, to vault over walls with the intent to nestle in the arms of a princess, despite the watchful eye of a husband who zealously kept her far away from those languid arms. Or would Harun ar-Rashid prefer to move about the tents looking for human rubble instead of visiting a lady?

At the head of the caliphate for twenty-five years, Harun ar-Rashid had slipped anonymously among merchants, beggars, and travelers, always upsetting the courtiers who distorted reality to prevent him from gathering at the source the outpourings of the heart, the intrigues, the schemes of his people. Harun was insatiable. He would challenge the denizens of the marketplace to tell him of their dramas, to speak about the reigning sovereign whose face they had never seen. He tested his own humanity by listening to the flurry of imprecations, offenses, sacrilegious expressions that accused him, in rustic fashion, of being a despot indifferent to the fate of the poor. And although he was verbally scourged by the unhappy throng, no commentary shook his conviction that he was loved by his people, who in centuries to come would weep at his memory.

Jasmine suspects his motives. A turban on his head, worn sandals on his feet, once again disguised, Harun ar-Rashid, the representative of an arrogant ilk, wished to correct an injustice by submitting himself to the judgment of the people. But when had he promulgated laws favorable to his own? How far had he gone along the scale of poverty and expiation, despite the garb of Bedouin and supplicant? Had he by any chance taken food from some beggar's bowl merely for the experience of sharing intimacy with the masses? Were his incursions into Baghdad only a grotesque farce?

Threatened with so much, Jasmine sweetens her mouth with a date. She is hungry, anguished, caught between voluptuousness and fear. She reins in her imagination, expunging Harun's ghost. She still maintains the hope of hearing in some nook a dervish telling the same stories another had recounted in the past to Harun ar-Rashid, making him forever the captive of his characters.

38

She has not learned to love the Caliph or to be touched by his tormented past. Beneath the veils covering her face, Scheherazade's chameleon-like gaze observes the manifestations of his unlimited power.

The sovereign's movements are slow, lacking any ecstasy. Bored in recent times by a power that endows him with the crown of divinity, he governs indifferently. But if he becomes irritated, it is enough for him to brandish several scimitars against invisible enemies. In his determination of the fate of others, no emotion on his face identifies him with common mortals. He is convinced of the rightness of his measures; there is in him no place for error.

Like a scorpion crawling over scalding stones, he glides along the marble floors, trying to understand the transformations that both Scheherazade and time have wrought on him. He resents the hourglass that marks the passage of an interrogatory time. Approaching the chambers, he slows his pace, giving time for the Vizier's daughters to prostrate themselves in keeping with the demands of protocol. He doesn't exempt them from paying him homage. He learned from his father, as a necessary guide for exercising power, the need to reconcile reason with the Muslim faith. A reason, however, that strikes him as replete with mystery, forever beyond his grasp. It had shaken him to discover at a young age his aversion to the blood welling from a sword wound. So disturbed by the sight of blood, he sometimes felt he was about to faint in front of his subjects. Had his father known, it would have been sufficient to remove him from the line of succession. Under such a threat and wishing to expunge the blemish of cowardice while simultaneously overcoming an area totally incomprehensible to him, he opted for actions that rived his sense of decency and would bring no regret in the future.

When he was being trained in the art of warfare, without apparent motive he challenged a subordinate to a fight without quarter, relying on his advantage over an opponent cowed by his presence. Upon seeing the wound spilling blood before death, the prince felt the urge to vomit, almost fainting. But he continued to behold the object of his horror until becoming inured to the dying man's glassy stare, fixed on a vague point on the horizon as if signaling his imminent departure. In that same instant, the crown prince removed from its sheath the dagger encrusted with rubies and emeralds and delivered the coup de grace.

In the intimacy of the chambers, the Caliph does not behave improperly or waste time. Reducing the temptation of power, he forces himself to prove to the Vizier's daughters that he is a tired man returning home, expecting affection and support. Like a common peasant, he awaits a dish of lentils and chunks of lamb. But he says nothing. He nods his head and accepts the cheese, the yogurt, the bread, the grapes, the figs, the honey.

He savors the breeze from the garden, while displaying tedium with other pleasures. He does not hurry to make use of the women. In the past he had professed the desire to emulate the deeds of Harun ar-Rashid and become the successor to his line. Having in mind this ambition, which the illustrious Abbasid embodied, he had deceived himself about climbing the palace wall and disappearing in the direction of the market, a plan that encompassed embracing heroic and altruistic values, sleeping among the people and eating from their crumbs. Every day he promised himself to fulfill the design of being that sovereign who had become immortal, a figure who, though vanished, the people even today resurrected. Ever since Harun's death, Baghdad wept at his memory. Evoking his myth, all repeated his name, waiting for him to suddenly return among them, capturing the intrigues of daily life.

According to what the Caliph had been told, Harun would roam among the tents of the marketplace disguised as a beggar in order to hear random tales. Far from the throne, peeling an orange, he would collect the palpitations of common feelings.

Masquerading as various characters, he followed the scent of recondite passions, amused at those who withheld the truth from him. It is believed that Harun attributed a basic portion of any story to lies, perhaps because he had removed his princely garments and no longer knew how to measure the truth. But through the nervous tics of each subject, he quickly unmasked what was kept under lock and key. The old, nearing death, provoked his compassion. He listened to those who were almost ready to depart, their words sibilant because of their lack of teeth.

A descendant of the dynasty of Harun ar-Rashid, the Caliph had since childhood been enchanted by the legends and speculations surrounding the Abbasid ruler who lived on in memory because of the love he inspired in his subjects. But were those stories believable, capable of serving as examples for the good ruler? Was it prudent for a caliph to trust his people to the extreme of yielding his heart to them? Wouldn't such devotion display weakness that might inspire rebellion, in which case wasn't it better to use intimidation, a feeling kindred to terror?

Walking through the medina, Jasmine enumerates reasons for erasing the attraction she felt for Harun, which now disturbs her sense of morality. She is suspicious of the behavior of that prince who was nothing but a fraud vis-à-vis his people. How far had he acted in bad faith, in inspiring unconditional love in them, forcing them to stop fighting for independence from his authoritarianism? Did his cunning affinity with commoners smother incipient centers of insubordination, while, disguised as a merchant, he obtained information?

On at least one occasion the Caliph had decided to follow Harun's footsteps. Dressed in rags, he went to the center of Baghdad. Moving through the streets, he judged himself briefly to have gained access to that strange way of life. But as the hours passed without his achieving the long-awaited sensation of happiness, he realized he preferred the dictates coming from the throne to being loved by the people. He would never relinquish the slightest speck of his majesty. That ancestral adventurer was no model for him as head of the caliphate. His suspicious nature would never believe the answers the people gave him.

After this decision, he had pushed Harun aside as example. Under the guise of justice for everyone, that hero had almost shaken the pillars of power. Harun's behavior had, after his passing, led his two sons, both of them confused by the social meaning of such messages, to battle over the legacy, a combat that resulted in the death of one of them.

Safe in his palace, the Caliph dreamed no more of Harun ar-Rashid. Surrounded by privilege, he admitted to himself that having aspired to be the new Harun was nothing more than a moment of uncertainty, from which he had emerged with furrowed brow, blocking out mercy and useless condescension. He had no reason to ever return to those foul-smelling streets. Not even the desire to regain the ideal of youth would make him turn back. Nor did he fear that the figure of his illustrious ancestor would disturb him by pointing to the collapse of his illusions.

Back in the chambers once more, he resisted confessing to the sisters that there, ensconced in his home, was a man overcome by fatigue, devoid of hope.

39

Dinazarda suffers. Closeness to the death that threatens Scheherazade affects her as well. She regrets the fate of her sister, whose
arrogance led her to come to the defense of the maidens of the
kingdom. She looks for signs of repentance in the other woman
now that she has survived the heroic phase of the first weeks. If
not from vanity, why had she succumbed to the temptation to confront the Caliph?

She makes her way through the garden. By order of the Caliph,
the walkways empty before her. She thinks about Scheherazade,
deprived of the power to lick the morning dew from the flowers.
And about her father, forbidden to visit his daughters, contenting
himself with the news, not always trustworthy, that reaches him.
She imagines him not knowing what to do, torn between paternal
love and his duties as vizier.

Despite his coldness, the sovereign is attentive. His marriage
to Scheherazade, which was to have lasted a single night, has
brought him no family responsibility. He doesn't feel part of that
clan. Nevertheless, he offers the sisters gifts and in no way rebukes
them. He leaves the rarefied site of the throne, where he is almost
always to be found, to lend ear to Scheherazade's expository talent. Outside this circumstance, he shows indifference to the sisters' plight, even when Dinazarda fixes her gaze on him in hopes
that he will free himself of the unmistakable proofs of his cruelty.

The Caliph underestimates the feminine gaze. He has always
suspected that beneath the delicate film of lyrical love attributed to
women lies a false transcendence. Behind the proclaimed fragility
of women, so convincing in its tenderness, can be found a fortress
whose objective is his annihilation. It is therefore necessary to
protect himself from the intimacy arising from frivolous copulation, so that no female, pretending to be his soul mate, can again

strike him a blow as the Sultana did. Despite such precautions, there remains the dilemma of reconciling this carnal alliance between him and women with his inhospitable, suspicious spirit, which feeds on power.

The years have accentuated his lethargy. The experience that comes from age has helped him resist the pressure of the lust that once confused him, when he wondered whether it was desirable for women to risk their life at his hands in exchange for jewels and hope.

As for Scheherazade, confined to the palace, her emotional range has narrowed since her arrival there. Her life is limited to the Caliph, her sister, and Jasmine, while the image of her father is slowly fading. As the result of such precariousness, she clings to the uncertainties that the sovereign himself engenders. She gives her characters hearts as unpredictable as the ruler's. And they, immersed in the same affliction as she, are obliged to know the fear that engulfs mortals. But even as she repudiates the Caliph, she does not overstep the bounds in judging what is eating away at the man's soul.

Slave to a preordained death, she waits for the Caliph to remind her at each sunrise that, while he can kill her, he is preserving her life for a few hours, only to threaten her anew in the immediate future. She resents this game and comes to hate him. What can she say to this successor of the Prophet, this imperfect poet of sarcasm, who dispenses with subterfuges and metaphors when speaking of her life and death?

She has plenty of time to think. The garden visible from the window, where Dinazarda is strolling at the moment, is a consolation set on the line of the horizon, a landscape that she quickly abandons in favor of introspection. To Scheherazade, cohabiting her own body in the course of a day's journey becomes a kind of passion.

She recognizes clearly the danger in prematurely satisfying the Caliph's intense curiosity. Every tale must meet the sovereign's expectations about the art of narration. Otherwise, without those stories long warmed in his imagination, how would he embrace the material unraveled by Scheherazade?

Unlike her sister, Dinazarda is used to giving orders and conveys to the others the instructions given her by the Caliph. Subject to the tribulations of the royal palace, she daily renews her faith in miracles, in prayers to Allah, to whom she directs requests. More than anything, she relies on the enthralling nature of her sister's stories to change the Caliph's insensitive heart and undermine his punitive ideas.

Less gifted than Scheherazade, Dinazarda has at her disposal pieces of stories that Jasmine has brought from her frequent trips to the marketplace. The slave returns from there reiterating her vows of confidence in the talent of a dervish whose name she doesn't know—a man, unmoved by her visits, who reticently denies her the outcome of the accounts he relates, despite the abundant coins that Jasmine drops onto his tin plate.

All too familiar with the ingratitude of others, Dinazarda accepts that the dervish rejects the coins that she provides by intermediation of the slave woman. With a soupçon of irony she observes the tactic the impoverished man uses, according to Jasmine, threatening to empty the arsenal of his stories. Especially when the dervish, wishing to punish her, confesses to the slave that the story he is now telling her is the next to last in his repertoire. These threats, even secondhand, fail to impress Dinazarda. Her reserves of story fragments, which she and Jasmine have accumulated during those weeks, will be enough. Scheherazade, thanks to her insolent sense of expression, will know how to grind up these pieces, making them disappear into her entrails.

Removed from the conspiracy headed by Dinazarda, Scheherazade allows her imagination to lay claim to the patrimony forged by Baghdad since its inception. The sheep of her flock, beckoned there, around her bed, are her reason for being. Because of these adventurous children of the Prophet, who are her characters, she recharges the narration machine from Monday to Sunday, without rest. And to keep the Caliph's interest from flagging, she implants in the enigmatic man a vice that prevents his freeing himself from the lust for hearing her stories.

40

As the night advances, Scheherazade stacks up the legacy of her stories in front of the bedazzled gaze of Jasmine, who reveres the stars before her eyes.

The Vizier's daughter unrolls for a weary Caliph the carpet of a sumptuous story line, whose knots and tassels come from the collective psyche of the people he governs, from a source originating in the merging of nomadic cultures that crossed desert and tundra. While she speaks, she parades the knowledge of a people who with every relocation carry on their backs their tent, their religion, their fables.

It was Fatima who stated that if Scheherazade wanted someday to tell a story so that everyone spoke through her, she should imbue every word with a choral timbre, and only then would she come to know what tradition required of her. By instilling in her such wariness, Fatima, to give meaning to her own life, had striven to have Scheherazade submit to the awareness of the people.

Sometimes during the day Scheherazade paces the chambers in all directions, with quick steps, fantasizing that she is traveling to Samarra, where she is convinced she once left her heart. It is a journey from which she returns obliged by the clamors of Baghdad, which whispers and bellows day and night.

Taken to the window by Dinazarda, Scheherazade leans on the parapet and inspects the horizon. With her fingernails she traces an illegible inscription in the dust. A powder from the desert, or from the golden-domed mosques and coming directly to her, had gone unnoticed and escaped the slaves' cleaning.

Jasmine joins her in her pacing. The women move about the relatively limited space of the chambers, by mutual accord testing the flavor of the exotic lands that Scheherazade describes to them.

With Jasmine at the end of the cortege, their identical forms merge into a single feminine body. But the one who speaks, babbles, murmurs, is Scheherazade, who celebrates the love of the Arab people for the desert—a love so intense that it taught them to view life as ephemeral, fleeting matter destined to fade away at nightfall. It taught them that life is temporary, and precious.

Through the hours, scenes alternate without major interruption until the visit by the sovereign, who after sex and ablutions makes himself comfortable on the divan. He readily trades the pleasures of copulation for those of the stories, sipping the warm tisane in the expectation that Scheherazade's heroes will introduce some incertitude into his daily life, everything, in short, that the young woman saves for night in order to light the fire of imagination. Scheherazade is unaware that Jasmine, after visiting the market that afternoon, has given Dinazarda phrases dictated by the dervish. Some of these, long and eloquent, cited a beggar who, on the way to Mosul, far from Baghdad, believed he had found at the entrance to the city a treasure that held great hope for humanity. The story line, replete with details, was broken off by the dervish before its conclusion, notwithstanding Jasmine's insistence that he finish. But from what Jasmine had heard, the dervish's story ran contrary to that of Scheherazade, who by coincidence had dealt with the same theme the night before—namely, a prince who, disguised as a commoner and having vowed never to resume the privileges of his class, has the misfortune to fall in love with a princess from Karbala, from whom he must hide the social station he has renounced, with no right to the happiness the young woman can offer him.

The dervish's tale, transmitted to Dinazarda in an Arabic dialect and with the appearance of truth, had surely emerged from the inhabitants of Baghdad, admirers of dramatic and romantic outcomes. It was clearly a story to be taken to Scheherazade, who if she found it of interest would promptly make it her own. Dinazarda was prepared to cede to her sister those parts with sufficient value to merit her attention.

Sitting on the carpet in a lotus position, the Caliph wears a white tunic of Egyptian cotton, which gives him a jovial air and also serves to hide any involuntary erection. He breathes the air of that January and begins his prayer. It relieves him to know he has already met his obligation of pilgrimage to Mecca and can remain in the palace, complying in good faith with the precepts of the Qur'an, even though it's difficult for him to fall to the ground five times a day, facing toward the holy city, to pray to Allah. But because his authority comes from God, he submits humbly to Allah and his messenger Muhammad. And he holds in unrestricted reverence the holy book, which has been revealed to him and whose lawmaking basis, in questions of both morality and customs, buttresses his temporal power. Except for a few sins that there is no need to mention, the Caliph dictates edicts and demands subordination following the command of the Prophet.

During the discourse, Scheherazade rises a few times, as if each movement fuels the tale of a princess who, transformed into a stone, has caused profound commotion in her father's kingdom. And as she speaks to them of the event considered an evil omen for the princess's subjects, Scheherazade measures her listeners' distress. Although dominating the story's details, she moves ahead slowly, laden with doubts, as if her mind is unable to supply the necessary material. She pretends that her slowness stems from taking pains to establish beforehand in the Caliph's mind the coordinates of a complex story line.

Although Scheherazade does not vacillate, her sudden paleness disturbs Dinazarda, who pictures her practically on her way to the scaffold, and has no means to help her. But then, in a total reversal, her face suddenly lights up, resulting in enraptured happiness as if a distant, intangible perfection is finally within her grasp. All of this because she has the feeling that by some miracle she has advanced along the path of her art. As she speaks of the princess enchanted by a witch, words now flow so smoothly that she is certain of having succeeded at last. Her memory, though hard-pressed by abundance, hasn't failed her; it has simply let fall to the ground what is left over from the princess's story.

After such a feat, Scheherazade withdraws, not permitting herself to be deceived by an unwonted contentment. For it is prudent to mistrust the forces of evil that dupe human beings through vanity. Master of her trade or not, she mustn't satiate the ruler's curiosity. It is better to divide the narrative parsimoniously, putting off the denouement, until the moment comes to tie the Caliph's heart with a tangled knot to what she is relating. Only by means of such pains can she solicit extra hours of life.

41

The music coming from the distance moves Scheherazade to commingle the living with the beings she invents at night, to offer them the sound of the lute overcoming the palace walls to reach her.

She fills her days with the other women in mutual watchfulness. To combat boredom, she resorts to the intrigues of the courtiers who, gnawed by envy, destroy anyone close to power. Some go to the extreme of picking up bread crumbs the Caliph drops on the floor, lest servants outside the circle of power come into the sovereign's sight.

These degrading acts by the courtiers arouse Scheherazade's curiosity. As she had been told by Fatima, they had much to do with the adventures hatched around the Abbasids. Intending to lead her pupil deep into human darkness, Fatima had not hesitated to mention the source from which some of those sinister plots sprang.

The young women look at each other. Enclosed in the royal chambers, they are suffocating in the monotony of afternoon. But so they may appreciate certain episodes involving the Abbasids, Scheherazade recounts in detail the private lives of that imperial clan. She takes on both male and female roles with the idea of better understanding those immortals. She hopes in this way to compensate her companions for the hardships suffered in their confined quarters, from which they can discern the shadow of the scaffold on the wall.

She has much to tell them. In these reminiscences, she evokes the slander so common among the courtiers, from whom they live separated by express order of the sovereign. She hesitates, however, about where to begin, overcome by the emotion awakened in her by the lute, a delicate six-stringed instrument whose sound, coaxed forth by the feather of an eagle felled by a pitiless hunter's arrow, enters from the corridor. From childhood, she has wept and smiled at the musical lament from the pear-shaped form strangely reminiscent of the female seen from behind.

Dinazarda, tense at the slow pace of the conversation, urges her sister to hurry, before the Caliph arrives. Dependent on the resources of her memory, Scheherazade refrains from worrying, concentrating instead on the lute, which had flourished both in the court and in the desert, as Islam planted its roots in Arab culture. Its sound box generated dolorous sentiments, becoming an indispensable presence at poetry recitals such as those held frequently among the Bedouins. It had been perfected by the time of the Abbasids, who surrounded themselves with the best musicians in the caliphate, especially in the reign of Harun ar-Rashid, who had the talent of Zeriab at his service.

Under the mandate of her nomadic imagination, Scheherazade pretends to follow the chords of the lute as the instrument crossed the whitecap waves of the Indian Ocean, indistinctly navigated the Tigris and Euphrates to visit villages until settling in Baghdad, where Zeriab had grown up strumming his strings. From a family of musicians, he would close his eyes in full romantic transport, concentrating on drawing from the sound a pained sadness, as if to say he had long been removed from human closeness. The man's musicality, however, upon surmounting the palace walls and conquering the recesses of the city, penetrated to the center of the mosques and huts, rousing fervent emotions wherever it passed. He was deeply convinced that the language of his music was addressed to Allah.

Any mortal hearing him succumbed to emotion. Caliph Harun ar-Rashid himself, conflicted, had designated the musician the panacea for all ills. Such enthusiasm aroused envy, especially in Ishaq al-Mawsili, the official court musician. Seized by raging jealousy in view of the growing success of his disciple, he vowed to silence the artist who was overshadowing him and threatening his position with the caliph. Acting swiftly, he first thought of killing the man but found no way of doing so without suspicion falling on him. He decided the best solution was to create enmity between the artist and the caliph, thereby neutralizing his influence and preparing the way for his banishment.

Ishaq knew how Harun ar-Rashid, despite his apparently altruistic and adventurous spirit, reacted when confronted with vital questions, as when he inflicted a merciless death on Musa al-Kazin, a great religious leader. And how delighted he was to stimulate animosity between his sons Amin and Ma'mun, not foreseeing that after his passing this would result in a war to the death between the brothers, with Ma'mun achieving final victory.

Relying on the caliph's moral frailty, Ishaq al-Mawsili acted so shrewdly and insidiously that Harun, yielding to the slander of the court master, decreed Zeriab's downfall. Taken by surprise and faced with a punishment that expelled him from the caliph's domain, the musician found himself unable to muster his defense and was forbidden to set foot in the land where he was born and his music had prospered.

Zeriab succumbed to the pain. Drowned in lamentations, he wandered aimlessly about Baghdad, saying farewell to the beloved landscape. Eyes wide, blinking incessantly, he filed away every detail around him, in fear of forgetting the repertoire of his life and without the consolation of being able at least to replace it in the future with some other good.

Out of control, he wept in the streets, on the balconies from which he contemplated the golden twilight at the time of prayer, his heart about to break, avows Scheherazade as she relates his misfortunes. Feeling sympathy for the artist, she inverts the hourglass to return to the era of Harun ar-Rashid and witness the slow agony that had beset the musician before he went into exile, bearing his sparse belongings, watching him take his last steps in Baghdad as he relinquished the world that was his reason to live—a setting without which he could barely conceive another reality that he would come to experience in other lands.

Dinazarda also suffers for the art of a man who, in addition to having dominated the melodic possibilities of his instrument, had striven to generate in his listeners altered states of mind, a growing scale of passion and emotional release. She regrets that Scheherazade's words describing him cannot be heard by Zeriab himself, who, thinking only of obeying the order to leave Baghdad, was ready to head for Al-Andaluz, on the other side of the sea, where in their zeal to expand power and culture the Arabs had recently installed themselves. And while he planned to land in the caliphate of Córdoba, under the rule of the Omayyads, he doubted in his heart the possibility of making his art grow there. Hurt by his teacher's betrayal, he could now aspire only to overcome the malevolence of fate and hope that the new lands where he would disembark might afford him a musical system impregnated with Persian, Greek, and Arab elements, a musical skill to become the target for obligatory consultation for the compositions of the time.

Zeriab tried to make out the future through the tenuous sandalwood smoke burning in his room as he meditated, far from guessing that he was about to influence the foundations of music spreading on the rim of the Mediterranean and to make an impact on the Andalusian centers under strong Sufi influence. Or that, with his lute as its source, he would construct a musical discourse with love as its dominant theme. But how could he have known that in the future he would have as accomplices a band of poets who, wandering through sunny lands and the region of aromatic herbs, would strum in his style the strings of an instrument similar to his own, while attempting to seduce the ears of women in castles with the song of their poetry? And never did these minstrels of courtly love recognize the debt owed to Zeriab's music.

Dinazarda asks her sister to tell them of the diabolical trap set by Ishaq al-Mawsili, who before yielding to envy must surely have loved his disciple Zeriab. But without letting Scheherazade speak, she aligns suppositions about the final destiny of the artist on that barbaric continent where the Arabs were beginning to create an incipient empire.

Scheherazade is surprised at the episode's strong effect on her sister. Unfortunately, she has no way of detailing the circumstances preceding the artist's departure. She knows only that, in order to comply with the time limit conceded by the caliph, Zeriab had hastily joined the first caravan leaving Baghdad, beginning a journey that left him at the edge of the Andalusian world after crossing Egypt, Libya, Tunisia, and Morocco.

Raised to contemplate the vastness of the desert before coming to Baghdad, Zeriab found the sight of the sea that divided two continents to be a balm for his mourning. That blue mystery, in the form of billows, waves, tides coming and going, helped him leave his homeland behind. At the edge of the Mediterranean, with a soft breeze wafting, he invented himself, using the clay of fear and hope.

Scheherazade describes the musician with dramatic flourishes. Familiar with the world of travel, she assigns him setbacks, encounters, menaces, the fear of never reaching Andalusia alive. She tells how, after boarding the fragile vessel for the relatively short sea crossing, he disembarked on a shore whose dunes reminded him of the desert, understanding at once why the first Arabs ventured into those burning lands with the intention of staying.

Battered by the emotion of exile, his voice grew hoarse. Its timbre, as if craggy, inspired him to adjust to his lute the song that now came from his throat. Voice and strings intoned a deep song that gave out poignant cries, which scratched his throat and forced him to lengthen syllables, to stretch the musical notes in his chest until they broke. Such effort, seemingly harmful to his voice, nevertheless produced a surprisingly emotional effect.

Zeriab took unexpected encouragement from this musical path born of his nostalgia for Baghdad, based on the threat of music and timbre becoming frozen in the air in abrupt paralysis, as if to promise that in Andalusia he was to find a new ideal of beauty.

Still in the chambers, Dinazarda asks Scheherazade to tell of Zeriab's end, whether he had found a love with Levantine features reminding him of the Arabian nights or whether he had died wretchedly, without a friendly hand to take his as he breathed his last. Dinazarda struggles to unveil the future of the musician without giving her sister time to develop the concepts of the injustices visited upon Zeriab. She doesn't let her say that the musician and she herself, a simple storyteller, both belong to a category sacrificed on the altar of cruelty. Or that for incorruptible hearts, whether in Baghdad or in Andalusia, life has always hung by a thread.

42

The Caliph is distracted, appearing to absent himself from the palace. It is difficult to follow his route. He has the wings that Scheherazade has given him. It is not easy to dislodge him from the places he visits, stimulated by the imagination of the young woman who offers him daily lessons.

Back in the reality of the chambers, he penetrates the Vizier's daughter indifferently, so that, under the terror of possible death, she will not become overly comfortable and will sustain the emotion and the curiosity he demands of her.

The sovereign's insolence is constant, but Scheherazade doesn't respond. Beneath the Caliph's thick beard, which hides cruel secrets, she records the skill with which he rips out her soul. The sovereign's long, convex fingernails bear traces of blood. Without altering his expression, he chews the dates slowly and deliberately, the forewarning of turmoil. And when he expels the seeds with the tip of his tongue, he keeps the plate close to his chest.

Scheherazade avoids observing how he satisfies his hunger. With her stories she strikes back at his parsimonious gestures, fattened on the abuse of power. It is as if she tells him that he cannot intimidate one who sacrifices herself daily for others, who voluntarily places her head on the block to please the executioner.

Her revenge consists of opening the drawer of imagination to him and establishing narrative chaos in his mind, of instilling in the man parallel and circular story lines, some begun in Baghdad, some ending in Singapore. Stories from which he cannot free himself, much less forget, so that he breathes only through a filter that purifies the air with the aid of voluptuous words originating in fantasy. And, were it not so, what more could this ruler aspire to, besides death, whenever he steps down from the throne and stands on the wrinkled tassels of the carpet inherited from his grandfather?

Scheherazade restrains her indignation. She needs to sustain the verbal entanglement and mystery with which she has captured the Caliph. She knows well that any plot depends on the faith of the listener. And she cannot forgo the credulity or blind confidence of the Caliph, Dinazarda, and Jasmine in the artifices of her craft. Without their cooperation, it would be useless to infuse the stories with the indispensable ingredients for elaborating what springs from her impulses.

Her intelligence, renewed at twilight, must afford Scheherazade persistence. Thanks to this, under the impact of so many variants, almost foundering, everything in her suddenly falls into place, as if the characters themselves have taken command of the action.

As a listener, Dinazarda waits anxiously for the Caliph to leave for the throne room, then showers Scheherazade with gifts as recompense for emerging from the vastness of words and saving herself. She does so also to express to her sister her admiration, as if they were both in the bazaar, free of the entanglements of the court and she were saluting Scheherazade, with the same verbal threads used that afternoon to confect her nightly story.

Since childhood Scheherazade had been accustomed to repeating aloud parts of a story, with the idea, perhaps, of softening the guttural sounds of the language, permanently clashing with one another, while she imparted order to words that mankind had randomly combined. In this way, dreaming of transforming what had been born imperfect, she erected images and consecrated them with poetry and emotion.

Whenever she felt disoriented, Scheherazade remembered Fatima, from whom she had acquired her sense of adventure. By secretly examining the hiding places of the Vizier's palace, she had become accustomed to other flights of fancy. It was common for them, sitting placidly around the fountain in the courtyard, calmed by the falling water, to exercise the art of flight. Pretending to have left the palace, already on their way to Samarkand, they were grateful for the breeze coming from the Euphrates in the presence of palms sown by the wind. They were sure to return home one day laden with unusual tales.

Fatima assured her she had been born with the art of storytelling in her heart. But to obtain good results she must blindly collect everything, straying from a story line only by an act of will or as the result of unforeseen inattention to the craft—as if she no longer wanted to go on living.

Fatima's eyes shone again after weeping. But Scheherazade mustn't concern herself with such disturbances. Her talent was so genuine that it would easily storm the tabernacle of another soul and exact what she needed, to illuminate what had foundered in the sea of so many ideas.

Despite the difference in age between Fatima and the Vizier's daughter, both saw the world as a caravan following the route dictated by the women's dreams. On such a journey, if Scheherazade tended to the storytelling Fatima would guide her through the labyrinths of the land.

Scheherazade suffered because of Fatima's absence. She looked for her in every corner and held her father responsible for the loss. Years before, when she was still in her father's home, the Vizier took pity on Fatima's growing difficulty in walking, caused by the pain from her swollen legs. He offered her regal conditions for retiring, including a house as a gift, for he didn't want Fatima, to whom he owed so much, burdened with work and unprotected.

Her father's proposal had angered Scheherazade. How dare he deprive her of the company of Fatima, who had been with her since birth, and whom she pictured at her side till death? She moderated her reaction only because she was certain Fatima would refuse to leave her, as she considered Scheherazade to be like a daughter. But to her surprise, Fatima unhesitatingly accepted the Vizier's offer. After all, she had never had a house where she could cook, prepare the fire, milk the goat, and console herself with the fantasies that she had produced all those years for Scheherazade's benefit.

When she said good-bye, Fatima refused to say where she was going to live, adding only that it would be far from Baghdad, amid sheep and camels, near a tribe that liked to tell stories that reminded her of Scheherazade. Even though they insisted on asking about her destination, she would confide only the itinerary of her life. She had told Scheherazade in detail how to arrive at the small house, with the hope of one day being with her for as long as she liked. The nursemaid had never loved anyone as much as Scheherazade.

Scheherazade had wept in the weeks that followed, until she became accustomed to reading the signals that Fatima sent from afar with the intention of helping her. Fatima's voice sometimes came to her clear, at other times in a whisper, but never without the echo of love at the mention of her name.

Seated now on the edge of the divan, with Jasmine massaging her feet, Scheherazade honors the new day she has won. On certain afternoons she questions whether she will have the strength to go on sharing the Caliph's bed, subjecting herself to his caprices. When she is asked why she narrates, she hesitates to answer, then decides it doesn't matter. She knows only that, at that moment, she narrates with the intention of driving away the shadow of future victims of the vengeful Caliph falling on the platform where the scaffold imposingly stands.

43

The lovers' nights are spent in the chambers of the palace, an edifice close to the mosque. This is the geography in which the two of them play out the drama of life and death, with the Caliph seeming to conciliate hurried coitus with the adventures described by Scheherazade. Erotic duty, linked to entertainment, doesn't interfere with what Scheherazade has to say.

Upon finishing his tasks of governing, the Caliph usually feels restless, beset by a moral dimension that forces him to seek out the Vizier's daughter merely for having spared her life that morning, to return to this temporary home to listen to tales and repeat the sex of the night before until his virility flags.

Thus, the yoking of the woman's words and carnal desire, rather than making him happy, merely wrenches the Caliph from the clutches of reality. It creates in him an expectation that at the end of his audiences takes him back to Scheherazade's stories, whose conclusion he longs to know. In their daily life, they share the tacit recognition that Scheherazade is the wife whose life he saves each morning and with whom he fulfills the rituals of matrimony.

It is not easy for him to counteract the plan he delineated after the Sultana's betrayal. It pains the Caliph to disrespect the sentence of death that hovers over each young woman, its origin in a proclamation known throughout the kingdom, whose sinister nature even today terrorized the parents of any maiden at risk of public sacrifice.

Scheherazade was the first to interrupt the sequence of killings, when the Caliph found himself unable to follow the precept of the law, always frustrating the executioner waiting at the entrance to the chambers by denying him his sacrificial victim. This suddenly imposed period of inactivity left the headsman desperate when he thought that marital happiness was responsible for the failure to apply the law the Caliph himself had promulgated.

The courtiers also found his love for Scheherazade odd, which led the Caliph to relegate his favorites to the saddest of fates. For since the Vizier's daughter had arrived, he no longer summoned women to the royal bed, giving rise to countless hypotheses, none convincing in the end. Faced with his heavy silence, the courtiers found that it did no good to hint to the Caliph the desirability of his returning to the harem.

Corpulent, with an aquiline nose, the sovereign had yielded to the young woman's fascination. He had practically given up the seat of power for fantasy. And, like any of his people, he aspired to be something other than himself, to usurp another's identity by illusion. Perhaps he would fill his loneliness by stealing the appearance of one of Scheherazade's characters, to merge the reality of the kingdom with the woman's stories, convinced now that through storytelling he would broaden his life.

Without abandoning the palace or renouncing the privileges of the throne, he had for some minutes assumed the role of Sinbad, exhaustively explored by Scheherazade, and experienced delightful adventures. In the name of the mariner, the Caliph witnessed first-hand the cunning of that distinguished liar, whom destiny intended for every kind of adventure—a fraud that enhanced his pleasure.

Upon becoming Sinbad, if only for moments, he decided to give the sailor a Hindu partner, Shiva, whom Scheherazade had not foreseen. Soon he was vying with this recently created woman for the right to transform the sailor's ambivalences without taking into account how such an act might affect Scheherazade's story. Through this artifice he also thought to grant himself temporary wisdom.

Hurt by this intrusion, Scheherazade refused to continue, claiming a sudden loss of voice. In ceasing to embroil the Caliph in her plot, and consequently interrupting his transport to realms where his regal humanity had never been, she trusted that such a ploy would produce the desired result.

The truth was that the Caliph was distancing himself from the administration of the caliphate to accommodate himself to the young woman, to such an extent that the courtiers asked in whispers how the Caliph, after the death of the Sultana, spent the nights with Scheherazade. This was a man who on that occasion had stressed his disdain for women, whom he held responsible for the ruin of his feelings, and who had therefore sealed his heart so that nothing could sprout and thrive there. Considering that world so illusory, why was he exposing himself to such danger? Was this excess of fantasy provided by Scheherazade having an effect on him?

The Caliph suffered from a serious dilemma. Merely because on his own he had tried to impose on Scheherazade a character till then nonexistent, thinking that it would foment the young woman's erotic storytelling, he was now at risk of adulterating her narrative aims. Or he might even silence her, a decision that would hand her over to the executioner. And, further, he would suffer the grievance of Scheherazade's depriving him of a pleasure he had never before experienced.

Beyond a doubt he had acted rashly in inventing Shiva. He had cast a shadow on Scheherazade's talent, perhaps motivated by envy. But, in that case, wouldn't this fantasy of his be occupying the space reserved till then for cruelty?

He had always feared uncontrolled actions, feared changing to the point of suddenly dividing up the crown jewels among the beggars, distributing acts of clemency among the criminals of Baghdad, all in the name of misguided kindness. It was not in his interest to tear down the wall erected to protect him from his subjects and his enemies, or anyone who might try to forcibly take his soul. No other threat, however, appeared as serious as Scheherazade's face darkened by the mystery of imagination.

Scheherazade keeps him in sight, interpreting the furrows in his soul. She has learned to cast light on the Caliph's mask, by adding and subtracting words not always in the desired order but with the intention of destabilizing the sovereign's reign. The battle between them has been raging for some time. But this day, after suffering his constant threats for so long, Scheherazade is amused to observe the Caliph's discomposure. Nevertheless, not wishing to marginalize him in relation to Dinazarda and Jasmine, she minimizes the discord between them by concealing what she knows about him. To dissemble, she thanks Dinazarda for the succulent dates she has brought the ruler.

Following this gesture of solidarity, Jasmine also pays attention to the Caliph. All that is missing is for him to order the storytelling to begin. But the sovereign, appearing tired, shows no haste. And even though he might be at the threshold of death, he does not, as a farewell, acclaim Scheherazade's talent or lift the sentence hanging over her.

The clash between the two personalities exhausts Dinazarda, moving her to tears. She would like to disappear over the horizon, riding Aladdin's flying carpet. But she regains her composure thanks to the plot that, from its opening moments, is so enchanting that it is impossible to forgo the ensuing sequences. Instinctively, she closes her eyes, following the trail of the characters. Through Scheherazade's persistent words, Dinazarda is introduced to Harun ar-Rashid, disguised as a merchant who, trying to attract her, follows her everywhere.

As Scheherazade proceeds, Dinazarda suspects Harun's intentions, which aspire both to her and to the love of his people. In general, he will not allow himself to be defrauded. But, for reasons she doesn't understand, as the two walk toward the medina, she feels for the expatriate caliph a dark and cursed desire. Still, she resists this ghost whose aura of sin makes her tremble. And when Scheherazade interrupts the story at daybreak, Dinazarda continues thinking about the Abbasid. In the hours that follow, she struggles to conjure his form, but as a participant in this game she regrets not having his turgid flesh and dark eyes among the living. Except that Harun, instead of sheltering her, covers a stranger's body in a corner of the market. In the darkness, the woman's moans as she is penetrated by Harun ar-Rashid resound in the emptiness, passing beyond the walls to merge with Dinazarda's sighs in the silence of night.

Scheherazade insists on barraging her listeners with the feats of her brave creatures. She surmises the thrill that grips her sister when she describes Harun as lord of the people's heart, a man who, long dead, still lays claim to her body and sets it throbbing. But as the one responsible for Dinazarda's present state of mind, Scheherazade tightens the strings of her nerves to make them vibrate. Obeying the laws of the story, Harun stalks Dinazarda, busying himself with her and with others at the same time. With nothing more than a look, he would include Scheherazade in his list of conquests, envelop her in his circle of fire, though the young woman, in thrall to her imagination, concentrates only on accumulating resources to continue her narrative task.

44

Sitting on the floor, his legs crossed in the lotus position pre-scribed for reading the Qur'an, the old man proffers words to passersby, drawing them to his plight. He is rigid, near death, catching Jasmine's attention.

She doesn't know what to say to attract him. She fears her tawny skin and curly hair will offend the man with bitter memo-ries. Obeying the dictates of her heart, she kneels beside him. In total silence, she listens to him.

The dervish pretends to ignore her presence but, trusting his honed instinct, shows he is aware of the reason for her visit. He doesn't need the boy in his service to alert him about the young woman for whom his words add savor to her food. What could a woman without litter or slaves, wandering alone in the bazaar, want of him?

With an incisive gesture, he insists she speak and not inflict on him a silence that is his prerogative alone. Jasmine sees that it is best to confess that she has come to ask something of him. She alternates lies and truth until finally admitting that she is there in search of exciting tales. She needs to hear adventures that she can take home in her bags like fresh bread. She has come with the hope of hearing what he would say to Harun ar-Rashid himself if the Abbasid ruler were still alive.

Jasmine has chosen him from the many poor because of his blindness. Drawing near, she notes the expression of cupidity that sweeps over the old man's face as he hears her promises. The man loves the gold that the stories can bring him. The loss of inno-cence adds a certain perversity and realism to his storytelling gifts. To entice him, the slave drops a few dinars into his tin plate.

The dervish is startled by the sound of the rattling coins, even though he doesn't prick his ears in time to know the value of the contribution, how many meals those coins will buy. He picks up a coin and caresses it with a delight coming perhaps from his blindness, a blindness that had been visited on him as punishment. Many years before, in the desert en route to Samarra, he had bet he could stray from the caravan without getting lost, relying on his talent for finding his way back. Without measuring the consequences of such an impetuous act, he wandered away amid derisive laughter. Soon, after much stumbling through the sands, he was crying for help. Aimless, with growing difficulty in seeing his surroundings, he couldn't find his way back to the caravan. When much later a nomadic tribe found him, he had lost his sight. His burnt eyes resembled empty craters. When they left him in Baghdad, where he had never been before, he was plunged into the deepest poverty.

He interrupts his account of the facts to confess to Jasmine that when he discovered he was blind, he wept and lamented. In addition to being afflicted with absolute blackness, he was poor and uneducated, devoid of the knowledge to be found in centers of study in the Islamic cities.

At first he had thought of killing himself. He had cursed furiously against men, sparing not even Muhammad. Totally desperate, he implored the holy man to grant him some talent capable of once more linking him to life. For left to his own devices, one more beggar among Baghdad's many, it was difficult for him to understand what was behind the punishment.

He waited a week for the Prophet to answer him. One morning, when he awoke, hungry and dirty, an unusual feeling of encouragement swelled inside him. Suddenly there surged from within him a man to whom Muhammad, forgiving his offenses, offered unexpected resources. He was given the ability to glean precious details from the reality around him, to resolve hitherto insoluble enigmas, to unveil the secret nature of men and objects even without being able to see them, to relate stories while avoiding sorry summaries that, once begun, would quickly exhaust themselves.

And a voice told him to listen above all to the imperative howling of his imagination. From this came his ability to speak for hours with no sign of weariness.

But which story would now captivate a woman who paid him even before he stipulated the price of his work? Although his repertoire had increased in recent years, he knew his limitations. Frequently, because of his meager familiarity with the medina, he avoided setting his characters in the caliphate, not daring to describe the urban configuration of Baghdad, which he knew only from descriptions. In his stories the characters roamed only along the four basic routes that provided access to the city, the eastern part known as Rusafa, and going as far as the estuary of the Tigris.

For the good price she has paid, Jasmine expects value for her money. However, pressed by a feminine curiosity that demands from him, besides a story, details preceding his blindness, the old man reveals to her his earlier life as a potter, an artisan who complained about privation and the clay sticking to his skin. Since adolescence he had harbored a bitterness reflected in the quality of his work, which made him turn out pots, plates, and platters that broke at the merest touch, to the point that he was no longer able to sell them. Despite his paltry talent he indulged the whim of scratching into the surface of the clay, as an artistic expression, calligraphic lines, with results that had nothing to do with the Islamic art of writing.

He doesn't tell her, though, that like the trade of potter, his present trade of storyteller obliges him to combine words, to embed them into the clay of fantasy and take them to the kiln. He is forever in search of figures, ranging from fishes, horses, and precious stones to the feminine contour, that will give rise to the creation of symbols that, with no apparent function, represent metaphors or the perfecting of mystical experiences like those of the Sufis.

The dervish's poverty leads him to publicly lament his fate, as if, forgetting the gifts received, he has lost faith in the Prophet who acted in his favor. As he speaks, he barely stirs. With limited movements, anxious to exploit Jasmine's emotion, he runs the back of his hands several times over his sun-scorched eyes, calling attention to the source of his pain.

Attentive to the dervish's suffering, Jasmine controls her thirst. She waits for him to begin the account, but tells him she is in a hurry, for her husband is waiting at home. He is a suspicious man who demands constant proof of her fidelity.

The dervish, in whose ears still rings the sound of the gold coins falling onto his tin plate, takes a deep breath, hoping for more coins to fill his stomach. As he starts to narrate, his voice comes out sharp, without the desired timbre. He softens his tone, for the moment demands a whisper. His goal is to arrive at the end and merit the payment Jasmine has afforded him.

45

Scheherazade feels like an adolescent again as she recalls how she would move about Baghdad with her hands darkened by coal, leaning on a staff. A simple strategy by which Fatima, taking pains in the art of disguise, hid Scheherazade's delicate features, the blue veins standing out in her snowy skin. The two of them could not afford to take any chances.

At Dinazarda's side in the royal chambers, she remembers the various trips to the marketplace, Fatima dragging her through the narrow streets like a blind woman, when she bumped into strangers, pretending not to know where she was going. While being led, Scheherazade quickly breathed in the musk of the male gazelle, perfumes originating in India, in China, everywhere, whose scents emanated from the small stores that supplied Baghdad.

On returning from these flights, each requiring a different type of disguise, Scheherazade would hide in her rooms so no one would see her burning gaze, her impassioned face. She never confessed to her father that she had gone to the center of life and had nothing of which to complain. He would not understand the advantages gained by venturing into lands impregnated with poverty and illusion. Devoted to his position in court, he could never bear his daughter's sullying herself among the rabble, with which he himself did not mix. At home, with the exception of Fatima, he treated everyone distantly, avoiding eye contact with the slaves, perhaps fearful that they would evoke pity in him.

Beside the fountain, whose gushing water sprinkled her face, Scheherazade, with Fatima at her side, would relive the Baghdad market, the true setting for the stories she created. In that conglomeration of humanity, the mingling of languages, dialects, imprecations, and private expressions was an infernal hidden tongue and a disturbing smell, a turbulence thanks to which she was reaching the heart of the craft of invention by renouncing her own soul for those of others.

While she was still in the cradle, Fatima would touch her, converting the smallest movement into a soft caress. Such was her anxiety to offer stimulating pieces of life that Scheherazade's own mother, though devoted to her children, yielded part of her love to Fatima, as if she foresaw her own early death.

Fatima had inherited Scheherazade after her mother's death. The nursemaid helped the orphaned girl to dream by providing her with a land peopled with beings whose intrigues reflected the sordidness of daily life, whether an opulent prince who had turned into a ruthless assassin or a mistreated lamp vendor who despite his poverty accorded his paramour all the delights of love.

On the trips to the medina, making her way through the narrow lanes, Scheherazade feared that any lapse would cause the stalls to vanish and, as punishment, she would be taken to a palace swept by the winds of evil, where she would be told that the reality of the bazaar was nothing but illusion.

Fatima always kept her in sight. She would bring her back to herself by refusing to let her yield totally to the power of fantasy, which had become her access to the real. With ties to Scheherazade as strong as if she had given birth to her, Fatima all but kept her lashed to her waist as she armed her with elements to broaden the territory of her stories.

An enviable zeal ran in the girl's veins. Each visit to the bazaar was like crossing the desert riding a camel, coming to know crystalline grottoes as part of the glorious lie that was fantasy. Fatima interpreted for her anything that till then had been distant from her understanding. When they were alone she would whisper words imbued with unknown meaning, representing a veritable document of emancipation. What truly mattered to the two of them belonged to the sphere of emotion and tears.

Dauntless, Fatima confronted the Vizier's tentacles, which

extended through all of Baghdad and could reach her at the slightest misstep. Her life, however, had meaning only in Scheherazade's service. She had never before seen anyone hurl flames with her gaze and her words, anyone who through this gift confirmed the existence somewhere of a universe within the reach of storytelling. Driven by such fervor, Fatima would have died for her. It would be worth following her to the scaffold, if that were the price to be paid for her happiness. It was natural that such a talent should carry a ballast of blood, the sacrifice of someone, for Scheherazade to be able to hoist the sail of the ship of imagination and cross the ocean.

Through her visits to the marketplace, Scheherazade discovered that despite her nobility she had come from the people huddling in the labyrinths of Baghdad. She kept this genealogy in mind in order not to lose sight of the stories she was beginning to bring together. She certainly didn't record any distance between her clan and the anonymous vagrants that peopled her imagination. They all pleased her, exhibiting in their carnality an equal dose of delirium.

46

Scheherazade hopes to defeat the Caliph, to break his will and return safely to her father's palace, to contemplate the flowers in the garden that have resisted the change of season in anticipation of her homecoming.

The tiles around the windows cool the area and serve as her mirror. Looking at herself in the dull stains of the enameled surface, she imagines that she is in the litter borne by the slaves, crossing the gates of the royal domain and going to meet her father. In her reverie, Dinazarda is sitting at her side, and both are anxious to arrive at the fountain in the courtyard of their home. In her dreams, Dinazarda commands the practical tasks, ordering the litter, under the watchful eye of the Caliph's guard, before going further, to take her to the market, where everything palpitates insouciantly. In recompense for Scheherazade's recent suffering Dinazarda has her visit the territory of the artisans, scribes, judges, police inspectors, soothsayers, barbers, beggars, vendors of oils, charlatans, where all live in equality.

Jasmine is also included in her daydream, protecting Scheherazade and holding her left hand. The litter moves slowly, giving her time for adventures. In the fog of reverie, the slave's form looms ever larger. Wherever she may go, Scheherazade plans to take Jasmine. She would never leave her in the palace, subject to the Caliph's violence, like an object he discards without a second thought. To gain her emancipation she would argue personally with the Caliph, imploring if necessary that he give her the slave as a form of payment for the stories that so entertained him, a payment merited by her long exile in the palace to serve him. And isn't it true that her tales were worth dinars, gold, emeralds? In case the sovereign doubted it, let him ask some foreign potentate how much he would be willing to pay for her. It was natural to charge for a mortal like Jasmine after regaling him with her immortal characters. She would not countenance Jasmine's once again suffering the pain of separation, the loss of those she loved. How could she avert her eyes from the gaze of the slave who, more than anyone, dominated the art of entreaty?

In her imagination, the litter stops in the square. Scheherazade draws the curtain slightly aside to see the parade of the human landscape that torments her heart. The swirl echoes inside the litter, bringing back her senses, refining them. Amid the merchants, supplicants, and vagrants returning to the dwelling of the soul that is Baghdad, she fills in the internal voids with the resources at her disposal.

In the Caliph's chambers, Dinazarda avoids her sister's gaze, respecting her absence. Scheherazade's imagination gives her ongoing reasons for fading away from there, leaving behind only her body. Even while dreaming, she absorbs the imperceptible heartbeats from someone passing close to the litter and wonders whether they come from a woman or a man.

Confined to the palace, Scheherazade feels the breeze on her face, which quickly changes to rain. Nature stirs her emotions, offering her an opportunity to imagine other, contradictory, realities. She has abundant time to dream. In her mind, she abandons the litter to review the tumultuous urban scene. When she sets foot on the burning Baghdad earth, everything appears fleeting. The excess of fantasy, almost a vice, strips away her princely garb and replaces it with the lust of the passersby. But she no longer wishes for anonymous gazes, in the midst of her dreams, to trouble her femininity, to penetrate her sex without measuring the consequences of that mortal embrace.

Back in the chambers, she realizes that each feigned return to her father's palace, or to the medina, allows her to experience ways of life that exhaust her. Surrendered to this burden, she demands her soul back. At the same time, despite the disillusionment of these exercises, she experiences the miracle of being in so many places without leaving the Caliph's palace. It was good, therefore, to continue with these occasional flights of fancy, even if she emerged from them with a lacerated heart. And to travel once again with Fatima, if she accepted leaving her secret place of refuge. In that case, they would choose the same ravine where the genie in the bottle had granted his liberator three wishes. After this and other duties, Fatima and Scheherazade would rest in a tent with the magical property of making them happy, as they had been promised.

But was it reasonable for her, in spite of living in the Caliph's domain, to discourse on the human story without at least visiting the places the magic carpet took her? After all, where did she have greater need to go without the sensation of having been there before?

47

Scheherazade learns to survive. The rules of life are unwritten, and she must reinvent them at each dawn.

It has been useful for her to live with the Caliph, who has made of dissimulation a tool, a sword, a dagger. She absorbs his silence, the radiations from a cruel gaze rarely altered by tenderness as it judges the world. To mollify the sovereign, to remove him from the center of his internal empire, will take years of effort in an almost certainly futile battle.

While the Caliph visits her body with increasing tedium, Scheherazade absents herself. Nothing interrupts the dictates of her account. She is confident of her art, which has proved itself superior to the revelries of the flesh. In their case, the clash between storytelling and lust has lost its meaning.

She has always told her stories without interruption. Her obsessive nature, which has not lessened, would keep Fatima from sleeping in order to add what had been missing the night before. This inclination gives her no peace but sustains her courage, obliging her to set a stage on which her characters born of illusion can firmly step. Almost real, they bear names indicating who they are and how they behave. It is no surprise that Ali Baba's servant woman, recently introduced to the Caliph, acts unwaveringly in defense of her ingenuous master, and that she moves easily through the corridors of the palace, behaving as if in the service of the Caliph. This because of the manner in which the servant sips tea directly from Dinazarda's cup and vies with Jasmine for the chunk of lamb roasting over the coals.

Scheherazade is unaware that her stories have inspired followers, with Jasmine her most ardent disciple. In front of the crystal, she copies certain characteristics and imprints them directly on her own soul. She tilts her head, sure that she has inherited Scheherazade's narrative temperament. With the mirror as supporting player, Jasmine promises to accompany Ali Baba in his flight through the desert. Who more than she knows of the terrible hardships of that region, with the advantage of being willing to sacrifice herself for him?

Scheherazade senses that Dinazarda is beset by a misfortune whose origin is unknown to her. Does her sister perhaps think herself replaced by Jasmine, who has been courting Scheherazade in recent days? Although ignorant of her motives, Scheherazade understands the tumult of a wounded heart tempted to cry out and act cruelly at the same time. She also notices in her sister contradictory feelings of envy, affection, remorse, and solidarity. But these sisterly distresses, instead of affecting her personally, make her understand the ambiguity that instills insecurity into the action of her story and torment into her characters.

Commiserating, Scheherazade seeks to reconcile Dinazarda to the forces of the unforeseen, which bring joy and sincere laughter. Her gaze asks her sister to say what she can do for her. Dinazarda notices her sister's effort to make her forget the times Scheherazade, with the object of searing the Caliph's untamed breast with the burning coals of words, had unwittingly wounded her and Jasmine as well. She decides, then, to disguise the hurt and distract her. Scheherazade must carry on with her craft and win the race against death.

Relieved by Dinazarda's smile, Scheherazade once again feels immune to small tragedies. She concerns herself now with affording pleasure to her listeners, adopting a rhythm compatible with the emotions of each episode. She is cautious in the choice of any phrase that might make her anticipate the denouement of the story before daybreak. Menaced by such a misstep, she intensifies the heat of her words, adding savor to the circumstances that yield surprising twists. With Dinazarda's help she forces her characters, pursued by assassins' daggers, to take refuge in boats on the banks of the Tigris, albeit at the risk of being dragged away by the river's currents, all with the goal of prolonging the stories.

Jasmine divines that Scheherazade's essential functions are falling behind. The princess can save herself only if the sovereign considers her tales indispensable, if memory, awakened by the princess, yields him continuous benefits. Jasmine is moved when she imagines Scheherazade's anguish upon being faced with the sterile and scattered material of life that she must encapsulate into a modest account. She has the urge to attend her with water and bread, to delve into a soul so firmly affixed to its dream.

The Vizier's daughters have been lavish in their desire to make her happy. The slave responds by providing them with the beauty within her grasp. She brings from the kitchen delicate pastries laced with honey that, piled one on another, resemble Scheherazade's narrative layers. She does it all to warrant the praise that she has lacked her entire life, not realizing that Dinazarda, feeling displaced because of these initiatives, sends her away with an authoritarian gesture that she immediately regrets.

The feelings that permeate the chambers unite the young women. Submerged in conflicts, Dinazarda does not venture to assist Scheherazade with a story. The act of improvising in such circumstances, besides painful and solitary, has the additional factor of being highly dramatic. Her poor sister, on the threshold of death, doesn't know beforehand how many hours remain for her to fortify her calling, to organize the subject now in her mind, to embed pauses for breath into what she relates to the sovereign—in short, to foresee with ingenuity and calm the outcome of a plot.

Urged to understand her own drama, Scheherazade draws back, avoiding any admission to Dinazarda about the true nature of her resources. She denies her information pertinent to the mystery of her art. All that matters to her now is to rely on the solitary skill of narration. Thanks to that, and contrary to the malicious insinuations of the courtiers that she owes her life to her dexterous performance in bed, she has escaped the scaffold.

Removed from them all, however, she doesn't notice the recently opened flower that Jasmine has placed in the opal vase.

48

Scheherazade sips the mint tea and barely touches the little cakes. Uneasy about the small twists in her story, she doesn't enjoy the delicacies that Jasmine offers.

The material of imagination that hours before had seemed intriguing now appears halting. So she fences with the aloof characters who are trying to take control of their lives without considering Scheherazade's interests.

Generously, she gives ear to their voices. The heartbeats of those wronged creatures accuse her of having assembled an imprecise panorama devoid of charm, as if she must respond to the weaknesses, verging on hopelessness, that stagger about the souls of Sinbad, Zoneida, and Ali Baba.

The duel between her and her creatures is worsening. The rebellion occurred in the very middle of the plot, when it was most painful to repair the damage or provide them with a sense of honor. Coming upon this private war, Scheherazade wants to instill reason in them. She raises her voice, imposing obedience. Who ever saw a disagreement that would divide them permanently? And hadn't they been born together, like Siamese twins?

Dinazarda follows the disharmony of those rebels clamoring for emancipation. Her sister's problems are evident to her, though the noises coming from her stories are difficult to capture. So she calls her sister's attention to the principal danger, asking her to please interrupt the unreal dialogue with her characters. Nevertheless, she is confused because Scheherazade proves as unruly as any of her creations, at whose hands she suffers as if feeling pleasure, as if her ability to improvise depends on such protest.

Naturally, Dinazarda is upset. She wonders how to engender solutions using the remnants of a rebellious heart like her sister's, who heeds good and evil like conjoined and inseparable entities. Even if Scheherazade's lapses go unnoticed by the Caliph, they do not escape her sister, who, after all, is skilled at finding overlooked dust in some corner of the palace. When she foresees Scheherazade's imminent failure, she loses her breath, thinks herself in the desert suffering the cold nights of December. She closes her eyes, her lashes trembling nervously, making it hard to grasp the meaning of things.

Scheherazade, however, contrary to Dinazarda's fear, smiles. She is unafraid of drowning or fishing debris from the bottom of the sea. Many times, amid danger, she returns to the surface with bubbles in her mouth but with a renewed vocabulary. Exposed to death, as the night before, she is able to use poetic artifice, and quite well, to gain one more day. She had learned survival among the poor of the earth, the human castoffs of Baghdad. With these people she justifies her decisions and abstains from yielding to the egoism of the Caliph, the unforgiving enemy of her dreams.

Dinazarda concentrates on Scheherazade's verbal collapse. She fears that her sister, despite constant flow from her creative center, will finally surrender to the misery of daily life and exhaust herself, no longer replenishing the mystery she sips at every meal. Feeling pity at Scheherazade's loneliness, Dinazarda leads her to the bed following her bath and tells her to rest now that the Caliph has granted her another day.

Her exhaustion is such that Scheherazade falls wearily onto the bed, not caring at that moment if she awakens in prison, if that be her punishment. Hours later, when she opens her eyes, she finds Dinazarda leaning over her, examining her features. Her whole being is unhappy and withdrawn, and she was gasping softly in her sleep. Had Scheherazade by any chance dreamed? Dinazarda wonders. And if so, where had she journeyed? Has she now actually returned to the royal chambers? Or were her dreams the epic forged by each individual to gain the stature of hero and be happy?

49

It is not necessary to ask permission to enter Scheherazade's unpredictable realm. In her pleasant cove she yearns to be loved. Unfinished stories await her with the expectation that her valiant sense of invention will bring closure.

When Scheherazade speaks, Dinazarda fears that her memory will fail her, that her tongue will falter, and that her gaze, drawn by the false horizon line, will come to rest on an oasis far from Baghdad. The details of this voyage induce in her the illusion of not wanting to prolong her plots as before. Nothing in the caliphate deserves her efforts to honor the deeds of a petrified past.

Dinazarda finds the idea vexing. In a scathing tone she demands that her sister continue to defend her life. And that in pursuing that objective she bring to the surface the singularity that emerges from all things. Distressed by Scheherazade's fate, she softens her voice and infuses it with courage. She promises to free her from that prison, trusting that Scheherazade's narrative power will awe the Caliph, arouse his enchantment, turn his spirit around.

Some days are especially cruel. In expectation of the Caliph's fatal pronouncement at dawn, Dinazarda sometimes loses the will to live. When she hears the echoes of the prayers coming from the minarets of Baghdad, it pains her to face the verdict. The Caliph's expression remains immutable, however, before his declaration, as he accepts the ablutions and the hot tea. It is still early to deal with affairs of state or to outwit the sisters. Back in the chambers, which he had left in the middle of the night, he shows no appreciation of the feelings of others. And when he finally spares Scheherazade with a wink, the Caliph yields to the agony of which he too is prisoner.

Scheherazade does not lose control or react. The Caliph's despotic act is born of the universal understanding that he believes he possesses of the kingdom and from the right to defend his wounded honor. She, however, resists such villainy, refusing to celebrate a victory achieved at the cost of her fear. She sleeps with the enemy but doesn't accept his plans. In reprisal, she has declared open season on the sovereign. She looks for gasping characters, genies in bottles, to poison her adversary.

Scheherazade's effort to survive is moving. She deserves to be treated like a queen, with petals strewn wherever she walks. But Dinazarda, subject to the volatility of her own feelings, sometimes loves her greatly, sometimes thinks about leaving her to her fate and saving herself while she can. She sees no reason to link her life to that of Scheherazade, a false vigilante who in the name of personal glory has cast father, sister, and Jasmine onto the bonfire of her ambition.

She pulls violently away from her sister, refusing to look at her. She takes refuge in the garden but soon returns to the chambers, for fear that Scheherazade will be taken away to the scaffold and she will never see her again. The pain of her possible death assails Dinazarda day after day. She foresees that if memory pretends to forget the dead, love, housed in the heart and ever vigilant, at the slightest sign lashes whoever survives the memories. Dinazarda goes to the window, her eyes brimming with tears. Her sister is living on the edge of an abyss, traversing an intangible path beyond her control. She wonders whether it is worth the effort to try to save her, whether she should continue sending Jasmine to the market to gather accounts wherever she finds them, to make use of resources that Scheherazade herself, so certain of victory, would repudiate. Perhaps she should confess to her sister what, with Jasmine's help, she has been doing to supply her with the modest tales provided by the blind dervish.

Jasmine detects the atmosphere of tension, which inspires her, even in daylight, to ensconce the sisters in the bed where the night before the Caliph's desire had swelled. They yield to her wish.

Hours later, forgetting the drama, they awaken enthusiastic. Scheherazade, amid murmurs, dried fruit, and sips of sweet wine from Madagascar, unearths the plot to be presented to the Caliph. Commanded by some recently invented character, she seeks solutions for the different stages of the account. She confesses to the other women that she is at a crossroads that forces her to shape the new story when, faced with so many options, she scarcely knows what path to take.

Fear of losing her sister becomes an obsession for Dinazarda. Invested with unexpected authority, she urges Scheherazade to mount the pulpit of Arab imagination, as glowing as the stars in the heavens. Where better to stand and speak to Arabs committed to interminable accounts? And to describe to the multitudes the pageantry of stories peopled with scheming merchants, poor and opportunistic adventurers?

Encouraged by her own words, Dinazarda continues. Isn't it true that creatures gone astray are Scheherazade's favorites? And that in her anxiety to shape their passionate faces and retouch their emotions, to display their lust, doesn't Scheherazade wave her arms as if her every gesture erects tents and palaces, accelerating the tense and subtle, almost desperate, imagination?

Jasmine is diligent. She serves the sisters tea as they debate. She feels she is saving the storyteller. Impulsively, the slave brings the young woman's hand to her forehead and transmits her heat to the other. She is honoring a tribal tradition from the desert, come from her mother, her grandmother, of warming children, the old, the snouts of sheep, with the softness of the skin.

Occupied with observing Scheherazade, Dinazarda doesn't censure the slave's gesture. But she calls the attention of her sister, who, hastening to compose the outline of the story, acts as if it is easy to invent without having to worry about the finishing touches. Is she by any chance neglecting her art, no longer caring to make use of the details that spring from the recesses of memory? Dinazarda quickly regrets her criticisms, recognizing that her moral weakness often allows petty feelings to emerge. She had envied her sister even while admiring her. Was that the underlying conflict between them?

Jasmine respectfully moves away. She has strong legs from having so long overcome the golden dunes of the desert. Back in the kitchen, she sees to the sisters' meal with the naturalness of one born to scarcity, and then lays out on the pillows the clothes Dinazarda has chosen for Scheherazade to wear that night. Such simple procedures help Scheherazade establish a connection between the slave's daily life and her own. The proximity of the banal, despite the prison in which they live, makes them a single flesh housing their intense humanity.

The tale that Scheherazade is preparing this afternoon departs from the pattern of her earlier stories. This presents her with problems in judging how long it will last. She knows that the success of any account rests with the Caliph. It is a sign of his interest when he plays with the hairs of his faded beard, which he weaves like a rug, and presses the back of his hand against his lips while slowly sipping wine with half-closed eyes like a dreaming poet.

No story, whose length sometimes is that of a ballad executed on the lute, can reach its conclusion before the sky begins to lighten. To achieve her ends, Scheherazade is obliged to create tricks and ruses in the empty spaces of the plots. As it grows dark, before the sovereign arrives, she fills the minutes with false leads—this so that Dinazarda and Jasmine will not think it an easy matter to close a gaping hole, the size of a story, with lame words not always associated with the dazzling beauty of the desert.

That night, ready to receive the Caliph, Scheherazade presents herself in clothes of the finest weave. Among all three women in the chambers the pact of mutual assistance endures, an alliance like that between Scheherazade and the story itself, which seeks the human essence of the characters. Thus any story line, however tentative at the outset, becomes energized by the accumulated plots to which Scheherazade adds chimeras, sometimes bathed in blood.

A similar gift, manifest in Scheherazade, had come from the lineage of her mother, who died so young. Wonderful things were said about the maternal clan. Their familiar voices coming from the desert in the mornings, after they drank goat's milk, would free their tongues to utter lies and speak of dreams. These spontaneous imprecations, rich in vocabulary, had no one target. In compensation, their prayers, directed toward Mecca, exalted the Prophet and nature, from whence came meat, grain, and yeast. This people had learned to turn the world into a fable, which could well be why Scheherazade introduced into her accounts motivations typical of the nomadic race from which she descended on her mother's side.

50

The course Scheherazade had chosen to follow beginning her first night in the palace allows her no repose. In the princess's body Jasmine foresees the dangers. She massages muscles taut from fear, but they resist her caresses. The veins throb from the wonders that spring from Scheherazade's mouth in the form of words and saliva.

After attempting in vain to make the young woman feel pleasure, Jasmine heads to the market. It is Friday, a feast day interspersed with prayers. Passing by the mosque, she hears the echo of the weekly sermons, after the muezzin, from the height of the minaret, has convoked the faithful to worship Allah. As a woman and a slave, she is forbidden to climb the tower stairs to the skylight and observe the filtered light falling on walls embellished with geometric patterns and calligraphic signs, or to have access to the secrets of a calligraphy that contains the verses of the Qur'an, the words revealed to the Prophet by Allah over the course of two decades. The epigraphic setting, the base of Arabic art, eschewing representation of the human figure, which was forbidden, translated the enigmas peculiar to the religious sphere.

Even before she came to Baghdad, Jasmine aspired to copy the writing that utilized those angular characters to express thought. Some of the calligraphy in the Caliph's palace enhanced the beauty of the rooms by preserving in their entirety verses of religious origin.

As she crosses the bazaar, a sensation of failure suddenly strikes her. She fears once more, on yet another visit to the dervish, offering Dinazarda an unusable message that, however hard she tries to memorize it, will serve for nothing, for at no time has she heard from Scheherazade's mouth any reference to the work of the blind dervish. This reinforces her suspicion that perhaps these accounts brought from the market are useless in Dinazarda's eyes.

As a consequence of such frustration, Jasmine falters in her mission. She no longer remembers precisely what he tells her, even running the risk of Dinazarda's severely rebuking her. At such times Dinazarda uses the art of insult as few can, pointing out Jasmine's shortcomings. Sometimes she accuses the slave of jeopardizing her sister's life, especially when the dervish's offerings do not entirely fit into Scheherazade's inventions.

Restricted to the chambers, Scheherazade, distant from the sudden animosity of Dinazarda scolding Jasmine, tests her limits, curious to know her future. What will become of her, without destination and without stories, if the sovereign spares her life? Perhaps the image of a woman changed into a swan, a turtle, an anemone? She knows full well that there is no mercy in his heart. She finds nothing of encouragement in the tyrant's steely gaze. It simply warns the young woman of the necessity to fight against his protracted melancholy and transform him, to his delight, into the genie in the bottle.

The Caliph asked nothing of her but an existence attainable only with her help. An initiative that emboldened him and reawakened, as when he desired to be Harun ar-Rashid, the wish to become part of the gallery of popular mythology. Since childhood, driven by his ambitious father, he had dreamed of riding through the desert, furiously combating the infidels, and also observing closely some pious man who, in total obedience to the Qur'an, cleansed his sins through difficult sacrifices.

Only Scheherazade showered him with sumptuous words, introduced him to other cultures, other beings, such as Solomon, who built a magnificent temple, or Ulysses, clever and shrewd. She brought him such knowledge without causing him to succumb to heretical doctrines like, for example, those of the Fatimids.

Detached from the scene, the Caliph orders them to bring him the life to be found in a glass of wine. He savors each velvety drop as if it were the last. Attentive to his wishes, Scheherazade doesn't notice that following coitus, Jasmine had covered her with a crudely knotted blanket from Palestine. Freed by the sovereign to begin her tale, she proceeds, uncertain of salvation. Everything in the Caliph's universe conspires against the spirit of adventure that she disseminates. But to avoid tripping over words along this journey, she must invent heroes with the stuff of warriors.

Scheherazade needs to know where she is heading. It is necessary to give her creatures a status pleasing to the ruler. Can they be heroes and villains at the same time, living with the precarious notions of good and evil that torment Baghdad? As she continues to speak, she encounters an obstacle. She has carelessly introduced a heroine in a conflict planned to erupt later, an error she would notice only through the promise to take her safely to the plains where her relatives were pasturing sheep until sundown.

After correcting this oversight, Scheherazade introduces her listeners to the combinations that govern the real and the mythic in her characters. She subjects herself to the apathetic and drowsy Caliph, who closes his eyes. Lying on the colorful cushions, he barely moves, sipping the cup of mint tea that Jasmine continuously refills. The sovereign's apparent indifference frightens Dinazarda, who notes her sister's imperceptible confusion but doesn't know what to do to placate the insatiable ruler. She perhaps asks herself what further punishment remains for Scheherazade to suffer.

Scheherazade's fate is to continue the story at any cost. To air the plot while the breeze from the arched windows cools the chambers. Fatima's teachings always foretold that no salvation was possible for the heroines who wore mourning in the sight of all, victims of the shackles of affection. Reinvigorated by the memory of her nursemaid, Scheherazade again faces the Caliph, who, now awake, stares at her, penetrating the walls of her soul.

On a permanent voyage of the imagination that transports her far from everyone, Scheherazade fortifies her imperiled characters. She takes the Caliph to places he has never been. Thus her listeners pass through Petra, kingdom of the camel drivers, which in the past had piqued the imagination of a map-loving Roman known as Pliny the Elder. Scheherazade incorporates the residents of the chambers into the caravans that leave Damascus and journey to Southeast Asia, to the plains of Mesopotamia, to the banks of the Tigris, which merged in the gulf with the Euphrates, some twenty miles from Baghdad, until returning to the city that the brave Abbasid Abu Jafar, also known as Al-Mansur, founded on the western bank of the Tigris. Round in shape, Baghdad, which she so loved, was protected by three concentric walls, each offering, to those entering and leaving, the four doors that Al-Mansur had thought indispensable for communication with the outside world. Of them all, the favorite was the northeastern door, at which, after one crossed the wooden bridge over the river, began the road leading to Khurasan. This road went to the palace that his heir, Al-Mahdi, would finish building.

Lodged in Baghdad, vigilant, her characters commiserate about their poverty. Exhausted, however, from the many voyages that Scheherazade has imposed on them, they sometimes take hours to return to the scene, to collaborate on the embellishment of the account. Forceful measures must be enacted against this rebellion. Hurt by such ingratitude, she grabs her magic carpet and unrolls it before the sovereign, inviting her listeners to fly over Baghdad in search of the fugitives until they find the rebellious characters crouching on the ground, waiting for them, besmeared with watermelon juice.

Her continual effort forces her to ask herself how many more lives she will possess to drag this flock of hers to the Caliph and to provide the sovereign, with them in tow, the carnality, the playful spirit, the calumny and intrigue of her people. It is all to prove to him that it is possible to mix them in with the princes who, to a man, long for the adventures of the poor.

The Caliph makes sure that, despite the upsets caused by the situation in which the two of them live, Scheherazade remains at his side. The woman's blood circulates through his veins. Thanks to her soft voice, he has fed on her demons, princesses, and beggars. Now, though, she seems distracted, as if far from the chambers, and he wonders exactly where she has gone, so he could follow her. But, try as he might, he cannot gaze into her heart. He sees only the Vizier's daughter facing the sword of power, confident that the blade hanging pitilessly over her will at last show mercy.

The sky begins to lighten. And Scheherazade, like other Muslims, offers her morning prayers. For some moments she dissociates herself from the death that, despite her portentous adventures, can come from the Caliph without warning.

51

Each night is a sacrifice. Like Persephone on her visit to Hades, in vassalage to Pluto, Scheherazade too, in the service of conjugal duties, journeys to the subterranean world, from which she emerges with the hope that the Caliph will grant her life at the first rays of the sun.

After she sips the last of the tea that Jasmine offers her, imminent death alights on her features with grave gentleness. The facial contractions that surface soon disappear, part of the drama being staged.

Jasmine doesn't leave her side. Her sharp sense of smell breathes in the voluptuous poison of the bodies that shortly before had copulated on the royal bed. She sprinkles essences, incense, and myrrh on the crumpled sheets. Later, hidden behind the screen, her imagination aflame, she rubs her nipples. Taking advantage of Dinazarda's absence, she yields to her growing desire by licking her fingers as if her tongue were not her own. Then her hand descends to her sex, from which drips a mucus that takes her into herself and does not expel her as she moves along the walls as if excavating them. Under the impact of continuous waves and convulsive rhythm, disoriented, the slave has the sensation of having lost the world where she was born, prior to her captivity. She shudders as her body finally opens in sudden explosion.

The Caliph, in turn, preparing to proffer the morning sentence, is captive to the narrative. Although he rejects his dependency on the young woman, his eagerness to hear her is so intense that he doesn't leave the palace even to oversee a kingdom that demands his presence. The emergence of dark circles under his eyes, signs of chronic fatigue, are proof of his attachment to the storyteller's words. The disheveled eyebrows and grizzly beard that he sees reflected in the crystal call his attention. He is invaded by the vague notion that ever since his first copulation with Scheherazade, followed by her incessant lies, he has neglected his appearance and sacrificed sleep for nights on end.

Scheherazade parades before the Caliph a succession of miseries, linking him to the misfortune of her characters. His face shows no reaction. The moral posture of the sovereign exacerbates her repudiation of him. She cannot understand how, in spite of his cruelty, he throws himself onto the mat in the direction of Mecca for his daily prayers, in hopes of pleasing Allah.

The Caliph remains silent. He protects himself from letting the young woman see his new feelings. In recent weeks, as a dangerous precedent, he has allowed himself to be fascinated by the possibility of investigating the mystery of Scheherazade, of listening to her laments, of discovering the opening in her spirit through which one day he will advance and defeat her forevermore.

The simple idea of fighting Scheherazade through certain resources excites the Caliph. He is no longer willing to submit passively to that which springs from the young woman. For a variety of reasons, he must not allow this enchantment with her to prevent his honoring the vow made after the Sultana's betrayal. Still, he is surprised by the nature of his emotions. Though he is heir to the throne by the will of Muhammad, it is difficult for him to free himself from one who now seems indispensable.

His voice assumes an inflection of irritation. Scheherazade's spell hinders his liberty to go to the harem and bring a favorite to the bed now occupied by her. Unconsciously, he has abdicated his prerogatives by aping the female practice of behaving according to dictates imposed by the master. His life has taken on an uncomfortable strangeness. His everyday routine, though affording him a sense of adventure, has now deprived him of his earlier existence. As a consequence, navigating Scheherazade's verbal world has sapped his inclination to concern himself with his royal functions, to accept life without imaginary happenings.

Scheherazade notes his secret tremors. Though master of an art replete with meanderings and subterfuges, she bends every effort to gather gold, silver, tin, and salt to offer him, to shower him with a life that he seems not to have. She shelters worldly goods in her imagination but can no longer bear having her belongings extorted by the sovereign.

Indifferent to the judgment the Caliph may form about her, she isn't tempted to share her innermost beliefs and ideas with him or, through the power of enchantment she exerts, to breach the limits imposed by the court. At the same time, she knows she is not the only one to offer herself for others. There are women who have gone before her, and others who follow her example. She had learned that Polixena, from ancient Greek times, offered her breast to Neoptolemus, son of the headstrong Achilles, for the ultimate sacrifice. Burdened by her suffering, the daughter of King Priam accepted paying with her life for the fall of Troy. And although as she stood before her executioner she designated the part of her body that merited the dagger as instrument of her death, she was not permitted to defy tradition. The Greeks, unlike other peoples, forbade piercing the chest of a woman, perhaps in the belief that death should not come from the bosom, from whose breasts humanity suckled milk and love.

Faithful to the Hellenic view, which had consecrated the custom of burying the dagger in the throat, Neoptolemus plunged the blade into the woman. The symbolic dimension of the gesture was implicit recognition of woman's aphasia, of extinguishing for all time words that leave an insidious trail as they narrate the story of the murder.

As if by common accord, Scheherazade and the Caliph mutually comply with the rituals that precede death, both indifferent to the fact that the Greek Homer and the Roman Virgil, in their respective poetic voices, were in opposite camps with respect to women. But what could have motivated Virgil, in open resistance to Polixena's refusal and opposed to the bard Homer, to choose the woman's breast to succumb to the fury of Neoptolemus?

As Scheherazade narrates the misfortunes of her characters, the words of the fictional truth fortify her. Like Polixena, there sprang from her breast a cry that, with the dagger at her throat, threatened never to be extinguished.

52

The Caliph doesn't know what he is feeling. But he fears nothing and nurtures hopelessness without remorse. Protected by boredom, he resists allowing his body to be stolen. He doesn't consider Scheherazade a threat. He sighs, relieved that in his favor is the power to send her to her death. It is, of course, a plan that he has delayed implementing, for instead of handing her over to the executioner and putting an end to his long agony, he invariably returns to his encounter with the young woman.

Scheherazade is equally cautious. Her face shows the same cloudy smile as when she saw him leave the chambers in the morning, after her life was spared. Her expression, identical to the day before, conceals the young woman's emotions and forbids intimacy.

The Caliph settles onto his throne, to him a common chair where he receives foreign rulers with due pomp. He knows he is pursued by the curse that falls on the Abbasids when the crown is contested by some malcontent heir-in-waiting and disposed to treason. Nevertheless, it seems natural to him that to win Baghdad even the blood of one's father should be shed. In the midst of the whirlwind of state interests, brought to his attention by the Vizier, the sovereign keeps thinking about the daughters of the chancellor at his side. The Vizier is unaware that the ruler, in reviewing the list of his holdings, does not count among them a family that he recognizes as his own, despite his children by many women. Perhaps that is why, in a moment of weakness, by designating Scheherazade and Dinazarda as a kind of family, he creates a tie with them that he interprets as a home.

It bothers him, however, to think of an emotional bond that ignores the pain of his victims and of which he is prepared to rid himself without pity. On the other hand, what kind of family is it that wouldn't love him despite his cruelty? With a few words, the sovereign transfers the administrative tasks to the Vizier and, without excusing himself, leaves the room, where the objects gleam in the incoming sunlight. Followed by his guard, he steps up his pace, taking a route different from his customary one. He leads his companions to think that he plans to head that same afternoon to an oasis near Baghdad, which he had stopped visiting in favor of Scheherazade's stories.

His gilded slippers, the work of an artisan who lived in the servants' quarters of the palace at his exclusive service, scintillate from afar, announcing his approach. In the polished marble along which he glides he sees his likeness diffusely reflected. He is several men in one. He advances, taken by the illusion that one day he will depart and forget the way home, a thought doubtlessly inspired by what Scheherazade has been relating. It would never occur to him to try that kind of roving life. He approaches the curve by the harem, a forbidden wing whose architecture constitutes a trap for the unwary.

The Caliph stops at the entrance to the seraglio, indifferent to the commotion that announcement of his arrival provokes among the women enclosed in that area. The favorites, deprived of his company, fear the future, the day on which they are told of the death of the ruler. In the gestures that take place at the entrance to the harem, no one dares admonish the Caliph about his obligation to those women. He should at least ask how they are, find out their mood after a painful abandonment, and promise to visit them soon.

The door to the harem remains under seal as a sign that despite his absence they still belong to him. That part of the palace, under constant watch, could be visited by him alone, the only one authorized to enjoy the flesh of rare consistency of the women he had personally chosen over the years. This territory of male fantasy, which he had inherited while still an adolescent, excused him from the battle of seduction, as he needed only to point a finger at the woman who would accompany him to the bedchambers.

In skirting past the seraglio and opting for the chambers where Scheherazade lives, he not only commits a grave fault, offending a tradition laid down by his peers, but he also demonstrates discourtesy to the concubines, ignorant of what fate awaits them. In those months of abstinence, he had not even sent his favorites a kind note or words of comfort. Nor had they had received a message that might have let them know his intention of experiencing in the next few days the delights of those bodies that he had long denied for reasons of state.

It would not have been difficult for him to excuse himself with them, or to mention his obligations. But, alien to female understanding, perhaps he wondered what those women would know about a kingdom in expansion, under frequent threat from enemies, and whose borders harbored caravans bringing seeds of evil and discord from inhospitable lands—harmful ideas with the goal of humiliating Baghdad, of putting a halt to the religious temperament of the Islamic people.

Although he was the only man allowed to enter the harem, except for the castrates, he did not plan to transfer to the Vizier the task of communicating to the women that on certain lonely nights he would repeat their names, imagining himself swallowed up by thighs avid to grant him blind and unconditional love. The Vizier wasn't the right man to promise that he would soon return to frequent their beds—pointless rhetoric, since he had both deprived them of his message and done nothing to prevent the palace community from spreading word of his assiduousness vis-à-vis Scheherazade. Neither had he taken steps to prevent talk about the diligence of Dinazarda, who of her own initiative had introduced significant changes into the routine of the court. Some of the improvements were designed to benefit the slaves. And the young woman had not hesitated to complain to the royal cooks about the insipid taste of their food, criticizing their disregard for spices. Didn't they know that a pinch of herb converted a tasteless dish into an unforgettable delicacy?

Unresigned to the role she played at Scheherazade's side,

Dinazarda had established for herself progressive steps, with the idea of accentuating her gift for command. So, when she would run into some courtier at the entrance to the royal gardens, she would cause delicate questions to surface, merely to demonstrate her knowledge, carefully leaving in the air observations to be completed later, as soon as she consulted her sister. She dared develop certain themes through consultation with Scheherazade, who would fill in any lacunae. With a degree of conceit inherited from her father, Dinazarda would discourse with the Caliph about the skill with which the peoples of the Far East used fire and cooking pots. The subject won the sovereign's immediate approval, to the point that sometimes, from so much culinary description, he would refrain from eating in the hours that followed, sated by the fantasies of Dinazarda's recipes.

The Caliph's esteem for her sister was no threat to Scheherazade. She often thought about how to repay Dinazarda's love, evident even when they disagreed. She recognized her debt to her sister—thanks to her, Scheherazade had fought for her life. With the intent to divert any bitter feeling toward Dinazarda, she lauded her talent. In fact, for the first time she noted the subtlety with which her sister discussed the effects of aromas and the ever-changing amount of salt and sugar in the food, initiatives that surely embraced the idiosyncrasies of other peoples.

Dinazarda too, since arriving at the palace, had made every effort to accept Scheherazade's rebellion relative to certain matters. She couldn't bear for her sister to make a decision of any sort without consulting her, as if she were the master of her acts and her accounts. She was always ready to intervene in the core of Scheherazade's stories, the essence of the characters, and anything else without asking permission.

The misunderstandings between the sisters, having reached the ears of the Caliph, revealed the degree of intrigue that the young women aroused among courtiers and slaves, two groups dedicated to sowing lies. The occurrence had led the sovereign to astonishment at the petty infamies and to an understanding of the extent to which these slanders served to vent woes and to incite resentments.

Without doubt, the Vizier's daughters evinced the same ambiguity as the characters did, deviations in behavior that, although confined to a small space like the chambers, still exercised over the Caliph an attraction without which he could no longer live.

53

Distant from the arched windows, the lovers' bed occupies a large space. The slave women, in fleeting intimacy, gravitate to it. As do the Vizier's daughters, who, like the servants, take part in the ruses that envelop everyone in a finely woven net.

Even though they share a bed, and are amused by mild erotic games, the Caliph and Scheherazade address each other with deference, never neglecting reverential treatment. During copulation, they partially remove their clothing. And despite the mingling of bodily fluids, they avoid looking at the traces left by sex as a lustful footprint on the silken sheets. They do not exchange glances, for the gaze of each of them has no need of speech. Scheherazade's words alone suggest the limits established between them. In this case, it behooves the sovereign to act according to the dictates of his phallus, said in the markets of Baghdad to be impatient.

Before becoming the Caliph's wife, Scheherazade lacked sexual experience. Her upbringing had not included the art of love. And on the occasions when she explored her own body, she had reached climax without passion. But not even now, when her womb had become the recipient of royal sperm, had she given free rein to her instinct. Everything about her deadened and extinguished the Caliph's desire. However, following Dinazarda's instructions, she would open and close her legs around the sovereign's voluminous body so the royal member could reach her uterus, without allowing this maneuver to impel the phallus into the depths of her insides. But at the same time that she listened to her sister, Scheherazade feared that this behavior might displease the sovereign and damage the circumspect modesty that both maintained.

Dinazarda didn't know how to convince her of the need to

gratify the ruler, who was more and more reticent. But Scheherazade, feigning obedience to her husband, was certain that under the circumstances cupidity was not the best weapon to defeat him. Her storytelling, full of eroticism, dedicated to the libido of her characters, seemed sufficient to revitalize the Caliph's worn body.

He carried out his conjugal duty tediously. After having experienced every perverse form of sex, he was drained by the landscape of the female body. The years had damped any internal fury, and he contented himself simply with a fast, effortless orgasm. At that stage of life he was little concerned with defending his reputation as fornicator. This was happening precisely when Scheherazade, always coy, prevented him from eliciting from her body proof of pleasure, even though he felt it moisten.

Different from other women he'd had in bed, she abstained from amorous revel, overly concentrated on her narrative voyages. The Caliph, however, was unconcerned that her hips didn't move or that her body was slow to synchronize with his. Intent on the pleasure coming from Scheherazade's accounts, he felt redeemed by the characters that took him from a dark, internal life to mold him into almost another being. From such delight emerged an enjoyment that rescued him from the inferno of the throne, where there was no place for reveries, while sharpening his perception, his senses. He was thrust into a state of excitement, as if he were anticipating the revelation coming at the end of each story, when, curling the strands of his beard between his fingers, he showed evidence of pleasure.

He peacefully accepted that the sisters exchanged secrets between themselves and abused his apparent tolerance. Possibly they even conspired against him, wishing to cast him into the shifting territory of lust, surround him with fog and miasma, from which he could not escape. And why shouldn't it be that way? Weren't his mouth and his sex an essential topic in Baghdad?

The suspicions imprinted on the sovereign's face now draw Scheherazade from the false vigil of love with which she had distracted herself, feigning that the Caliph's orgasm had affected her. Alert to the dangers, Dinazarda reacts to banish that farce that could cost her sister's life. With a powerful impetus, she ushers Scheherazade into the realm of words, where she must operate. She will win the gift of another day only if her listeners, accustomed to stories, absorb her talent and attain another sense of life.

54

The sun appears in the windows. The glow of morning comes first to the Caliph's face. The early light brings to a close Scheherazade's narrative adventures shortly before she emphasizes the rebellious and emotional aspects of Sinbad.

On the cushions, resigned to her fate, Scheherazade awaits the sovereign's verdict. She dreams of returning to her father's house, erasing the memory of those endless nights, a yoke she can no longer bear. She is mute before the approaching drama, but soon the Caliph, with a simple wave of his hand, grants her one more day.

On her feet now, she moves about the chambers, walking repeatedly around the bed already free of any sign of the coupling that took place on the sheets. Her gesture hints at going to the windows and leaping out, never to return to the Caliph's palace.

Leaning against the parapet, she admires the luminous garden with its changing colors, not caring if the Caliph, when he returns, senses in her the rebellion that blooms among the flowers. She realizes that her undertaking has increasing costs, that she sacrifices the duties of the bed, scene of her captivity, in service of words so pleasing to the sovereign. But why would he criticize his master in the art of the unexpected? With whom, if not her, has he been learning the sense of adventure, the madness of being in the wilderness at the mercy of the unforeseen?

The ruler must understand the reason she sometimes speaks rapidly when, to dramatize the accounts, she becomes agitated and points to the faraway horizon, so distant from them. These gestures are intended to wrench from deep inside herself situations that convoke ghosts, goblins, and wizards common among the inhabitants of Baghdad, all to give him and these creatures eternal life.

As she paces the chambers like some tireless wanderer, Scheherazade crosses cities, deserts, oceans, the everlasting Tigris. She sees enemy feudal domains, erected in the past for the purpose of attacking the people of Islam. In her role as narrator, she is not unacquainted with the fate of those who take up arms and kill. They too bear troubles embedded in their hearts and shed tears.

Suddenly, nervous about the direction of a scene in which Sinbad grasps a weapon before the planned time, Scheherazade turns her back on the Caliph, in violation of ceremonial custom. The Abbasid dynasty had established this protocol with the objective of hierarchical clarity. She bows, asking forgiveness. Her gaze, veiled but insistent, assures him that the trespass was unintended. It was committed by someone raised far from court who lacked the occasion to see the Caliph close at hand, or even to attend a school of advanced learning, in Baghdad reserved for the elite. She would know little of the norms that govern the subjects of the caliphate. But please let it be remembered that this same character, recalcitrant and modestly dressed, embodies noteworthy virtues and that her boldness survives thanks to her imagination.

Her eyes fixed on the garden, Scheherazade pictures before her an exuberantly colorful magic carpet whose carefully tied knots keep it from damage from the wind. The artifact allows her to fly above the merchants' stalls, steal a bunch of grapes, and drop them into the lap of a beggar. From these heights tiny details of the city loom gigantic, and everything pulsates with the emotion of its inhabitants.

On this flight she sees, through the windows of Aladdin's house, his mother baking bread and cooking a piece of sheep fat that contaminates the air. Farther on, she watches Ali Baba's servant girl heating in a vat in the courtyard the oil she plans to use to kill the forty thieves. Though she is convinced of the rightness of her action, fear grips her heart. If the plan fails, she will die immediately at the blade of the merciless bandits.

After gaining another day of life, Scheherazade imagines herself in Tikrit, having arrived in time to accompany Prince Zaruz as he is about to leave his tribe. He has no place to go now that his father has banished him from his domain. It all happened because he had defied the will of his father, who wanted him to marry a princess from a friendly tribe but discovered to his dismay that his son had taken as a wife an Ethiopian slave. The prince, confronted with his father's wrath and the new reality of punishment, is desperate. Not knowing his whereabouts, he wanders through the desert, eating scorpions, locusts, a young gazelle. A situation of difficult resolution for Scheherazade, so crafty in the denouement of her stories and seeking happiness for all.

She is expanding her reveries when Dinazarda, fearing that such unruly imagination will end by hastening her death, restrains her verbal frenzy. She insists that Scheherazade rest in the same bed where the Caliph appears every night intending to kill her, even if in the end he concedes her temporary freedom at dawn.

55

The Caliph does not make life easier for her. He is sparing in the gifts he offers her, except for the jewels and clothes accumulating in the chambers, barely fitting into the space set aside for the purpose.

He never suggests to Scheherazade, on nights when the moon bathes the palace and inflames the hearts of its occupants, a stroll in the garden, holding hands and discovering the buds of flowers behind the bushes, born thanks to the channels through which the water flows soundlessly. Nor does he take her to see the fountain at the center of the garden. For its construction, his Abbasid grandfather summoned from afar specialists in the art of redistributing water in continuous movement, in the form of powerful jets that made the foaming liquid attain unheard-of heights and fall onto the ground, where it rose again and hurled itself upward in a dance of rare beauty.

He doesn't take Scheherazade to see the royal treasures, comprising pieces accumulated by his forebears, zealous in their display of power and wealth. The Caliph is insensitive to her seclusion, her unhappy countenance as he lives in the moment of the words raining from her lips, words that he gathers up like one more possession in his immense fortune. The sovereign's boredom seems to assure the young woman that it would be of no avail to become acquainted with artistic works if she had too little time left to appreciate them. Standing before the scaffold, she would lament leaving behind her belief that human beings, despite the cruelty rooted in their hearts, were also capable of responding to talent's outpouring of art.

The Caliph's caution relative to the Abbasid treasure was well known. He feared that some neighbor's cupidity would lead him to steal the artistic wonders kept under lock and key. He did enjoy, however, describing certain pieces as if about to offer them to some dignitary visiting Baghdad. But his words were without effect and fell into the void.

Instead of affording the sisters some pleasure within his reach, the sovereign keeps Scheherazade tightly restrained, and nothing makes her laugh. She accepts the daily order of imprisonment as part of the system it is her task to destroy, if she wants someday to win. A victory would mean she could leave the palace, say good-bye to the medina, walk through the gates of the round walls, board a vessel on the bank of the Tigris, murmur to the boatman the name of the place she is to be taken, not precisely her final des-tination, from which she would never return.

The idea of flight is becoming an obsession. For no apparent reason, the theme began to emerge in her accounts and in her con-versations with Dinazarda and Jasmine. Not once, however, has she manifested an inclination to leave the palace, even under a vow to return. It is as if Scheherazade is resigned to the limits of her prison, knowing that inside her is something that Baghdad cannot offer. Aware also that the Caliph cannot add to her that which she rejects in her inner being, she finds that there grows in her the desire not to see him again, to leave the chambers stealthily, with-out communicating in writing that she has been forced to depart in search of dreams long delayed. It would do no good for the Caliph, impulsively, to kneel before her in a desperate attempt to forestall her plan.

She accepts that the sovereign possesses her body as if it were some other woman's. After copulating, however, all her muscles contract to expel him.

The sovereign also takes pleasure in distancing himself from her flesh. The only interest he has in Scheherazade is the tales through which he becomes excited about the poor of Baghdad, those vagabonds into whom the young woman has breathed the appearance of life, supplying them with whatever they need to fulfill their destiny. And while he meditates about the intensity of this spasm that surpasses coitus, Scheherazade vows never to hurt her characters. She refuses to attribute false ideologies to them or to go against their way of being, for they are simply creatures obeying a complex and adventurous nature, who, though born from her, are neither people of her blood nor copies of herself. They cannot proclaim themselves children of Scheherazade or mirror her anxieties. If the Caliph were to ask her to characterize herself as an artist, expecting a straightforward reply, she would tell him it was an enigma even to her. By this she would mean that the actions of her characters depend on circumstances not always the product of her own viscera. As a simple storyteller, yes, she is at the service of the adversity and the unexpected that reflect her own darkness and that of others.

And as she speaks, she confesses her futile effort to instill tenderness in Sinbad and Zoneida, to make them part of a repertoire corresponding to every human want. But even if she rarely meets those goals, Ali Baba and Aladdin are there, always at her orders—not as replicas of the Vizier's daughter but to shine in the sovereign's eyes.

Following the line of thinking developed by Scheherazade, Dinazarda hopes she will tell her who her favorite character is, the one who most resembles her. As she asks the question mischievously, she shows her teeth, assuring her sister that there is no point in lying. She is certain that at least one of them dwells in the dark morass of her heart, dense and imprudent like that of other mortals.

Scheherazade abstains from unveiling a mystery that in the final analysis resides as much in her as in the one who asks the question. Is not each individual responsible for his own personal enigma, sealed for all eternity? Dinazarda is irritated that after her sacrifice for her, Scheherazade still withholds such a confession, because she wants to deceive Dinazarda, and roams about the chambers, staring first at Jasmine, then at the portion of the heavens visible from the window.

Jasmine's bronze color, which outshines the metals lying on the table, dims as night falls. The involuntary object of dispute between the sisters, she observes sadly that the storyteller, her nerves in shreds, is ready to break free of the shackles that bind her to that strange family headed by the Caliph. But can Scheherazade's exhaustion be so great that she is thinking of one day abandoning them, of fleeing on one of her flying carpets, caring nothing about the consequences of her precipitous act?

She wants to oppose this caste that took away her freedom. Her status as slave entitles her to renounce them. Both because of her background of poverty and her knowledge stemming from the voices of the desert, Jasmine feels clad in a popular mandate. Having assumed this persona, she presents herself to Scheherazade as someone of value in moments of crisis.

Disguising her uneasiness, Scheherazade asks for a respite from those around her. She is moved looking at Jasmine, whose ingenuous slyness comes from the same roots as that of Ali Baba, Zoneida, and their flock. She identifies affectionate characteristics in the slave who follows her around the chambers. She does not, however, want to feel compassion for someone who may be on the eve of death. Scheherazade has no way of answering for the slave, of removing her from her servile state and returning her to her tribe, today scattered and cursed. Trying to compensate for her suffering, she offers effusively colored garments that accentuate her beauty. She obliges her to sound out her own mystery in the dark center of the mirror, which falls in love with Jasmine's harmonious features. Scheherazade helps her to imprint tracks on feelings, to observe the universe without being seen, so that in the future everything in her may perhaps acquire a revolutionary perspective.

The Caliph, in turn, pursued by the shade of Scheherazade, who arouses in him the desire to escape from himself, finds no peace in power. He suddenly leaves the throne room and walks through the palace, avoiding the gardens. He doesn't wish to see the scaffold that dominates the landscape. When he arrives at the chambers, Scheherazade is startled, not by his melancholy appearance but by the chain of new ideas that the sovereign's presence provokes. She continually asks herself how she can submit to a man who despite his noble stripe seems like a vulgar assassin. Drowning in the flow of words, she wonders what right she has to orient Jasmine when without protest she would allow the ruler to rip out pieces of her soul.

She knows her situation is delicate. Her body is at risk in confronting the power of the Caliph. It strengthens her to think that, notwithstanding some of her plots having been lent by anonymous storytellers of Baghdad, the majority arise out of her personal flights of imagination, bearing traces of her mother's family, a dynasty more fecund than her father's. How often, without knowing where to go in the future if she survives, she has pretended to mount a spirited, slow-trotting Arabian horse. Her strategy is to gain time and soften the Caliph's stony heart, to have him rescind the curse cast upon the young women of the realm, and only then to flee.

The Caliph's whims suffocate her. It becomes more and more difficult to design the duration of the story under the threat of dawn catching her unawares. She does not have the luxury of counting the minutes, for time is both fleeting and tense. It avails her nothing to determine the route of the story if the Caliph doesn't comprehend what she narrates. He bestows authorship on her without any sense of courtesy, and always with the expectation of condemning her to martyrdom. Though she is attentive to the enemy embodied by the Caliph, in her pulsates once again the passion that weighs heavily upon her, simultaneously provoking fear and splendor.

56

The Caliph is on familiar terms with Dinazarda, the guardian of his conjugal intimacy, without considering her an adversary. He doesn't accuse her of forming an alliance with her sister to dominate him. At no time has he threatened to make her his wife following the death of Scheherazade. Nonetheless, even without considering this hypothesis, he has learned from the storyteller that reality is unpredictable.

Concerned with avoiding conflict in the chambers that could suddenly spread to other areas in the palace, the Caliph neither rebuffs nor confides in her. His disillusionments, albeit kept to himself, appear on his face.

He recognizes that under the circumstances Dinazarda is useful to him. She is zealous, for example, in taking care of the wing reserved for the young women, though she moves about pretending that he hasn't handed over that corner of the palace to her care. She seems so at ease with the world around her that the Caliph has thought about using her alongside her father, one more helper amid many, among whom he has sowed discord in keeping with the ancient Abbasid tradition. For some time now, in fact, he has detected strong signs of fatigue in the Vizier, owing perhaps to excess of work and an administrative routine without major compensations. The Vizier, no doubt about it, has aged in the last few months, surely because of his younger daughter, now temporarily the Caliph's wife. The sovereign can even calculate which wrinkles in the Vizier's face are accountable to his daughter's drama.

Among other virtues he admires in Dinazarda is her discretion. At the first hint of his moving toward the bed, the Vizier's firstborn will take refuge behind the screen. This procedure has not been imposed on her, for he cares little if the slaves or his favorites see him fornicating. He merely appreciates someone who is able to sacrifice curiosity in the name of moderation.

In the few minutes that the sovereign grants her to speak, Dinazarda emphasizes aspects of Scheherazade's accounts that he may not have noted the previous night, minutiae that escape amid the abundance. He is surprised to find that a plot of such apparent simplicity can house allusions evident only through such considerations.

Amid shock and apprehension, he learns that these accounts, though of popular origin, insofar as they relate to Scheherazade have as their sole reason for being whether he approves of them, whether the young woman introduces him to mysteries that he has hitherto thought nonexistent.

This perception of the world, which only recently has emerged in him, translates with unconsidered virulence the dual nature in him and in each story. He can see that there is a fierce opposition in certain narrative elements corresponding, in the practice of the men of Baghdad and of the desert, to the battle of good and evil that no Muslim is excepted from fighting in his inner being.

He walks through the palace, the problems of the caliphate merging with those raised by Scheherazade's accounts. And it seems to him there is in some of them a false dissidence, because in speaking of the administration of the state he might end up mentioning men from some story.

The Caliph suspects that below the surface of those stories lies a secret layer, attainable only by his complete surrender. That is, to the degree that he abandons his disbelief he will gain the conditions needed to attack Scheherazade at the very heart of her invention. For the only thing the woman's persistent voice demands of him, in exchange for everything given him, is to identify with the hungry of Baghdad, without asking thoughtless questions. Above all, he should let himself be taken by the magnetism of the muleteer who trod the streets of Baghdad buying old lamps.

Like a refrain, Scheherazade's words, heard at night, pursue him to the throne. Together with what the Vizier tells him in defense of the kingdom, they form a flood with which he identifies in the illusion of promptly ridding himself of that persecution, of being free of a certain uncomfortable grandeur in competition with his own, for he nurtures the hope of one day narrating also.

Such a plan, however, strikes him as a long way off, as he lacks the integration with his subjects capable of creating an ecstasy equivalent to copulation, an emotion without which no narrative truth could endure. Before meeting Scheherazade, he had never formulated these ideas, was unaware that to admit the veracity of a character it was necessary to accept the life of the most humble of his vassals, to explore, often tripping along the way, the secret labyrinth of the popular mind. How could he rule if he had never noticed the color of their eyes?

The Caliph foresees the danger. As he debates with himself, his answers contradict what as ruler he defends. The excursion into art by Scheherazade, at the same time that it evokes wonders with every sentence, makes him vulnerable, weakens his reign, for it exposes, even in the form of a narrative, the soul he bears in secret.

The signs of age are becoming more evident. As if it is not enough for his body to neglect the offerings that wealth presents, the heady inventiveness of Scheherazade underscores the lacks in his upbringing. Ever since she came to live at his side, he has begun to distrust his human plan. For, in all those years ruling the kingdom, he never exercised a certain kindness dictated by the heart, which he found in the young woman's eyes, in her manner of telling stories. He had never thanked anyone at all for the gifts placed at the foot of the throne—as if awareness of his noble extraction, so powerful in him, exempted him from courtesy to others or from honoring the minimal formalities that cement relations among people. It was all because of believing that his subjects owed him their pitiful lives. And wasn't it true that he could demand them back simply by decree?

His Abbasid father had been unwavering in his personal dealings. For him, the logic of a ruler was guided by the interests of the throne. The norms of power prevented their submitting to the laws that govern love and gratitude. Simple feelings, nourished in the kitchen and in bed, were things of the people, who were capable of hating, stealing, killing, and even, amid tears of repentance, of effusively embracing.

Once, some of the ruler's advisers took advantage of the Vizier's absence to express unfavorable opinions of Dinazarda, a veiled censure stemming from the influence she exerted on the sovereign's wife, not to mention her meddling in areas beyond her competence. Such comments surprised the Caliph. What could be so wrong about wanting to improve conditions of palace life, long neglected by indolent courtiers? In fact, he had observed lately the beneficial influence of a friendly hand on the details of daily life. Only now did he learn that these benefits were because of Dinazarda, who had never mentioned the matter. Such modesty surely spoke well of her.

While still in her father's house, Dinazarda had shown a gift for command. Her sharp glance would examine every corner of the house in search of flaws. At first the Vizier tried to forestall her calling, but finally he accepted her practicing on family property that which she aspired to do in the future in the royal palace.

The Caliph reacted to the attacks. Beset by the sudden desire for justice, he declared that henceforth Dinazarda would be charged with certain administrative tasks. As a result of the trap set for her, wherever she went Dinazarda, now invested with power, began to accumulate proofs of neglect, of diversion of funds, of acts that impoverished the public exchequer, causing an increase in taxes. But, although defending the royal treasury, she investigated cautiously, fearful of incriminating her own father.

Involved in so many tasks, Dinazarda had forgotten in recent days to pay attention to the sovereign as he listened to Scheherazade, thus giving cause for the Caliph's somber temperament to come to the surface. He was assailed by the sensation of having made a mistake in granting so much power to the two sisters. It seemed to him that the playful enchantment earlier present in the

Vizier's daughters was fading away. This fact coincided with the discovery that he had failed, in all those years, to observe and interpret the universe of woman.

Since childhood, the Caliph had ignored the signs of a daily routine that women forged in his life and that now suddenly emerged, clad in sacred trappings and worthy of celebrating. Thanks to the Vizier's daughters and the slave Jasmine, he was slowly deciphering the meaningless smiles he saw on women's faces at all hours of the day. It seemed to be a kind of happiness that let them put aside a reality injurious to both their body and their dignity.

Now, contrary to habit, the Caliph approaches the window. The gardens bring to memory the grandfather who had passed his intransigence to his son, who in turn had not spared his heir. A chain of power that drove away any trace of the affection found in his favorites and in the Vizier's daughters. For the first time, the Caliph admits to himself that he cannot do without the moral strength of those women, or the ingenious montage so natural to their kind.

On those hot days, which cause him sweat and uncertainty, the sovereign seems resigned to mere females, prisoners in the chambers, guiding his steps and dictating rules. He also notes that Scheherazade, through her stories, drains his energy, submitting him to a path that could have easily been avoided from the beginning if he, disguised as Harun ar-Rashid, had gone to the medina.

Recently the Caliph has been strangely confusing Dinazarda's timbre with Scheherazade's. He can barely distinguish, until the fourth or fifth sentence, who is relating the story. Scheherazade, entranced by the plot woven by her imagination, is surprised by the unselfishness of Dinazarda, who, talented in all things, has never mentioned in public her role in the accounts. After all, since coming to the palace, the Vizier's other daughter, at her side, has daily climbed the stairs leading to the sacrificial altar without complaining or stabbing her in the back. For this reason alone, Scheherazade has a powerful desire to weep and flee the palace.

57

Scheherazade alternates between feminine and masculine roles. She feels at ease describing the genitalia of both sexes. She throbs, pulsates, swells, grows, hardens, according to the anatomy she represents in her tales. When she tires of being a man, forgetting what it means to be a woman in the court of Baghdad, she feels disdain for a humanity immersed in filth and illusion.

Hers is a resilient vitality. Her voice displays no weariness as she describes the feats of Sinbad. She does everything to make Zoneida's body compatible with the adventures attributed to her. And how was she to clip the wings of these creatures who wanted to fly? But in order to exist among these diverse ways of life, she has learned to emphasize her vocal modulation so that the sound, coming from her diaphragm, arrives at her brain a fraction of a second before she hears her own timbre.

Throughout her time in the palace, she has accentuated certain fancies. Caught between the Caliph, her sister, and Jasmine, each of them sucking her blood, she finds that her sensitivity has become debilitated, and she has undergone changes. Anticipating conflict, she foresees an ill-starred future. She can no longer bear her confinement. She wants to one day join a caravan and leave the sovereign behind, to go far away. But before disappearing beyond the dunes, she will go to the bazaar in a farewell, scooping up in her cupped hands the sounds coming from the hearts of the characters who, having no place to grow except Baghdad, live in her imagination.

She has become so accustomed to inventing that at times, for amusement, as if visiting some century not her own, she assumes in bed the posture of a celebrated courtesan who, suffering from advanced tuberculosis, reviews her life while stressing that she has experienced and loved much in her years. A courtesan, played by Scheherazade, whose persuasive song is abruptly cut short from lack of breath from coughing. But to help her performance, she sits down on the bed, which allows her to continue with her laments until her strength flags once more, obliging her to finish her song lying down, proof of the graveness of her condition.

In this playacting, Scheherazade imagines having been born in Babylon, or even Samarkand. And, uncertain of where the woman had first seen the light of day, she remembers, in that bed of countless sins, how happy the courtesan had been in the company of her lover in a village not far from there, from which the father of her fiancé had all but expelled her to protect the family fortune and honor, finally convincing her to reject his son. But as she lies there, dying and desperate, the father repents of the sacrifice he has demanded of her. To her surprise, her lover unexpectedly appears and bends anxiously over her, sobbing, quickly followed by his father. Both have come in time for the final farewell.

The story, which was made up in the presence of Dinazarda in order to satisfy her with the intricate misfortune of others, is similar to her own, although at the moment she does not see the points of convergence. Nevertheless, in a comparison of her fate to the courtesan's, she would be unable to say which was more dramatic.

This woman she has invented is not always of use when she has to precisely measure time, occasionally failing her. In the hourglass beside her in the dark, the sand slips imprecisely away. But she looks to the stars in the expectation that they will tell the truth. Dinazarda also scrutinizes the night for some sign indicating the passing of the hours.

Jasmine accompanies the sisters. She has a sundial inside her that radiates the heat and cold of the desert. Her people, coming from the dunes, know better than anyone which stars to reckon in the heavens before proudly announcing the seconds until sunset. Or what breeze blows the flame of the lamp in anticipation of dawn.

Scheherazade is troubled by the progress of the account. She needs to know how many minutes remain for her to advance the story in which she is now engaged and which she cannot allow to cool even if it burns her hands, lest she compromise the next scene. She consults her sister. The code between them, imperceptible to others, consists of blinking and scratching the forehead with the index finger. The strange dialogue has an immediate effect, for Scheherazade quickly accelerates what she is saying, forcing the young character and his loved one to hasten their carnal consummation as the enemy's boots creak menacingly outside the bedroom. He barely has time to kiss his lover before leaping out the window to the courtyard, at risk of breaking his bones, and setting out across the ravine, after which he will be at the mercy of the snares of fate.

While the rueful lovers escape from the sultan's men, Scheherazade, under pressure from the Caliph, develops measures for survival. At the first sign of danger, a fire ignites inside her and lights the way to follow in order not to perish. And in this fashion, by mediating dream and reality, she sees the first ray of sunlight reach the Caliph's face as he moves toward the executioner, posted behind the door, to pass sentence of life or death.

58

In the half shadow of night, Scheherazade wears the cloak of uncertainty. She has been entrusted with secrets anointed by the hands of a god who wandered the desert and the narrow banks of the Tigris, and she feels lost. The gray, distant sight of Baghdad cannot rescue her from the darkness.

Despite the burning lamps, memory sometimes becomes confused, undoing deeds, remaking characters, softening the action, replacing settings. Scheherazade wearily yields to sleep, watched alternately by Dinazarda and Jasmine. The Caliph, who had fallen asleep beside her, awakens, demanding that the story continue. Despite her drowsiness, she is dauntless, immediately resuming the web of intrigue in the tale interrupted by fatigue and fear.

The night is long and menacing. The vigil frightens men and beasts. In her zeal for justice, Scheherazade frees Ali Baba and Zoneida to speak their minds. She removes their implacable doubts, their temporary heroism. How can one be the hero of his own terror?

This night, like all the others, Scheherazade must outdo herself, probe the deeper meanings of Ali Baba and Zoneida and grant them, in the name of protection, the entities that each of them secretly reveres. While Jasmine, the Caliph's slave, had engendered gods adapted to the inclemency of the desert, venerated by men, camels, and lizards, Dinazarda had inherited religious reverence and a sense of drama. The Caliph himself, a simulacrum of the divine, would surreptitiously resort to the favors of a god to rescue him from catastrophe. Who but each person's god stands between him and chaos?

In the medina or the throne room, courtiers and common folk alike await the coming of the sun. Together they commemorate the brightness of another day. In some distant spot, perhaps in Samarra, Tikrit, Mosul, or along the Tigris and Euphrates, believers prostrate themselves in the direction of Mecca, uttering fervent prayers.

The storyteller, as she invokes the Prophet, remembers Fatima. What would she say if she learned of her beloved Scheherazade at the mercy of the Caliph? But she remains silent. She is pained by the absence of Fatima, who had made her try the milk of a snow-white goat brought especially from the desert for the newborn child. She doesn't want her nursemaid in the chambers even as a memory, witnessing a humiliating copulation. In the final analysis, Scheherazade has ceded to the Caliph's demands in furtherance of a just cause and has no grounds for complaint. It matters little that he never modifies the swift joining of their bodies, or that both of them yawn, knowing that the lamp flame will not betray their mutual tedium.

She celebrates such disinterest. The sovereign's decline favors her. While he is no longer the same in bed, the passing of the nocturnal hours arouses in her the will to defeat him, to intone chants to the moon, to exalt the combat undertaken by his scorned ego. Fortified with the energy that springs from first light, Scheherazade slowly plots against the Caliph, weaving a plan that will offend him and lead to her freedom.

On whom could Scheherazade count in this final battle? She thinks seriously of Jasmine, she of the burning flesh and a slave. By some chance, motivated by glory, would she accept taking Scheherazade's place in the Caliph's bed, without his realizing whose body he held in his arms? For in the darkness everyone pants in agony and desire, in the parity of sexual torment, wanting to forcibly rid themselves of the secretions of passion.

She would have to convince the slave, to promise her, in addition to earthly tribute, the privileges of paradise. Elicit from her the loyalty inherited from the inhospitable desert and living every day amid poverty. She wished to persuade her, however, without deadly impositions, and Jasmine was free to reject the proposal.

But she should weigh the convenience of becoming the Caliph's favorite, if he approved of the delights of a tawny body burnt from grazing the scorching sand, enchanted by a vulva from a region where the sovereign's sex had never been.

Naturally, there were risks implicit in that action. But hadn't she always desired to imitate Scheherazade? So much so that in the mornings she would extract from her both her smell and her talent, not failing to notice the abstraction stamped on the story-teller's face—an expression that sowed in everyone the suspicion that she had long since departed from the chambers, if not for the artifices of her craft.

But wasn't Jasmine doing the same thing? Wasn't she now weaving her own account by observing Scheherazade moving across the marble floor like a gazelle that keeps in its heart the secret fierceness of a caged tiger seen in the market in Baghdad?

59

Scheherazade can no longer bear the shackles that bind her to the Caliph in the form of coitus. After rejecting the idea of having one of the slave women replace her in bed, she considers the possibility of bringing from the harem a favorite experienced in erotic duty to take her place, without the knowledge of the sovereign.

She thinks about the reaction of Dinazarda, her accomplice since their arrival in the palace. She cannot keep her ignorant of the scheme growing apace in her, occupying all her time. After the ablutions ministered by Jasmine, she reveals to her sister the depth of her anguish. She waits for Dinazarda to ask for the details of the trap she is preparing for the Caliph.

Dinazarda is startled by the possible end of an adventure that has brought them so close together and that seemed like a simulation of happiness. Looking at Scheherazade, she immediately rejects a plan she deems destined to fail. She has no faith in the Caliph's benevolence if he discovers the fraud, and much less in his inattentiveness. He had been raised to distrust the acts of others and reprove them without justification: whoever the other might be, he was essentially a foe. How, then, to make him forget the flavor of her sister's flesh, the salt he had been tasting for so many nights, how to deceive a palate accustomed to distinguishing delicacies and have him accept a strange body in bed pretending to be Scheherazade?

Despite Scheherazade's irritation, Dinazarda censures an undertaking that would quickly lead to death. Why take such a risk? But as she speaks, Dinazarda feels her arguments wane, as if Scheherazade's proposal is not entirely senseless but could even represent a historic turnabout in their lives.

To Scheherazade, her sister's feeble arguments go against her interests. Her voice, mildly altered, rises above the music from the banquet room where the Caliph is entertaining foreign guests. She states firmly that the Caliph needs a change. Recently he had confided to a noble that he could no longer bear the monotony of an utterly predictable daily routine.

As selfish as he was, the Caliph would scarcely care who was in his bed. All he wanted from Scheherazade was the specific piece of her heart that told endless stories. He had no interest other than that coming from the adventures and absurdities of mankind, a taste he had cultivated since Scheherazade's arrival. Furthermore, who would rely on the love of a man known for his inability to love? In his lengthy reign there was no record of even a single love over which he had rent his garments or manuscripts or had sprinkled ashes on his head as a sign of mourning.

In her eagerness to convince Dinazarda, she suggests that the exchange of young women in the bed, before the Caliph's arrival in the chambers, be done at nightfall. Darkness, unfolding in shadows and false images, facilitated misidentification and welcomed monsters and fantasies, serving the interests of lovers and assassins.

Scheherazade especially loved the epiphany of those hours when, by candlelight, the men of the caliphate likened nocturnal shrewdness to the nature of woman, from whom they could expect every kind of allurement, lies, and illusion. The Caliph himself believed in the demonic ability of the female to incite in him the ruin of his flesh, to thwart his virility, to devour his phallus. Perhaps that was why it was common in the Islamic world to name women Laila, which means "night" in Arabic.

Scheherazade was not the only one to respect the dangers of night in her stories. For a long time, caliphs and paupers alike shared a fear of darkness and the vulva, which they associated with one another. Even the court poets were not free of the curse. Interpreters of the sentiments of love, bordering on chaos, used the female and twilight as primordial sources in their odes.

While still a child, Scheherazade had studied Sufi mysticism.

Her teachers, with the benefit of metaphors that gave equal importance to fishes, water, horses, and women, defended the need to unite two or more mutually antagonistic elements in search of transcendence. Those mystics believed that because religious experience constituted a symbolic existence, dedicated to explaining the enigmas of the universe, it was natural for night, Laila, and woman herself, to coalesce with a hidden reality to which not even the most painstaking exegeses had access. Indissolubly merged, both would evoke a cosmic womb from which all had been born.

Surrounded by the small group of women, Scheherazade reviews in her mind the frightening and poetic symbolism of night. She recalls how, at Fatima's side, she had cried out against the dark areas of the palace, complaining of the secrets that were everywhere. Then she came to understand that religions, arbitrary and apprehensive, and men in general, with no loss of honor, join forces with darkness, the natural zone of sin and redemption.

Though forbidden to attend the university in Baghdad, Scheherazade had not been deprived of learning. Her teacher Abissena, who took pride in having roamed the earth for years in hopes of understanding man, conveyed to her in detail everything of the heated debates about philosophical and historical questions. Even now, wherever she went, his words followed her. With a hump like a camel, bent under the weight of the years, he accepted the delicacies she offered, which he seldom enjoyed. As he chewed lustily, spattering food on the table covered with manuscripts and scrolls, Abissena clarified for her that myth explained metaphorically the riddles of existence. It became a way of expressing other ideas, even occult ones still lacking definition.

He spoke to her in an almost inaudible voice, compelling trust. The sage, whose consciousness was affected by fear of the dark, unable to foresee that he would die in his garret without a friend beside him, attributed legends and enigmas to the night, without exhausting explanations. It was a legacy originating in ancestors frightened by the first signs of twilight, to whom dawn was beneficent.

Scheherazade's torments always began at night. The combat waged between night and day, both with their elevated charge of contradictions, sacrificed people, especially those who, audaciously choosing man as the central figure of the universe, dispensed with the notion of good and the existence of a god.

Consigned to the darkness that amplified the specter of the Caliph's cruelty, Scheherazade had no doubt that the man was the incarnation of evil. In the name of his wounded honor he had forgotten the doctrine of Islam, celebrated especially at Ramadan, the date when the archangel Gabriel had revealed to the prophet Muhammad the commandments now found in the Qur'an.

As night approaches, she joins the retinue of women suffering the effects of the hour of the wolf descending on mankind. At that difficult hour, ancestral memory deeply rooted in each individual remembers a past when everyone, huddling in caves, believed it impossible that they would ever see the light of another day. In her case, night is more dramatic, for thanks to the curse cast upon all young woman by the Caliph, Scheherazade prepares to die. On the chamber walls, where the scales of justice loom, are inscriptions warning her of the danger she faces. But before the angel of death comes for her, she begins a new story.

60

To Scheherazade's surprise, Dinazarda embraces her and asks whose silhouette might be mistaken for hers so that the Caliph would never suspect the substitution.

Dinazarda's action arouses her suspicions. What has made her sister yield to an undertaking as dangerous as the one that some time ago brought the two women to the Caliph's palace, where they have since remained? Seeing Dinazarda excited, taking up swords in her defense, Scheherazade regrets having harbored unjust thoughts about her. Dinazarda deserves her consideration, for she would never do Scheherazade harm. She has redeemed herself from suspicion by taking on the task of selecting the woman to replace Scheherazade in the Caliph's bed. Scheherazade herself would not know how to choose a face similar to hers or a body with dimensions that mirrored her own. She didn't know how to look at the surface of the crystal and memorize changing features that showed joy with each new day won and then retreated before an uncertain future.

Dinazarda had charged Jasmine with selecting the woman to play the role. After speaking with a young woman named Djauara, who shook with fear before a cruel destiny, she approved her amid continuous recapitulations of what she must do in the Caliph's presence. Only then did Dinazarda consult the stars to choose a dark and moonless night to reduce her sister's risk. Once the day was decided, Djauara was brought into the royal chambers, which she was entering for the first time. She was shown the bed where she would couple with the Caliph, and the final details were quickly reviewed for her benefit. Above all, she must never forget that she was forbidden to utter a single word, even if the Caliph insisted. The list of instructions ended with an emphasis on how to act now that she had become Princess Scheherazade.

Dinazarda put out the oil lamps, leaving only a flickering candle flame a short distance from the bed, intended to emphasize shadows and project the lovers' silhouettes against the wall. Scheherazade silently observes her sister, who hides behind one of the screens near the bed. And upon examining Djauara, whose name means "precious stone," she sees that she does in fact resemble her and is the same height.

Leaning against the pillows on the bed, the position specified by Dinazarda, Djauara is worried about how to make her body into that of Scheherazade, who had believed in the effectiveness of the plan from the beginning. It had been she who argued vehemently that the scheme, though risky, was in keeping with the essentially secret nature of all existence. In childhood she had learned that any reality had a fictional form. Wherever she looked, whether at her father the Vizier or at the Caliph's eunuch, life seemed to be made up of a harmoniously false fabric beneath which stirred gains and losses difficult to assess.

Guarding against anything unforeseen, Dinazarda prepared arguments to answer the sovereign's accusations in case he discovered the fraud. She herself moved about the bed to simulate a courage she didn't have, terrified at the consequences of an act considered high treason. At each step she rehearsed words to convince the ruler of her good intentions. The unwise initiative, she would argue, had sprung from her excess of zeal after perceiving the sacrifice to which the Caliph submitted in his efforts to remain faithful to his wife. For, since Scheherazade's arrival in the palace, he had come to dispense with his favorites, depriving himself of experiencing other flesh. Therefore, the situation that occasioned loss to the Caliph seemed unfair to Dinazarda, even if, as a result of her current enterprise, Scheherazade were to be deprived of exclusive access to his erection.

Djauara seemed docile. She behaved as if nothing was about to happen. Even though she was experienced sexually, having learned early how to please a man, she was forbidden to demonstrate this knowledge to the Caliph, so as to emulate the inexperienced Scheherazade. For this reason, Dinazarda had reminded her that after coitus she mustn't extend her stay there and should leave the chambers immediately.

When she found herself in bed with the Caliph, as silent as she, Djauara kept in mind Dinazarda's orders, which admitted of no mistakes. The coupling was fast, with the Caliph doing nothing to prolong it. During intercourse the young woman acted like Scheherazade, holding back the sexual impulse to delight the sovereign who, lying back on the pillows, awaited the basins with warm water for his ablutions as soon as Djauara hurriedly left the bed and was replaced by Scheherazade, who had hidden behind the screen.

Crouching near the bed during the coitus, Dinazarda was relieved, even though she still had to criticize Djauara. After the Caliph achieved orgasm, the young woman, holding her breath longer than she had foreseen, began panting rapidly, unlike Scheherazade's sober behavior in bed.

The presence of Djauara had brought Scheherazade temporary relief. Without confessing it to Dinazarda, she knew that this initiative represented the first step toward freedom, the plan to one day disappear and leave someone in her place. All that was missing was someone to substitute for her as storyteller.

Testing their luck, the sisters invited Djauara back, with the condition that she do away with the final sighs that threatened to ruin everything. Djauara, though conscious of her lack of sexual control, swore to obey. That night, at the end of the orgasm, she excelled in repressing any manifestation. And as soon as the Caliph fell exhausted beside her, closing his eyes as usual, the young woman abandoned the bedroom without a sound.

Thanks to this arrangement, Scheherazade was able to reduce her time with the sovereign. All but freed from conjugal duty, which at Dinazarda's insistence she had not renounced completely, she suddenly evoked the deceased Sultana. She knew little of the woman responsible for the series of deaths decreed by the Caliph, said to be of an almost angelic beauty, although her mild features concealed an insatiable lust. At the same time that the Sultana's deeds put her own life at risk, it was thanks to her that Scheherazade had experienced, alongside unhappiness, the pleasure of telling stories, without which the Caliph, and she herself, could no longer live.

61

While Scheherazade calms her spirit by thinking about the Sultana, whom she knows through the hatred the sovereign dedicates to her, the Caliph discovers that the fraud of which he has been the victim affords him a strange pleasure. The fact of the Vizier's daughters deceiving him with his tacit consent augurs the advent of an unusual emotion, a feeling that, although it leaves him exposed to himself, gives him the rare opportunity to review some of his decisions vis-à-vis the women.

Probing the repercussion of the fraud in his heart, he detects nothing that must be extirpated at the point of a dagger. He has suddenly come to view certain betrayals as irrelevant. Acts he would have previously judged as threatening now do not affect his equilibrium. As if he has sated his thirst for vengeance, punishment imposed on women does not bring the same joy as before. Thus the ghost of the Sultana, which has pursued him for so long, dissolves in his mind, and he almost misses the pain she evoked in the past.

The Caliph had long noticed Scheherazade's boredom with intercourse, which mirrored his own, a rejection that made it easier to understand her behavior and even to sympathize with her. Thanks to Scheherazade's imagination, he too had learned that the borders of the world opened as the veils of the visible were ripped away. Now he wishes for changes that, among other things, will release him from his wearying conjugal duty—without the risk, however, of losing the source of entertainment, the stories he hears each night, pieces of knowledge that add to his understanding of the world.

Even in the dark it had been easy to realize that the stranger in his bed, semi-nude, disguised as Scheherazade, was not his wife.

By the light of the only candle available, which confused his vision, the Caliph had confirmed his suspicion. What especially caught his attention was that when he penetrated her, with both close to orgasm, the young woman's breathing had accelerated, revealing a degree of emotion absent from the severe and austere character of Scheherazade.

In light of the discovery, he reacted to the deception without losing control. At no time did he rage, become furious, or give the sisters reason to believe he would use his humiliation to impose an appropriate punishment. He merely smiled complacently. What in the eyes of the law of the caliphate was a crime struck him as something abounding with attenuating circumstances, obliging him to review the moral aspects of the case. Besides which, thanks to that imposture, he had the chance to interrupt the tiring sequence of fornications. Most important, it freed him from the enormous task of visiting that vulva every night, with the advantage of this dispensation occurring now when the joints of his knees, which pained and impeded him, had started to creak, probably from lack of ointment. Furthermore, his member, at the time of coitus, already near the vulva, had started to retract and was slow to regain its virility. This caused him no suffering, as he had for some time been asking Allah to rid him of the obligation, dating back to adolescence, of daily visiting the sex of women.

The night the slave introduced herself into his bed, Allah, as if hearing his prayers, had given him the rare opportunity to repay the provocation on the part of the Vizier's daughters and abstain from sex at the same time, without the risk of losing Scheherazade's stories in the future. Beginning with that first visit, and followed by others, the sovereign would display his tiny teeth, imprinting on his sly smile a mischievousness never before evident on his face, an expression that surely corresponded to his most recent conviction. In the past, when confronted with insubordination or disloyalty by his courtiers, he would have reacted furiously, immediately sending the offender to the dungeon or the scaffold. At the mercy, for the moment, of the archangel Gabriel, he defended himself without thinking about death for the young women.

Faced with the fraud he has suffered, he takes time to meditate. Thus, when Djauara once again comes to his bed, replacing Scheherazade, the shrewd smile that rejuvenates him appears on his face. Without hesitating, he throws himself toward the young woman. But in contact with that tumescent flesh, his member, in total disobedience to his plan, hardens. Disconcerted by the unexpectedness of having his instrument poised in the direction of Djauara's sex, he covers her body and lies still over her, suffering his desire.

Djauara opens her legs to attract the Caliph. The royal member, however, active till now, instead of plunging into the depths of the uterus, shows no sign of life. Only his voluminous body, pressing upon her, causes such discomfort that Djauara, in continuous movement, rubs her body against him in order to resuscitate the Caliph's staff and free herself.

Mounted on her, the Caliph does everything to avoid his sex hardening. Trying to ignore the possibility of his member betraying him involuntarily, he begins stroking the woman's face, as if she were his Tatarian horse, untangling her hair with his fingertips like a comb, despite the awkward position, a gesture that, devoid of lust, leaves his inert phallus against Djauara's body and thus precludes any sexual union.

Djauara can barely breathe. Lacking air, she makes a muffled sound. The sisters, behind the screen, are troubled, unable to help her. The slave hesitates about pretending that the royal member, still erect, is nestled in her vulva, and wonders whether to voice false moans and sighs as proof of the pleasure the sovereign is giving her.

The Caliph amuses himself in the days that follow, pleased at sowing small disasters around him. Such retaliation, though initially leaving the sisters without recourse, leads him to ponder the failed scheme that he feels has victimized him. In later visits, still retaliating for the affront, he increases the time he spends over

Djauara. As he practices this malevolent exercise, the feeling of revenge begins to taste sour on his palate and he loses the desire to savor a triumph unworthy of his noble stripe. Perhaps because of this, he pushes Djauara to one corner of the bed and, in a voice audible to the Vizier's daughters, tells her to never return to the chambers.

Dinazarda turns pale, thinking herself lost. Instinctively, she places her body in front of her sister. Punishment should fall first on her. But to her surprise, Scheherazade throws herself onto the pillow previously occupied by Djauara, assuming blame for the crime. On the crumpled satin, she breathes the scent left by the young woman, which evokes the smell of Jasmine's desert.

She is comforted by the memory of that illusory place. The punishment about to befall them as a result of the switching of roles has become one more link in the chain of events that has afflicted her since she first confronted the Caliph. The imminence of a failure that has long threatened her perception of reality no longer matters. Having learned to live with the fatal sentence proffered daily by the Caliph, she sees no reason to fear the consequences of a different act that takes her to the scaffold. She is ready to offer her head to the executioner.

Amid the tumult following the expulsion of Djauara, Scheherazade, in addition to challenging the sovereign with her decision to die, appears proud of having completed a plan that would represent the man's defeat. So much so that the Caliph, enfeebled by this injurious game, exits without saying good-bye, leaving behind a trail of woe and defeat. Approaching the throne, he consoles himself by thinking that the sisters, awaiting the punishment to be inflicted on them, will suffer in expectation of his return to the chambers accompanied by the executioner.

Aware of the danger, the Vizier's daughters embrace as they hear the herald, whose voice, resounding in the distance, foretells their doom. They don't know what welcome to give the Caliph to evade the danger.

Enveloped by Jasmine's lamentations, they say their farewells to life. But in one final effort to move him, they exhibit, prostrate on the floor, the humility of servants.

The Caliph appears triumphantly in the chambers. He passes by the young women without acknowledging their sacrifice. He accommodates himself on the divan as if nothing had happened. He motions for Scheherazade to lie down and, without undressing or baring his phallus, covers her with his body. His gestures, simulating an energetic coitus, indicate his willingness to live a farce in exchange for the habitual compensation of Scheherazade's accounts.

62

Scheherazade awakens with fever. She feels exhausted. She makes an effort, but her body refuses, and she cannot rise from the bed. The Caliph, with an absentminded gesture, reading her reddish cheeks as pleasure, concedes her another day of life, a decision made as he was halfway out of the chambers. One that cost him nothing once he had overcome the urge to punish the women. But before he leaves, he looks back. He is moved by the young woman striving to apprehend the world with her words. And he wonders who after her, in case she dies or goes back to her father's palace, will tell him stories. For the first time, he formulates the possibility of losing her, without being able to feel pain or impede her departure.

Left by themselves and ignorant of the Caliph's inner transformations, the women yield to desperation. Each of them, gathered around the bed where the feverish Scheherazade lies, attempts to save her, applying purifying oils, herbs from the desert, anything capable of deterring the disease that threatens to spread throughout her body and prevent the young woman from defending herself from the intransigent Caliph.

The suggestion of appealing to the court doctor is rejected. Dinazarda fears that the courtiers, participants in a conspiracy under way, will poison the mint and hasten her sister's end. It would be easy for anyone in the palace to assassinate her and hide the evidence. Besides which, the number of courtiers and servants who envied Scheherazade's influence on the Caliph had grown. And that power is now enhanced by the responsibilities conferred on Dinazarda, charged with overseeing broad areas of the palace.

Removed from the drama going on around her, Scheherazade opens her eyes with difficulty, sees an opaque world and the evil that has deeply wounded her. Her febrile state, however, makes her excited, and from her thighs comes a warmth that burns and binds her to life. She makes discreet movements as if taking from the coffer of her body the ghosts, goblins, wizards, and enigmas that surround her spirit. She relies only on Dinazarda and Jasmine for alleviation of her sickness, which seems incurable. It is a burden, surely, for her sister, who deliberates about what to do before the Caliph returns to the chambers, expecting to hear the end of the latest story. The sovereign's reaction, seeing her still prostrate on the bed, unable to gladden his night, could aggravate the irritation he usually displays after the audiences and cause him to order her death in a sudden outburst of temper.

Dinazarda thinks about Fatima, who she knows lives somewhere far from Baghdad, and what she would do if she were still with them. Her proverbial shrewdness easily converted a snake into a frog, with the final acquiescence of the one she intended to fool. But what ruse would Fatima use to deceive the sovereign and protect Scheherazade? Or to achieve her sister's freedom, an end to her custody?

She had always suspected that the servant woman whom Ali Baba marries had been inspired by Fatima, as cunning and lively as that character. Scheherazade had not, however, named her Fatima, in order to protect her nursemaid and keep her distant from the circle where life and death are so lightly decided.

Willing to make use of some providential recourse, Dinazarda turns her attention to Jasmine, beautiful and firm of flesh, who frequently declares that she loves Scheherazade more than life itself. This love was never exclusive, for it extends also to the Vizier's other daughter. She shows herself ready to be sacrificed for them should it prove necessary. Her loving measures have always been intense and exaggerated.

Scheherazade's fever has not lessened. It is imperative to remove as quickly as possible the danger that the Caliph always represents. Hearing the laments of the slave kneeling beside Scheherazade's bed, declaring her willingness to die in her place, Dinazarda doesn't hesitate, nodding that she accepts her sacrifice. The time has come to put her to the test.

Jasmine bows her head, waiting to learn what is expected of her. Dinazarda takes her by both hands and orders her, without subterfuge. She demands that from that day forward she become the heroine of the stories spreading through Baghdad. She must measure up in real life to Scheherazade, this sister of hers who in her stories saves mariners, spares the shipwrecked, overcomes the raging tempest. And if in fact Jasmine has come to admire Sinbad, let her now vie with him for the scepter of courage. What could life offer more noble than to allow herself to be slain by the dagger's blade in order to save Scheherazade?

Her sentences need no tears to be convincing. Her eyes, fixed on Jasmine, have an uncompromising expression, with no trace of tenderness or consideration. She simply demands that the slave, beginning with the vow made between them, adopt the stance of a fearless warrior and that the two of them alter the course of the events that will take place in those chambers.

Jasmine nods assent. There is no need for Dinazarda to insist or prove there is no other choice. But Dinazarda, anguished over her sister, fails to notice the gesture. So, as if she has lost confidence in the slave's solidarity, she demands that Jasmine keep her sworn word. Faced with the possibility of losing Scheherazade, she forgets the slave's virtues, of which her sister so often spoke.

Jasmine casts herself to the floor, shaking with indignation. Under pain of death for her audacity, she defiantly confronts the gaze of her mistress. Who was this daughter of the Vizier who stole from her the innate virtues of the voices of the desert? She, who belonged to a tribe that acted according to sacred precepts that predated the Qur'an.

Dinazarda is confused, uncertain how to react. For the first time Jasmine surprises her and she realizes she does not know her. Has she perhaps underestimated the slave's strength and humiliated a friend, all in the name of Scheherazade, who would surely disapprove had she witnessed the scene?

She knows no way of checking Jasmine's sobbing. She would ask forgiveness, but her lips remain sealed. She leans forward, her breath almost mingling with the slave's, waiting for her to comprehend the language of a heart in distress. She doesn't know how to repair the damages of this drama. Her frustration grows, as does a sense of anticipatory mourning. This gives Jasmine, who is of a generous nature, time to compose herself. She doesn't want the Vizier's daughter to suffer because of her. Both of them, after all, are at the mercy of an evil that unites them. In a soft voice, Jasmine asks what is expected of her. There is little time left.

Dinazarda is slow to act. Jasmine, however, demonstrates her readiness, heading quickly to the market in search of herbs to save Scheherazade. She has in mind a mixture used by other tribes as nomadic as her own. She anxiously grabs leaves, tries ointments, drinks disgusting syrups. Back in the chambers, after Jasmine applies unguents to the young woman's chest and makes her drink a dark, slimy liquid, she is sure she has restored her to life.

Dinazarda wipes her sister's brow, gathers up the urine and feces and holds the material up to the sun to discover ills that earlier escaped her eyes. She has hopes that her sister will survive until nightfall. But who can take her place in the farce that will begin with the Caliph's arrival?

There is no need to wait for the hour of truth, for it does not exist. What has disappeared from the scene is the voice of the narrator, who now lies in bed with a fever. Couldn't someone equally eloquent come forth to replace Scheherazade, thus avoiding the waning of the story?

Dinazarda feels her sister's brow. The fever has subsided. In spite of her weakness, Scheherazade smiles. Her body is bathed in sweat. Jasmine dries her with balms and cloths, caressing her excitedly, believing she has saved her. And she is happy for Scheherazade to owe her for such a treasure, just as the Caliph will someday owe her for the stories she is to tell. But will it be exactly like that? Will Dinazarda accept sharing daily with Jasmine a life that both aspire to live with praise and passion?

Scheherazade removes the cloth from her head and the veil from her face, as if to promise that the moment has come to choose her successors and disappear from the Caliph's palace.

63

Jasmine brings him carefully selected dates. Absently, the Caliph sucks the fruit, chews on the fiber, and slowly removes the filaments. Only then does he expel the pit from his mouth.

Kneeling at his feet, Jasmine extends to him treatment reserved only for Scheherazade. Beautiful and delicate, she bends toward him like a palm tree in an oasis. But who is she, where did she come from? He doesn't remember ever hearing her voice. He thinks she might be mute, her tongue stolen from her before she had been bought to serve in the palace. Her silence might owe also to having heard in captivity the beauty of the Arabic language spoken in court and resentment of the tribal language of her family, replete with coarse expressions, although translating to perfection the needs of the desert as they drove their animals. That would be a good reason for hiding the metallic timbre, in which she would emit dissonant sounds. Her quietness, however, radiates a restiveness and indomitability of spirit. He detects a pent-up, irrational sensuality beneath her satiny skin.

He feels like sending her away and demanding that Scheherazade, miraculously recovered from fever, kneel and replace the servant. But he doesn't dare offend the Vizier's daughter. He turns his attention back to Jasmine. What would she tell him, were he to show interest in her turbulent past? Would the slave woman be capable of relating a story comparable to those he'd heard from Scheherazade? Or did Scheherazade's gift, exclusive to her, refuse to be shared with others, leaving the slave only the smallest portion of the enchantment of the Vizier's daughter?

Lately the Caliph had asked himself whether the moment had come to try living without Scheherazade, after replacing her with someone who, with talent similar to her own, was not simply a copy of her but demonstrated the ability to begin and end a story with pleasing results. Someone who was able to preserve throughout the narrative suspense propitious to both the emotion of the account and the storyteller as well.

The Caliph contemplated this change. He planned to drive away the loneliness that would come from losing Scheherazade by surrounding himself with the poor of Baghdad, brought to him without his leaving the palace. He could lie on his cushions, attended by beautiful slaves, feeling no need to wander the streets of the city to obtain his daily ration of storytelling.

After admiring Jasmine's face for so long, he felt an intolerance for human features that could be easily confused with those of a goat or camel. He rose, bent his legs, bringing his hands to the floor without the hoped-for result. By the gesture he had planned to wipe away uncomfortable memories. Forlorn, he let his body sink back into the cushions.

He listened to Scheherazade's story with his usual curiosity. It was a pleasure that was softening his heart in such a way that he was tempted to confess to her, shortly before dawn, that she would be excused from his verdict. That is, there would be no punishment for her. She was free to leave, to go wherever she wished, taking with her the guarantee that he would never again punish a young woman of Baghdad. For the first time, he felt that his accounts were settled with women and with life. Besides which, as a result of the recent scheme, which culminated with the slave Djauara, he had decided to reduce his sexual activity, without giving public notice of the fact. Even suspending for good his nightly coitus, after first ascertaining that such interruption would do him no harm, and thus freeing his joints of the obligation of fornicating in exchange for the creative reveries of some young woman soon to be recruited.

He said nothing to her. As if talking to himself, the sovereign recognized his culpability for excesses committed. Negligent with the sisters, especially with Scheherazade, he had made her suffer without the grace of having at least taught her the art of vanity.

He was, then, willing to forget the sisters' deceitful conduct. After all, it had been he who took them to the point of saturation, inspiring them to a beneficial farce, after which, by simulating coitus, both lovers could dispense with their mutual presence in bed. He could go on finding delight in the stories that, despite their lack of verisimilitude, took on the appearance of truth thanks to the words springing from Scheherazade's mouth like a gray-green toad from some hypothetical swamp.

Dinazarda resented the Caliph. What was she to think of the ruler who mounted her sister, convulsed over her fragile flesh only long enough to convince everyone that his phallus, quickly withdrawn, had penetrated the young woman and ejaculated, merely to make the others believe he had fulfilled his duty, when in fact he lacked the appetite to fornicate?

Using Jasmine as a sounding board, Dinazarda vented her griefs and fears. She felt danger was imminent. She needed for Jasmine, in her own way, to describe whether the sovereign, following the sham coupling with Scheherazade, displayed a distressed expression or some faint trace of lust. How had he reacted to Scheherazade's opening her legs so he could reach the depths of her uterus? Did he by chance act as if the body of the Vizier's daughter was merely a vessel for the sperm that had never taken root in her?

Jasmine followed her reasoning, looking for purpose in what Dinazarda told her. Perhaps the princess judged that the time had come for Scheherazade to break her ties to the sovereign and return to her father's home. To declare herself defeated once and for all, giving the Caliph the opportunity to recommence the shedding of young women's blood. Or perhaps Dinazarda planned to test him, to find out if he was in fact ready to pardon women for a crime they had not committed and renounce any revenge against Scheherazade by restoring her right to live.

Speaking almost to herself, Dinazarda insists on confirming the Caliph's intentions as he sips cups of mint tea. The Caliph had barely glanced at Scheherazade—just enough to be sure she was still at his side. He cared little whether instead of her sister some stranger occupied her place, with the specific task of not depriving him of the words that flowed like wine into his veins.

Dinazarda moves restlessly about the chambers. She goes to the garden to pick flowers, and has a sudden realization: The Caliph has given unmistakable indications of his willingness to free Scheherazade, to grant her safe conduct with which to visit his kingdom and choose the ideal place to settle and tell her stories. She could, if she wished, take a female slave with her, like Jasmine.

The moment had come for Scheherazade to depart. To begin her journey in accordance with her repressed desire, a relocation that coincided with her dreams. In the coming weeks, she would proceed through the desert until she reached Fatima's small house, a veritable oasis in the middle of the village. The description of the locale, which Fatima had given her before she left the Vizier's palace, would allow Scheherazade to arrive there without mistake. Both women, the nursemaid and the princess, had always known that after the long and painful separation they would poignantly embrace, bound by ties impossible to break, a reunion that promised to keep them together until death.

Filled with emotion, Dinazarda buried her head in her arms, not letting Jasmine see what was going on in her heart.

64

Dinazarda and Jasmine were ready to admit to the Caliph that Scheherazade had fled at morning, after he took his leave of the young women to return to the throne room. But perhaps he would ask nothing when he failed to find her that night in the chambers, indifferent to the fact that Scheherazade, weary of storytelling, had bidden farewell to the palace and embarked on an unknown adventure.

Scheherazade had long aspired to a life free from restraint and regulation, even at the risk of narrowing the paths of salvation. She could no longer bear being the wife of that man, forbidden to experience passion with anyone else. Her tedium would have resulted in disaster, had Dinazarda not taken drastic measures. For days, Dinazarda had foreseen the fatal consequences of her decline, even though Scheherazade went on telling her stories. Her latest inventions, however, were markedly pessimistic in tone, spoiling a plot whose initial sentences had promised a happy ending. She wasn't making her listeners smile as before. She seemed to prefer imposing on them a discomfiting melancholy, as if daily life in its most telling expressions demanded a flood of tears.

Scheherazade could no longer sustain the full bloom of her despair. It was only a matter of time before she would ask the Caliph, as a personal favor, to decree her death as a way to free herself from her destitute life. Dinazarda sensed this danger and sent a message to their father, who had been cowardly throughout this long period, and urged him to take severe measures. The Vizier had distanced himself from his daughters, who he thought deserved punishment for having disobeyed his orders, but now he realized he must redeem himself and become the hero of his family, so few in number. He must show the other courtiers the depth of his love for his daughter.

Since first coming to the Caliph's palace, Scheherazade had refused to involve her father in the drama, sparing him the unpleasantness of her asking for help and being rebuffed. She didn't want to see the disapproval in her father's face for her choice of turbulence instead of lasting happiness, and for being a daughter who had been incapable of foreseeing the pain that challenging the Caliph would bring her.

From behind the pergola, Dinazarda demanded that her father remove Scheherazade from the palace and take her far away from Baghdad. To prove her firmness, she promised to remain in her sister's place. After their father agreed, Dinazarda made the same declaration to Scheherazade. To her surprise, Scheherazade reacted with questions. How could she remain in her stead if, from the moment she had decided to save the young women of the kingdom, that fate was hers alone, and no one could rob her of her destiny? How could that happen, unless Dinazarda confessed to having long sought her place, to having always aspired to be queen and to surprising the aging Caliph with an heir to the throne.

If her sister admitted that she always desired to be where Scheherazade was, she would leave her in peace and accept their father's help. But Dinazarda said nothing, for it was not necessary. Her silence confirmed Scheherazade's suspicion. The conspiracy between Dinazarda and Jasmine had advanced to the point that they had divided their respective functions. Dinazarda would service the Caliph in bed while Jasmine, having recently discovered her calling as storyteller, would entertain the sovereign with stories that had been brewing for some time in her witch's cauldron. She would mix the herbs of her remembrances with fresh material from the dervish, relying on the limitless universe that Scheherazade, in her generosity, had opened to her as a gift.

With her father's promise to send Scheherazade wherever she wanted to go, and vigilant to any danger, Dinazarda made her plans. She had learned in recent days of several caravans leaving Baghdad, and Scheherazade had only to point out on a map her direction of choice. Transporting merchandise, these caravans would find nothing inconvenient about taking the princess and her precious belongings, which the Vizier planned to advance her as part of her inheritance. Scheherazade would cross the desert settled in a comfortable litter, surrounded by the animals she loved, especially the camel, whose beauty and usefulness had inspired her to compose odes in the past.

Scheherazade refused to specify her itinerary. Once she departed Baghdad she would leave no trace. Dinazarda insisted on knowing her destination: if she was to remain there in Scheherazade's place, risking the Caliph's cutting off her head, she would help decide the route.

Scheherazade had always known that if she left the palace alive, she would secretly take the caravan heading north. She knew the point at which she would leave the cortege, continue in a different direction, and, after some days of travel, knock on Fatima's door. She was convinced she would succeed. The house, by Fatima's account, was not large, but she would be able to spot it from a distance. Surrounded by vegetation, and even by olive groves, it had a room reserved for Scheherazade, and everything inside was organized with her in mind. Where else could her imagination flourish, and make up for lost time? And shouldn't that same imagination be abundant enough to invent any story line at all? To imagine a prince who in reality was only a teacher from the schools of Baghdad and whose heretical vocation, countering the prevailing religious precepts, had caused him to recently settle in the village, near Fatima's house? It could well be that in the future, the two young people, weary of the city and of the dangerous illusions springing from all things, might meet. And gradually learn that they were meant for each other. They would experience a grand love, and though it might become dulled by habit, each would make the other laugh.

Fatima would approve of the union. For this she was willing to give up space in her house in favor of a growing family, when the time came. Scheherazade and Fatima were in agreement about the simplicity of a life that left them free for the fantasy they both needed.

Was this, then, what would transpire after Scheherazade was

taken from the palace on a holy Friday and handed by the Vizier's emissary to a caravan told to obey her orders? Without her father ever knowing in what direction his daughter was to go, yet providing her with jewels, gold, coins, everything that she might need? Not forgetting to give her his loyal servant, Abu Hassam, long in his service, who had come to him with his tongue cut out by Bedouins who feared he might someday talk and put the safety of the tribe at risk?

To effect Scheherazade's flight, her father had to set the date. Dinazarda caught in Scheherazade's gaze the anticipated pleasure of the moment when she would cross the threshold of the chambers without looking back.

If her father, in alliance with Dinazarda, had not decided to remove her from there, Scheherazade would have thrown herself from the window in desperation. She could not bear the Caliph demanding of her more happy endings without promising her freedom in return. At no time did he confess to her that, as payment for so many favors, he was willing to see her depart. For, thanks to her rich descriptions, he had recovered his spirit for living, and the caliphate had come to seem less wearisome. But perhaps her greatest gift was that he had learned to forgive women as a result of Scheherazade's stories, which held men and women as narrative partners.

With the power the Caliph had granted her, Dinazarda moved through the palace giving orders, which were always obeyed. In her last meeting with her father, still at Scheherazade's behest, he seemed offended by his daughter's growing influence in areas under his command. But when he smelled the floral perfume emanating from her skin, it reminded him of his deceased wife, and he embraced her, his love for his daughter filling his entire being. She kissed her father's hand, having no wish to usurp his power. But she demanded that Scheherazade be taken safely to wherever she wished to go.

On the eve of the flight, Jasmine, multiplying her functions, incorporated the image of Scheherazade into her body. She was certain that the Caliph would soon forget the storyteller. And Dinazarda, the living remnant of a tribe on the verge of disappearing, would comply with what Scheherazade had taught them. Both were confident that the Caliph, in their company, would feel free once again to travel around the caliphate, frequenting his favorites and forgetting that he had been prisoner of the Vizier's younger daughter.

Scheherazade's flight, planned by the Vizier, went smoothly. Anyone who glanced at her would not have believed that she would leave through the rear gates of the palace dressed as a slave to meet her father's mute servant, who had been designated to assist her. The two were quickly received by the caravan, which was about to depart. Everything moved so rapidly that by twilight they were far from Baghdad, without Scheherazade ever looking back at the walls of the city. She barely had time to bid farewell to Dinazarda and Jasmine, both of them eager to take her place and fearful that her flight would be discovered sooner than expected.

Scheherazade had not seen her father. She didn't miss him, as if she had banished him from her life. She felt that, having made him into a character in a story that fit him like a glove, she would always have him at her side. Even if she never again saw her family, she would keep them near by sharing them with Fatima. And she hoped they would not consider her disloyal for reserving a discreet role for them in an account already forming in her mind.

The dunes before them were welcoming. She was finally seeing the desert near at hand. She heard the secret voices mingling with the fine grains of sand that pelted her skin. As the caravan proceeded on its way, Scheherazade was leaving behind a universe made up of her sister and Jasmine. Whenever she wept in years to come, she would console herself with the memory of them. And they would never lose her. Wasn't it true that what we experience, even as it dissolves into memory, is a point of resistance in the future?

The Caliph would not come after her. She had sensed his exhaustion, imploring her to leave his sight, as he had no wish to send her to the executioner. He had finally made peace with women and had put their betrayals in perspective. He had come to understand the necessity of preserving his legacy, and although it could not compare with that of the adventurous Harun ar-Rashid, it could not be denied that it had been he who obliged Scheherazade to tell the best stories in all the kingdom in an effort to save herself. Because of his tyranny, the history of his people would be consecrated forever in a verbal edifice more powerful than any mosque or palace built with stone, lime, and sweat. What Scheherazade had sown in the chambers would never vanish. To ensure this, Jasmine and Dinazarda, her disciples, would repeat each tale to exhaustion. Neither they nor their successors would allow the essence of the Arab soul to die, even if he and the young women never heard the new stories Scheherazade was surely sharing with Fatima, who had received her with open arms when she arrived at her home, dusty, hungry, and happy.

A Note About the Author

Nélida Piñon is a native of Rio de Janeiro, where she still lives. A former professor at the University of Miami, she has also been a visiting writer at Harvard, Columbia, Georgetown, and Johns Hopkins universities. Among the Brazilian literary prizes she has received are the Golden Dolphin and the Mário de Andrade Award. International prizes include Juan Rulfo (Mexico), Jorge Isaacs (Colombia), Rosalía de Castro (Spain), Gabriela Mistral (Chile), and Menéndez Pelayo (Spain). In 1996 she became the first woman elected president of the Brazilian Academy of Letters.

A Note on the Type

Pierre Simon Fournier *le jeune,* who designed the type used in this book, was both an originator and a collector of types. His services to the art of printing were his design of letters, his creation of ornaments and initials, and his standardization of type sizes. His types are old style in character and sharply cut. In 1764 and 1766 he published his *Manuel typographique,* a treatise on the history of French types and printing, on typefounding in all its details, and on what many consider his most important contribution to typography—the measurement of type by the point system.

Composed by North Market Street Graphics,
Lancaster, Pennsylvania

Printed and bound by R.R. Donnelley,
Harrisonburg, Virginia

Designed by Anthea Lingeman